A Life's Journey

from Sri Lanka to Hawaii

To my mother Lilo in loving memory

Claudia Ackermann

A Life's Journey

from

Sri Lanka to Hawaii

Originally translated from German by

Susanne Winsauer-Schrader

Translated by: Susanne Winsauer-Schrader

Edited by: Mark Mardon

Cover painting: Hansine Schwer

Cover design: Peter Wolf

ISBN: 9781657508385

"My life is like a river.

A river must flow.

If water stops flowing, it will become stale.

Only by flowing it will achieve clarity."

(Sooriya Kumar)

The telephone rang. For a moment I considered not answering because I was standing at the door and wanted to leave my apartment. Could be important, I thought, already dressed in warm outdoor clothes for a frosty winter day in Germany. I picked up the receiver.

"Hi, this is Sooriya calling from Hawaii."

I pulled off my woolen cap. Had I heard correctly? In about a quarter of a century I hadn't heard anything of Sooriya. But when he continued talking, his voice sounded as familiar as on the day when we had to part in Colombo, Sri Lanka's capital city.

I had never forgotten my experiences during my stay in Sri Lanka and meeting Sooriya. Back in Germany, I often asked myself how his life had fared after he had to leave his home country for the USA because of the civil war.

The memory of it all had been haunting me for years, so finally I wrote a book about how I got to know Sooriya Kumar in Sri Lanka, never expecting to hear from him again.

"How are you?" his warmhearted voice asked. "Does life treat you well?"

I learned that he had been living in Hawaii for many years.

"I've seen your book," he revealed. "And often I have thought of you and Arugam Bay."

As if it was the most natural thing in the world, he told me that an old friend from Switzerland had given him my book while on a trip to sacred Arunachala Mountain in the Indian state of Tamil Nadu.

"Sooriya, did you know that a book has been written about you in German?'" he recalled his friend's words.

"Immediately I knew it was you," Sooriya confessed, "even though your surname has changed in the meantime."

1

After so many years since we last met, I pondered he must have found my current phone number through the Internet.

"No," Sooriya surprised me. "Do you remember the little torn-off piece of an envelope that you gave to me in the cave? You had scribbled on it your mother's phone number. I found it. You had given it to me in 1984. We were so young then..."

Yes, I had been young. Totally inexperienced and blue-eyed when I started my journey to Asia, I could not imagine then all the future events that would accompany me my whole life after meeting Sooriya.

As soon as Sooriya hung up, I found and opened the book I had written – that I hadn't looked at in years. It kickstarted the journey once more, if only in my imagination ...

Chapter 1

This was my first flight ever. I had never crossed European borders, nor had I ever traveled on my own. I had spent all my previous life in the small South German town where I was born. It was the summer of 1983.

Now, I was sitting in an economy-class seat in a Boeing on its way to Asia.

I had known Sri Lanka only from books and, of course, from Marcus' tales. Marcus had been staying in my hometown for a few days. He told me about his various trips and journeys, especially about Sri Lanka, the former Ceylon. He described beaches bordered by palm trees; visions of endless tea plantations appeared in my mind. I imagined friendly, ever-smiling people in a foreign land full of secrets.

Then Marcus moved on. He never stopped anywhere for long. And me? I had to stay back home in my little town, but I was infected with Marcus' longing for far-away countries, and his homesickness for Sri Lanka. A kind of magic started pulling me there.

But now on the airplane, getting closer to the tropical island, I started to ask myself, what was I looking for on this foreign island? I had no idea how long I would be staying. My return ticket served as my insurance for a possible break-away at any time.

Maybe I just wanted to leave my stuffy hometown, to be free and independent, making my own way and seeing new things, but also, I wanted to be rid of Rainer. We had separated some time before and I needed a lot of distance from him. So, about five thousand miles seemed to be exactly right.

Below me, I could see a thick mat of clouds. As the Boeing started to descend for Colombo Airport, it dived into the clouds and seemed to sink into a bottomless sea. Rain started splashing against the windows. Beside the landing strip, a few blackbirds rose with a start, disturbed by our plane's landing. We touched ground somewhat rudely, but the passengers clapped, as if the pilot had performed a magic trick. Then the doors opened. Immediately, hot air crept into the air-conditioned plane. Soon every passenger including myself started sweating. I felt like I was having a sauna treatment, minus the smell of peppermint oil. Instead, there was a stale and foul stench to the outside air.

"Passport, please!"

The man behind the counter was looking me over with eyes so black that I couldn't distinguish iris from pupil.

"Tourist?"

I nodded, and he stamped and signed a three-month visa. The rain was still pouring when I left the airport building. I stood around, unable to decide what to do with myself during the coming weeks; meanwhile the other travelers shoved by me and into their waiting busses.

"Stop dreaming! The bus to Colombo is leaving shortly," a voice startled me. The German woman who addressed me pushed me aside. I had noticed her in our plane. Obviously, she was traveling on her own, like me, but in contrast to me, she seemed to be familiar with everything here. Unerringly, she crossed a parking lot and aimed at a bus stop.

On the other side of the road leading to downtown Colombo, I saw a red and rather rusty bus that looked like an import from an English scrapyard. I grabbed my backpack and followed the woman in a hurry. I was not even near the bus when the driver started the engine. My heavy backpack bumped my back painfully as I crossed the street. Rain soaked me, and my clothes clung to my body. The German woman had seated herself on one of the hard benches already, and I hauled myself next to her.

"I was lucky - just in time, I guess," I said to her, gasping for breath.

"This has nothing to do with luck," the tourist replied. "He does it every time."

Groaning and bumping across countless potholes, the bus worked itself along. Through the window, I could watch the rain patter unceasingly onto the tin roofs of the huts we passed. A skinny cow was trying to find some fodder in a garbage dump. Children in shorts ran barefoot through the warm rain, their legs smeared with light brown mud up to their knees. This sight bore no resemblance to the idyll Marcus had described to me. Meanwhile, my German neighbor on the bus introduced herself to me as Petra. She seemed to enjoy the scenery.

The bus moved with breathtaking speed through the flood-like rain despite the poor visibility through the front window; one wiper was missing completely, and the other was squeaking and spreading the mud across the glass. The driver hardly slowed down when we had to pass an oxcart; he even blew his horn! I perceived the shadow of a truck heading at us. Our bus and the truck missed each other by only a few inches, mirror to mirror.

I clung to my seat, scared to the bone. Obviously, nobody else felt as I did; neither the local people nor Petra seemed to mind the driver's way of getting ahead.

"First time in Sri Lanka?" she asked me with a broad grin. I gave her a nod.

I had been planning to rent a room in Colombo, but the closer we came to downtown Colombo, the less I liked this idea. The crowd of people in the streets was getting denser. Cyclists tried to worm their way between cars and busses. Motorized rickshaws, those small, rattling and stinking tin machines on three wheels, squeezed themselves through the traffic, blowing their horns. Although the rain still poured, the streets brimmed with countless people - their hair a deep black, eyes dark, and

5

skin tones ranging from light brown to near black. Some women wore colorful saris; some wore long, wraparound skirts and tight bodices, their waists uncovered. Businessmen dressed in long trousers and white shirts. Other locals wore sarongs, consisting of a skirt-like fabric, folded in front to fit all sizes.

On both roadsides, merchants tried to sell their soaked goods, and everywhere gracile women balanced heavy baskets on their heads.

A beggar dressed in rags sat on the ground between garbage and mud. He had lost his right arm, so he reached out his left hand to me for some money.

"I never stay longer in Colombo than necessary," Petra said after she noticed the shocked expression on my face.

"You simply have to get out of this mess and relax a little on the beach. I know a small and calm hotel in a fishing village near Hikkaduwa."

The cloudburst had flooded Colombo's bus station. We stepped out of the bus and right into a dirty, ankle-deep soup. Unfamiliar scents mingled with the musty stink of the puddles. At almost the same second, a motorized rickshaw stopped to pick us up.

"Tuk-tuk, Madam?" the driver asked. Not waiting for my answer, he jumped off the rickshaw and tried to grab my luggage. Unsuccessfully, I tried to tear my backpack from his hands. Now Petra took the initiative and stood up to the local man. The German woman was taller than the Sri Lankan man by almost a head's size, and she was rather stout as well. She simply pushed the man aside.

"Do you believe I will find a room in that quiet hotel on the beach?" I asked Petra.

"I am sure. We will find you a nice room to stay. The owner is a good friend of mine. And I know inhabitants of the village. I have come to this place for many years."

With determination, she ploughed her way through the crowd.

"We'll take the minibus to Hikkaduwa," she called toward me.

Petra was walking fast. It was difficult not to lose her with all those people standing around. At last we arrived at the minibus parking lot.

"Minibus" was no understatement. The vehicles were so small, it was impossible to keep an upright position within. Actually, they were made for ten sitting humans, however, they were stuffed with countless passengers crouched on benches, emergency seats or on the floor.

We tried to read the various destinations listed on every bus front, but these were printed in letters of the national language, which were unknown to me.

Drivers were yelling names of towns or villages out of every bus, unbelievably fast and in constant repetition.

Ratnapura, Ratnapura, Ratnapura," one Sri Lankan bus driver called loudly. From a further bus, we could hear another city name. Voices seemed to be competing. I was soaked by now and ran after Petra across the muddy square. Finally, she aimed at a certain minibus.

"Hikkaduwa, Hikkaduwa, Hikkaduwa," the man shouted with a powerful voice.

We stopped in front of the bus. Immediately, someone took our luggage and heaved it to the roof. My bulky backpack would never have fit in the packed interior. Luckily, Petra and I found room within. A woman on the floor took her child on her lap, and the passengers moved up even closer, so that we had a small gap to squeeze ourselves into.

Now, the man with the quick pronunciation jumped up. With one hand holding open the sliding door, he poked his head outside, despite the incessant rain. There was no way for him to stand upright. I was fascinated by his naked, dark-skinned feet standing near mine. He moved his toes apart like fingers to grip the floor when the bus took sharp bends.

A muggy stench of sweat and moist clothes permeated the air. The wet hair of the local woman sitting beside me smelled intensely of coconut oil. Loud music blared from a speaker. A woman was singing a melancholic melody in a nerve-killing, shrill voice. She was accompanied by monotonous sounds from strange instruments.

After the start of our speedy travel through Colombo's streets, we passed slums at the outskirts of the city. Our bus careened along the coastal road with breathtaking speed. Even when passing villages, the driver would not slow down, but instead he raced past the huts, blowing his horn; men, women and children had to jump out of our way.

When at last our conductor slowed down, we caught sight of a big white temple. The conductor stopped for one second and threw some cash into the offertory.

"They ask Buddha to protect our journey," Petra explained to me.

"Anything to protect us will be appropriate," I replied.

The locals scrutinized us throughout the trip. Petra, especially, seemed to get their whole attention. Due to her height and stoutness, she was a giantess compared to the petite local women. Petra's long blond hair hung into her face in strands. Her pale skin was studded by so many freckles that they seemed to combine into big spots. A little girl stared ceaselessly at Petra's face. She seemed to be afraid and wanted to get away from Petra, which, however, was impossible in the overcrowded bus.

Petra leaned back and relaxed, looking out the open sliding door. We spotted the sea behind palm trees and fishing huts. The water was gray and churned wildly beneath dark rain clouds. Big waves crashed onto bizarre rock formations rising from the sea. Petra had a content smile on her face and seemed to enjoy the bus trip very much.

I, on the other hand, hoped for an end to this torture. I was curled up on the floor because there was no way for me to stretch my legs. Whenever our bus took a bend, I had to find something to hold onto, trying desperately not to get hurled out of the open sliding door.

At last, after about three hours of driving, we reached our destination – a small fishing village called Akuralla. My bones had stiffened during the trip and getting up to leave the bus took considerable effort. The conductor threw down our drenched luggage from on top of the minibus. A second later, the driver continued on his way, hooting his horn loudly.

We had stopped in front of our hotel. The white, one-storey building sat picturesquely beneath mighty coconut palms. Petra was expected by a female friend.

A young local with pitch-black, curly hair smiled and said hello to us. He was the hotel manager.

Petra moved into her friend's two-bed room, but for me there was no further room left. I was told that this was the only hotel in close vicinity. The sun had already started to set, and I was exhausted after my long journey. So I was very relieved when the manager offered a private accommodation to me for one night. He promised to have a regular hotel room ready for me next day.

For tonight, I had to cross the street and enter a worn-down building consisting of one single room. Dampness and mold had penetrated the walls. Spider webs draped from pane-less window frames. Rain dripped from the palm-leaf-covered roof. One piece of furniture occupied the room: a bed whose mattress had a tattered green cover showing stains from previous guests.

Since the room was without electricity, the manager provided me with a candle. It was the same with the shower, meaning there was none, so he showed me a nearby well from which I was allowed to fetch water to bathe. It took only a little time for dusk to turn into dark night. I lit my candle and made my way to the well. Unknown, frightening sounds emanated from the thicket adjoining my outdoor bathroom. I couldn't shrug off the feeling that I was being observed, but with only my little candle, I was unable to recognize if it was a human or an animal hiding there. With a rope, I pulled up a bucket with dark-colored water from a black-colored well, or so it seemed in the dim light.

I continued observing the thicket and decided not to undress. Instead, I poured all the water over my head and my clothes. Then I pulled up another bucket from the dark hole. I dipped my towel into the water and raced back to my room.

Once inside, I hastily closed the wooden shutters; only now did I notice that the door had no lock. Awkwardly, I began to clean myself with the wet towel, much too afraid to take my eyes off the entrance.

Mosquitos kept buzzing by my ears. Geckos scurried up the walls and along the ceiling. Not enough yet, a huge cockroach tried to hide beneath my bed. I always had been afraid of spiders and other creatures with more than four legs, and thus was trying hard not to think of what further animals might be crawling about.

But I had asked for it, right? This was the kind of trip I had chosen when I had left Germany for Sri Lanka. Well, not exactly; I hadn't imagined strange animals in lonely huts. My ex-lover Rainer surely would not have shared this adventure with me. He had preferred holidays in comfortable hotels, and always persisted in his plans. But this time I was able to create my journey in my own way. For this night, I decided to accept my crawling friends. I blew out the candle and bravely closed my eyes.

*

The next morning, I woke up sweating, and was badly stung by many insects. But on this new day the rain was gone, the sun was beaming, and the sea, having abandoned yesterday's dark and threatening waters, was glittering a bright turquoise green.

My new room in the hotel across the street had been prepared for me. It was furnished in a simple way, and the walls were painted white. A mosquito net dangled from the ceiling; o, what luxury! A fan hummed gently above me. In a niche, I spotted a bathroom; finally I was able to take a shower!

Several guests were enjoying breakfast on the hotel's terrace. Among them, Petra was deeply absorbed in a conversation with her friend. At another table, two women were speaking in Swiss German. I joined them and ordered a glass of juice. Despite the fact that my English was quite decent, I enjoyed being able to speak some German.

"I wouldn't order that," the elder woman said to me." They mix it with water, which might make you sick."

I had not thought of that at all. The Swiss woman was scrutinizing me from head to toe.

"What happened to your skin?" she asked, shaking her head.

I had been shocked, too, after looking at myself in the mirror that morning. My skin was studded with stings resembling measles. Countless dots on my face and my body were getting red and growing large. The itch was becoming unbearable.

"You should have brought some insect repellent along," the Swiss woman lectured me. She went to her room and returned with a bag full to the brim with a lot of medication. She rummaged through its contents for quite a while and finally found the ointment she had been looking for.

"May I introduce my sister Brigitte," the younger woman asked. "Her profession: nurse. Her passion:

hypochondria. She loved talking about any kind of disease."

The younger girl's name was Kerstin. She was about my age – we both were in our beginning twenties.

Anura, the Sri Lankan who had introduced himself to me last night as the hotel manager, now took my order for breakfast. Apparently, by calling himself the manager, the young man made himself feel important. Brigitte informed me that, not being content to be merely a waiter, a cook, or a cleaner, Anura was all employees in one. The hotel had no further personnel.

Having finished our breakfast, Kerstin and I decided to spend the morning on the beach. Here, at last, I found the Sri Lanka Marcus had so enthusiastically described. The ocean was switching colors from a turquoise-blue to an emerald-green, and calm waves washed on the shore of an endless sandy beach. Palm trees swaying in the steady wind skirted our bay. Fishermen threw their nets into the water from colorful catamarans. All together, they returned from the sea and pulled their catch ashore, chanting monotonously. Dark-skinned children playing in the hot sand watched us white-skinned people with keen interest.

Kerstin and I seemed to be the only tourists on this part of the beach. Brigitte had preferred to stay in the shade of the hotel terrace and read a book.

By noon the sun was burning down from the sky, showing no mercy, so we went back to our hotel for lunch. Of course, I was not adjusted to the local cuisine. Brick-colored rice was being served in combination with immensely spicy-hot vegetable- and fish curries. Despite Anura's assurance that he had flavored the dishes with only a pinch of curry powder, the spices made me sweat right from the first mouthful. I gasped desperately; my gums felt as if I were on the verge of spitting fire. Petra and her friend were unfazed; they enjoyed the local cooking. This was not their first visit to Sri Lanka; they had had many occasions to develop a tolerance for hot chilies.

Our evenings in the little fishing village were quite eventless. After dark, the place seemed deserted. The huts of the local people had no electricity, nor was there street lighting. Our hotel was the only building with a generator. It provided electricity for light, and for cold drinks from the refrigerator, but it also produced much noise. Its loud hum drowned out the calm rush from the waves of the night sleeping ocean.

Kerstin had been so right: Brigitte's only topics were tropical diseases and dangers. She was telling horror tales of poisonous snakes, spiders and scorpions. As soon as the lights on the terrace attracted all kinds of insects, she retreated to her room and hid under her mosquito net.

Petra regularly closed the evening with a glass of arrack, a drink distilled from the juice of palm blossoms. Alcohol made the reserved Petra open up and talk and she visibly enjoyed sharing her travel experiences with Kerstin and me. She was older than either of us. I guessed her to be in her mid-thirties. Petra had seen quite a bit of Sri Lanka. For many years, she had been spending all of her holidays on this island.

"I know this country by now," she told us, slightly drunk. "In the beginning, I tried to stay near the tourists, of course. Later on, I visited the inner island, the ancient cities, the temples and the famous Buddha statues. Meanwhile, my favorite place is Akuralla. People there are not as spoiled yet as in Hikkaduwa or other tourist ghettos."

Enough drinks for Petra, and she rose from her chair heavily to go to bed.

I was dead tired myself. Since my arrival in Sri Lanka, I had been suffering from the heat and the moist air. The quiet hotel in Akuralla was exactly the right place to get used to the tropical climate.

After a few days I had adjusted somewhat, and my spirits started to get high again. So, I decided to make a trip to the tourist place, Hikkaduwa, which was not far away. Anura guided me to the roadside and held up a hand to stop the minibus.

"Hikkaduwa, Hikkaduwa?" the conductor was asking. I nodded and squeezed myself into the crowded bus. Those busses aren't made for tall people; so many passengers had to duck. Thank God, this time the sliding doors had been closed, so I wouldn't be in danger of getting hurled outside. For further "safety," the inside was so crowded, no one could fall over. After about half an hour, we arrived at Hikkaduwa.

A little boy addressed me the moment I departed from the vehicle. "Hotel, Madam? Souvenirs? Batik manufactures?"

As a matter of fact, I had planned to have a look around first. But there was no possibility stepping on the coastal path without being bothered by merchants. Hotels stood side-by-side, as well as restaurants and countless souvenir shops – like pearls on a necklace. Fortunately, there were no big hotel sites. Tall palm trees overtopped the small buildings.

In a teashop, I asked for the post office. I badly wanted to write a postcard to my mother. When I said goodbye, I had to promise her that she would hear from me at regular intervals. She was deeply worried that I might not return safely from all my dangerous adventures in Asia, traveling on my own.

Surely, she imagined me living in a jungle among wild natives, encircled by poisonous spiders and dangerous crocodiles. Possibly, I could be assaulted and robbed, or I might catch a bad tropical disease. My mother's lively fantasy was familiar to me.

Perhaps she was afraid that I might become the victim of a terrorist's bomb. I recalled that, a few days before I left home, German media had reported about political tumults in Sri Lanka. There were conflicts between the Hindu Tamils, living in the North and East of the island, and the Buddhist Sinhalese majority, governing the whole country. The Tamil minority was claiming more political participation. Since my arrival on this island, I hadn't seen or heard about any troubles. There was no reason for me to get upset. I was in good health, and I was staying in a peaceful place. It was essential to write this to my mother.

Hikkaduwa had a nice flair, the only disturbance being those pushy touts and traders. They were calling and pulling from all sides. They never tired of trying to have a conversation with you or lure you into their shops. The industrious young guys were asking the same questions over and over: "What's your name? What's your country? Are you traveling alone?"

"I can show you Hikkaduwa," one boy offered. "If you rent a motorbike, I will show you the whole island."

To make my irritation complete, he awkwardly fumbled about with his sarong. Then, making eyes at me, he whispered: "If you like, I will show you everything."

I was not interested in seeing "everything" and stepped into a shop to put an end to the discussion. Slowly, I adjusted to the darkness inside the hut, which had no windows. The air was thick with almost narcotizing scents from highly concentrated oils, Asian spices, and tropical fruit. Goods were stacked on shelves reaching up to the ceiling: all kinds of kitchenware, souvenirs, silver jewelry, and edibles.

An old man, who had been sitting in front of the shop, followed me inside. He paused for a moment in the doorway and watched me. Then he came in, handed me a glass of black tea and milk and invited me to sit down.

I accepted his offer and slowly sipped the tea, which was extremely sweet and steaming hot. He began to show me his goods, but I had no intention of buying anything. I looked around quite bored.

But then I discovered a ring that roused my interest. It was made exquisitely of silver with a big sapphire. I wanted to look at it more closely and picked it up. This was the signal for the old man to entangle me in a wide discussion about the price. He praised the high quality of the ring enthusiastically and looked through the sapphire, which caught the light that came in from the door. The sparkling was beautiful.

"Those sapphires are found in our country," he emphasized with pride, not missing a beat. "You will not get them at a lower price anywhere."

After he noticed my skeptical glance, he lowered the price: A special offer just for me. I had emptied my glass. The old man became increasingly pushy and insisted that I put the ring on one of my fingers. The price came down further – of course, only because it looked so beautiful on my hand. He would sell it to me at no profit, he complained.

Just at this moment, a new customer entered the shop. Against the light framing his body, I could see that he was wearing a sarong. The man's height was unusual compared to other locals; he was taller than the merchant by a head's size at least. Only when he was standing in front of me, I saw that he was no Sri Lankan. He was tanned almost as dark as the old man. His bare arm showed a tattoo shaped like a cannabis leaf and the fair, medium-length hair had been bleached by the sun and the saltwater. His deep-blue eyes studied me.

The shop owner seemed to know him and didn't look very happy about his visit. Immediately, he tried to push the young man into the corner with the food shelves.

Plain to see, he wanted to get rid of him to get on with our price arguments.

But the young tourist took his time examining the fruit and vegetables. I still held my empty tea glass, watching him. Suddenly he turned around and bent down beside me, whispering in my ear: "If you pay only half of what he wants, it will be too much even then."

He had spoken German. How had he known I was German? I hadn't said a single word since he entered the shop. He smiled, and his eyes twinkled at me. He handed some cash to the shop owner, who didn't even bargain, but returned the change.

I got up and left the disappointed old man, who was holding another steaming glass of tea in his hands. In the distance, I saw the German walk to the far end of Hikkaduwa, barefoot. No touts were followed him or tried to talk to him. Just a few local boys waved their hands at him from the opposite side of the street.

It would have been nice to spend the evening in one of Hikkaduwa's restaurants, but it was time to catch the bus back to Akuralla.

The sun was setting as I arrived at my hotel. The sky above the ocean was changing colors from full orange to blood-red, followed by a dark violet. My two Swiss sisters were already waiting for dinner, and I sat down at their table to join them.

Just then I caught sight of a local man approaching the hotel in fast steps. "Anura," he called out. Our manager left his kitchen and greeted the Sri Lankan with a friendly smile. But something must have happened. Anura's face suddenly expressed shock. As he listened to what the man had to say, both men stepped into the kitchen. We heard them argue excitedly in their language. After a while, the two of seemed to calm down a little. The visitor left, giving us a quick nod.

"There has been a terrible massacre," Anura reported to us a little later. "Tamil rebels have attacked a Sri Lankan army unit and killed thirteen Sinhalese soldiers. The public is very furious about it. The Sinhalese people will take revenge."

Hatred showed in his eyes. Anura was Sinhalese, as were most Sri Lankans living here on the Southwestern coast.

"You are in no danger," he assured us. "This assault has occurred in the North of our island. The Tamil rebels, who call themselves the Tamil Tigers, are living far away from here."

I was going on regular trips to Hikkaduwa now. A mixture of international travelers liked to meet in the restaurants and tea-shops there. They exchanged news and experiences, of which I had almost none. You could quickly make friends and have conversation, which was an advantage for people like me, traveling alone.

In one of those restaurants, I became acquainted with Maggie and Theresa. These English women came here every day. Maggie, the older one, was a vivacious person with lots of flair. She greeted everyone who sat down at her table. Her looks were quite remarkable. The hair was henna-red. Around her hips she had slung a colored scarf and she wore the kind of bodice the local women wore. The younger English woman, Theresa, was totally different. Most of the time, she sat quietly and shyly among the other guests. Theresa's dress code was simple and unimpressive. Her fair hair was bound in a plait down the back of her head.

I told the English girls that I was looking for a room in Hikkaduwa. I had hesitated until now because of the sales hustle on the beach. Maggie and Theresa suggested I look at their accommodation in Dodanduwa, a little fishing village within walking distance of Hikkaduwa. They said here was a room for rent.

We took the main street. Shortly after leaving behind the souvenir shops, restaurants, and hotels of Hikkaduwa, we could make out some huts of Dodanduwa. Here we found no touts and fewer tourists. The locals sitting in front of their huts showed no interest in us. The beach showing through the gaps between the little houses was deserted. No one was taking a swim.

We had reached our destination. From the street we discovered a small, hand-written "rooms for rent" sign. Between two little huts, a narrow path led to the beach. We walked along it and suddenly stood amid a beautiful tropical garden. Banana plants and fragrant flowers protected a little terrace, from which a few steps continued down to the beach.

Close by the steps stood three small houses, each painted light blue. A single table stood on the terrace; it was inhabited by a cat snoozing in the shade. A little boy was playing in the garden, and laundry was drying on a cord. At first, I had the impression that this was private premises, but Maggie and Theresa took a seat at the terrace table. Soon an old man stepped out of his own hut.

His hair was a dark gray. Walking wide-legged, he leaned back a little as he pushed his big, bare belly up, as if trying to prevent his sarong from slipping down. Together, we had some tea. The old man apologized that he had no cold drinks today, as the power supply had failed.

Mr. Sirisena put Maggie and Theresa up in one of the light-blue houses. The second house inhabited by a German who had left for Colombo for a few days. The third accommodation stood empty, so the owner was only too pleased to fetch the key and show it to me.

It was a light, single room with a bed and a table. In a separate niche, luckily, I found an indoor bathroom. A rusty pipe emerging from the wall appeared to be the shower. A gully channel crossed concrete floor, draining valuable water to the outside through a hole at the bottom of the wall, to the benefit of the garden. Right at the outlet grew opulent banana trees. The room had a big window allowing a beautiful sight onto the beach, and the breeze cooled down the heat pleasantly.

In a second, the proprietor and I settled our agreement. Then I went back to Akuralla to quit my room there. The next day, I moved to my green oasis in Dodanduwa.

*

The name of my new host was Mr. Sirisena. Together with his wife and his three children, he lived in a hut made from wood and woven palm leaves. It too had only one room, which served as living room and bedroom. The cooking was done outside on a stone stove on the bare ground. This area was separated from the garden by a bamboo fence.

The proprietor's elder son was hardly ever seen; apparently he had a job elsewhere. His daughter, however – a pretty and cheerful girl – liked to be in the garden. But as soon as we went out to the terrace, the girl retreated into the family hut. Occasionally, she took a nosy peek out of the hut to observe us. She seemed very interested in our way of dressing, which was quite unrestricted by any conventions. Whenever we saw her, we waved at her to join us at our table. Then she felt caught and smiled at us, feeling ashamed, and with an impish flash in her eyes hid again in her hut. This was a pity, because we would have enjoyed talking with her. Only now I became aware that my contacts with local people had been limited exclusively to males. The only conversation we had with a family member was with the youngest, a six-year-old boy who helped serve our meals.

Mr. Sirisena's wife, as well, stayed back, behaving modestly. She was an elderly, big-proportioned woman with gray hair, which she wore in a big bun on her neck. Just like her husband, she bent backwards slightly while walking, and her big, dark belly showed between her tightly buttoned bodice and her colorful wraparound skirt.

She went into the garden only after the guests had left the terrace. Sometimes I watched her from my room as she quietly went about her daily tasks: scrubbing laundry on a flat stone by the well or sweeping the sand off the stone slabs.

The Sinhalese woman didn't speak English. Upali, the youngest son, served as our translator. Mr. Sirisena's wife would utter a few English words only occasionally. Whenever the little boy tried to tell her our concerns, she would smile in a friendly manner and wiggle her head. In Sri Lanka this means that she consented. It was no nodding or shaking her head, but rather she would bend her head to one shoulder and then to the other repeatedly.

The family treated us quite informally. There was no menu; instead, Mr. Sirisena took his daily walk to the beach and bought for us fresh tuna, shark or smaller seafood, or whatever catches had been brought ashore that day by the fishermen. If we had no preference, the national dish consisting of rice and curry was served. In fact, at every meal we had at least five different very-hot vegetable curries, together with brown rice.

"It's not hot," Upali swore every time he set a dish in front of us. He didn't refer to the heat, of course, but to the spiciness. From a distance, he would observe us with some amusement as we started to sweat and gasp. For relief from the fire, Mrs. Sirisena had placed a big bowl of grated coconut on our table. The coconut helped soothe the burn, and we gratefully and generously made use of it.

Meanwhile, the six-year-old boy was nibbling chilies like sweets, grinning at us.

Every night, Mr. Sirisena stayed awake until his guests had retreated to their bedrooms. Only then did he lay down to sleep on the wooden table where earlier we had eaten our dinner. He assured us repeatedly that he slept better outside than in the stuffy family hut, but in fact I had the feeling he wanted to guard this place and his guests.

Sometimes the electricity went off at night, so I always had my flashlight at my side. Then I would listen to the various noises coming through the window from outside – rushing waves, rustling palm fronds, chirping crickets, barking dogs – and to Mr. Sirisena, who softly snored on the terrace. Finally, I fell into a deep sleep, feeling safe.

From morning till noon, I savored the calmness by the seaside. In Dodanduwa there were no souvenir shops, or touts pestering people. Only now and then did a tourist show up, usually on a walk along the shore from Hikkaduwa.

Lying in the sand, I watched a few skinny black cows doze in the shade of a palm tree. One of them was chewing a piece of newspaper. Theresa came to the terrace, and Maggie was jogging along the beach. She seemed to be in perpetual motion. Around noon, Maggie got bored, and so the three of us headed for Hikkaduwa on foot.

We strolled along the main street, which took quite some time. Again, the unavoidable boys besieged us. Theresa got angry, but Maggie had a provocative way of dealing with the pushy guys. She spoke to each to them in a seductive voice, and patiently answered their constantly repeated questions. The boys maneuvered her into every jewelry shop, batik shop, or boutique. Maggie bought nothing; she just liked to flirt with the boys. After they had run out of questions, it was her turn to make inquiries.

"Have you grown up in Hikkaduwa?" she asked a roughly eighteen-year-old jewelry merchant. He affirmed by wiggling his head.

"Surely you have a cute little girlfriend," Maggie looked him up and down.

"No, I don't have a girlfriend," the boy replied. "Our girls are different from the tourist girls from Western countries. Too bad!"

The young Sri Lankan was sticking with Maggie. He accompanied us to the entrance of the restaurant we had chosen. There, he could proceed no further. Jewelry merchants and other locals had to stay outside because the restaurant owners feared that their guests might feel disturbed or even molested.

Maggie had already forgotten the young beach boy. By now she was paying her sole attention to a fair-haired man from Colorado, sitting at the table next to us. After a little while she left Theresa and me and joined him. He ordered beer for both.

Beer meant luxury to the Sri Lankans. It came in big bottles, and waiters would pour it as if it were a delicate and expensive wine. Maggie seemed to be having lots of fun, enjoying the beer in generous amounts. The sun had set by now and Theresa was urging her to come along with us. Maggie wouldn't think of breaking away. The more her alcohol level increased, the more effort she put into her flirtation with the fair-haired American. So, Theresa and I got on our way home without her.

Once we had left behind the restaurants and shops, the road to Dodanduwa grew darker and darker. By nighttime, all the lights in the houses had been extinguished. Fortunately, Therese had taken along her flashlight.

Stray, hungry dogs with dirty fur followed us. One of them was bleeding from a head wound. The animal was limping and growled at us repeatedly. We tried to ignore it, but often Theresa had to direct the flashlight beam into its eyes to stop it from getting nearer. We were very relieved when we arrived safely at our guest house.

Maggie didn't return until noon the next day. Her henna-red hair dangled, and her face looked pale and tired after an obviously sleepless night. She looked at us as if we were strangers. Without speaking a word, she walked past us and into her room. When she showed up again in the afternoon, we could see she was feeling sick.

This night Maggie did not go to Hikkaduwa. She decided to spend a quiet evening on our terrace for a change.

"I bought a bottle of whisky from a tourist I met," Maggie revealed "We should spoil ourselves tonight," she suggested.

"Mr. Sirisena, please have a drink with us," she invited our host. "You won't have Scotch whisky in Sri Lanka very often!"

Mr. Sirisena refused disapprovingly. But after his wife and children had gone to bed, he joined us at the table.

"My family must not see me drinking," he whispered to us as the English woman poured our drinks. "I have to be an idol to my children. They don't know much about alcohol. They only see the tourists turn crazy now and then."

But he liked the Scotch whisky's taste on his tongue, and he emptied his glass in one big gulp.

"This tastes much better than arrack," Mr. Sirisena praised our whisky.

The drinks had their effect on Mr. Sirisena. Normally he was very reserved. But he was not used to alcohol. Getting sentimental, he started to tell tales about former times.

"When I was a little boy," he began, "Hikkaduwa was a sleepy little village. My father was a fisherman. We had almost no money, but always enough to eat. Fish we got from the sea and our mother planted bananas, mangos, papayas and vegetables in our garden. Being a good climber, I had to harvest coconuts from the top of the palm trees. And by trading fish with the peasants, we had enough rice in return."

Mr. Sirisena shoved his glass to Maggie to refill it.

"I remember the first tourists coming to Sri Lanka," he continued. "They arrived wearing their backpacks, the young white men having long hair and beards. Later, young women visited our island, wearing almost no clothes while having a swim in the ocean. From that moment my father forbade me to walk to the beach of Hikkaduwa. The young strangers spent their time lying in the sun. They were living with the fishermen and rice farmers and paid them well for food and accommodation. Some of the locals really liked to have them for their guests. My family never let rooms to tourists, because my father didn't approve of them. He was saying that they would spoil our way of thinking. And meanwhile, those strange visitors are dominating our way of life in and around Hikkaduwa. My father died a long time ago. Sometimes I am glad that he doesn't have to witness what is happening to our villages and their inhabitants."

"We tourists have not only done harm to your way of life," Maggie replied. "We bring money to you. And you and your family are living off your guests from other countries."

"This is correct," Mr. Sirisena agreed. "We are getting along well. But sometimes I worry about my children. I don't want my sons to become like those Hikkaduwa beach boys. They won't go to school any longer, and some of them are dealing with drugs. Many of them are even selling their bodies to the white visitors. We fathers are helpless. Those boys make as much money in one day as our fishermen or rice farmers earn after a month of work. This way of life is not good for our sons."

"You are only talking about your sons. What's about your daughter?" Maggie insisted. "We hardly ever see her. I know that she speaks English quite well. She is an educated young woman. I'd really like to talk to her, but she seems to avoid us."

"My daughter will marry soon," Mr. Sirisena replied. "Until then, she will be kept away from any guests. Girls who associate with foreigners too closely will not marry into good families. This marriage has already been arranged with the bridegroom's father. In a few days, my daughter will get to know her future husband. I have found a good husband for her. He is older than her and quite experienced."

"You have promised your daughter to a man older than her, and she does not even know him?! What, if she doesn't like him?!" Maggie said, really inflamed.

"She will have a good life at his side, if she behaves like a decent wife," Mr. Sirisena retorted. "In Sri Lanka, a lot of things are different from Europe."

Mr. Sirisena said thank you for the drinks and went to bed. This night, he did not sleep on the table on our terrace, but went to his family's hut.

Next morning, I felt this typical headache: good whisky but too much of it. My guts revolted, and my room was unbearably muggy. Much dazed, I opened the shutters, hoping that the fresh breeze from the sea might reset my brain to normal.

A young man wearing a sarong was strolling along the beach, looking towards the sea. Ocean spray was splashing on his feet.

His fair hair shone in the sun. I recognized the cannabis-leaf tattoo on his shoulder. It was the guy from the jewelry shop where I had seen the sapphire ring. He had to be Christian, living in the third little house owned by our host. Maggie had mentioned, that the German would return from Colombo today. And she had told me that Chris had been traveling through Sri Lanka and India for more than a year.

"Most of his time he spends with the local people," she said. "We don't see much of him."

Chris did not take breakfast with us, but with Mr. Sirisena at a little table beside the kitchen. While we were being served toast in the mornings, he would already have rice and dhal, an extremely hot curry dish of red lentils. According to local habits, he didn't use any cutlery. His right hand formed rice and soft-boiled lentils into little portions, which he shoved into his mouth. After breakfast, Upali placed a bowl of water and lemon bits on the table, so that their guest could clean his hand.

Chris spent a lot of time on our terrace. Now and then he went to Hikkaduwa, but he would not be gone for long. Maggie had watched him talk to the local boys there. The little touts seemed to know him well.

Like the local women, Chris did his laundry on a flat stone beside the well. In the evenings he ate rice and curry in Mr. Sirisena's company. Our host's wife and children took their meals inside the hut. Amazingly, to me, Chris didn't seem to mind the hot dishes.

"My taste has gotten used to the pungency," he once told me. "And besides, the spices protect you from various diseases."

In fact, when I took a bite from his meal, I had the feeling of really being disinfected.

Maggie tended to return from her patrols through Hikkaduwa's restaurants late at night. Theresa no longer accompanied her. She went to her room early in the evenings to read or write letters to people back home.

I had the impression that the girl was longing for her friends in England.

I often sat with Chris on the terrace. He told me that he, too, had recognized me immediately from the jewelry shop in Hikkaduwa, where to his amusement I had proven inexperienced in bargaining. He made gentle fun of my food sensitivity. The more we got to know each other, the more intriguing our evening conversations became.

While an oil lamp shined dimly, Chris told me about his journeys. He was fascinated by India, and particularly by the beach parties in Goa where travelers of many nationalities met at Christmas.

"You see a lot of people there, whom you have met previously somewhere in Asia," he reported. "Maybe spending Christmas in Goa is an opportunity for travelers and dropouts to avoid loneliness. This is a meeting place for those lonesome souls, who prefer having a party under some palm trees to singing under a Christmas tree."

Chris also described Northern India. He spoke of Rajasthan with its splendid temples, of camel rides in the Desert of Thar, of the desert itself and the women in brightly colored gowns – such a contrast to the endless beige of the sand dunes. But he was most enthused about a little fishing village on the Eastern shore of Sri Lanka, where you could live in palm-leaf huts for almost no money.

"I can't even describe what is pulling me towards this place. Maybe it's the gorgeous bay, or the peaceful life the people are leading there. There is not much you can do in Arugam Bay. But I am a dreamer; I can stand the boredom under palm trees." Chris would tell me about a special family with whom he had become acquainted in Arugam Bay.

28

"They are five Tamil brothers living in Sooriya's Beach Hut. They behave in a very special way compared to all the other Sri Lankan locals I've ever met – especially Sooriya, the oldest brother. Some magic emanates from him that I cannot explain. Sooriya has lots of friends all over the world, and they visit him at quite regular intervals."

Actually, I was unable to imagine what could be so special about this Tamil guy. But somehow, Chris' story roused my interest.

I wanted to stay a little longer in Dodanduwa, but later I would set out for the East Coast. Chris was just telling me about a religious celebration in Kataragama, which would start soon, when Maggie and Mr. Sirisena joined us.

"Actually, the Perahera is a Tamil celebration," Chris explained. "The Hindus will pray to their god, Murugan, in Kataragama, seeking to gain forgiveness for the bad deeds they have committed during the previous year. The believers will torment and mortify themselves, which is not a sight for sensitive souls to see."

"You really should attend it," Mr. Sirisena interjected. "Those Tamil believers should torment themselves even more for the harm they do to our country. But the temple grounds in Kataragama are also sacred to Buddhists and Muslims. During the Perahera period, all hostilities between Sinhalese people and the Tamils are being interrupted. Buddhists and Hindus celebrate together."

Maggie was listening, concentrating closely. She was fascinated by the description of men driving iron hooks through their own flesh, or walking across red-hot coals, having fallen into trance.

"Obviously this is not just another boring tourist event," she chimed in.

Maggie and I decided to go along to Kataragama with Chris. I would not return to Dodanduwa but travel northeastward to Arugam Bay after the festivities. Somehow, I was compelled to go there. Mr. Sirisena reacted with shock when I informed him.

"Arugam Bay is East Coast territory. This is Tamil area," he warned me. "The riots there are increasing. You are in no danger here in the West of the island. The Eastern territories are not safe for tourists any longer."

Indeed, I recently had heard about bombings in Colombo. Foreign travelers who had arrived only a few days ago told me. Media in their home countries had provided them with fresh news, while we tourists, who had come here weeks ago, had to depend on less reliable sources of information.

At Mr. Sirisena's place, we had no television, and none of us was able to interpret the Sinhalese radio news. Of course, the Sri Lankans avoided talking to tourists about politics. Nobody wanted to alarm their foreign guests. But in this case, Mr. Sirisena had decided, it was better to warn me.

"Northern Tamil territory has been closed to tourists by now," he reported. "And the East Coast has been declared a crisis area as well. It is inhabited by Tamils, Sinhalese people, and Muslims. Nobody can say at what time the riots will arrive there. It is much too dangerous to travel to Arugam Bay!"

After Mr. Sirisena had left to fetch fresh tea for us, Chris declared that he was not impressed in the least by those warnings.

"I've known this old Sinhalese for quite a long time," he said with a grin in his face. "Every time I have told him I was going to the East Coast, he would advise me against leaving. He wants to keep permanent guests. Once, he declared that the East Coast was expecting a cyclone that might destroy the whole area. He claimed that the whirlwind, although still hovering above the sea, could change its direction towards the island at any time. Another time he warned me that cholera had broken out in the East. Whenever I arrived in little Arugam Bay, everything was calm and safe. Never has anything unusual happened there. It is true, that people of various religious backgrounds are living in this place, but all of them get along peacefully. Only yesterday I met an acquaintance who has just returned from Arugam Bay. Don't worry. Everything will be alright there, as always."

*

By the time we left Dodanduwa, my backpack had lost some weight. Warm clothing such as jeans, a jacket, and a solid pair of shoes, I left behind with Mr. Sirisena. I would not need them in this island climate; they were unnecessary luggage.

My host took them from me only too gladly, now knowing that I would return.

Chris stopped the local bus and luckily, we got hold of a bench with enough space for Maggie, Chris, and me. We had a ride along the shore. The morning sun was reflecting in the smooth waves. Fishermen were pulling their multi-colored catamarans ashore.

After some time, we reached Galle, a town with an ancient harbor. From afar, we had been able to identify the fortress, whose wall was overgrown with grass. This wall surrounded the ancient town center. Towers and big white buildings from the Dutch colonial era were much taller than the yellow-brown houses with brick roofs. It still was early morning and already the bus station bustled with activity. Many goods were being dispatched on oxcarts or by men with long rods resting across their shoulders, loaded on either side. And quite a few women were balancing heavy baskets on their heads. Bicycles were overloaded in such a way that I wondered if they would ever reach their destinations.

Traders were offering refreshments and small dishes to the travelers in the busses. Only few tourists were there around this time of the day, so we were besieged immediately. Christian's fair hair and Maggie's tuft of glowing orange, attracted full attention.

Chris bought us some flatbread filled with hot spicy vegetables along with several bottles of soda water. The trader gave an unsatisfied grunt when Chris handed over the money. There was no time left for bargaining, because after just a few minutes, the bus continued its ride.

At every stop, people stepped in. The inside got more and more, and in addition I had the feeling that we were being observed crowded. The bus stopped in every village. At one point, the bus came to a halt so abruptly that riders could not grab hold of anything in time. A young guy got hurled to Maggie's lap. Hurriedly, he tried to get up again, but his sarong got entangled in the buckle of Maggie's belt. Hectically, he pulled at his cloth, which started to slip downwards. At last he was able to free himself and disappeared among the passengers, both his hands clinging to his sarong.

"I've always suspected that they're wearing nothing underneath," Maggie remarked with a grin.

A few stops later an elderly Buddhist monk mounted our bus. Carefully, he lifted his gown a little and slowly ascended, step by step. Respectfully, the passengers gave way to him. He walked straight towards us and came to a halt in front of Christian. Saying not a single word, he glanced out the window above our heads. I wondered why our bus didn't resume our journey. The driver was looking at us reproachfully. Also, all the other passengers were scrutinizing us.

With a sigh, Christian got up from his seat. His gaze went to a sign fixed to the wall above our seats. "For monks only," it said in Sri Lankan and English, meaning that our bench was to be kept free for monks. But now that Christian had left his seat, the monk still stood unmoving in front of us two women.

"He will not seat himself between two white women," Chris declared.

Maggie and I got up as well, the passengers moved together more closely, and we all tried to hold on. Finally, the monk sat down on the bench. Immediately, the bus continued on its way.

I was looking out the window next to me. Close to the shore, huge wooden posts rose from the sea. They must have been more than fifteen feet in height; halfway up, they had narrow crossbeams. On those branches, fishermen had taken a seat and thrown out their rods. Tourists stood around on the beach, taking pictures; a local boy collected some rupees for allowing them to do so.

By now it was midday and we had arrived at Hambantota. Here the bus driver took his break. Alongside the bus stop there was a tea shop. The passengers departed and entered the wooden hut. Chris, Maggie, and I followed them. We sat down at a table where already a family with their little daughter had taken seats. Shyly, the girl moved closer to her mother, but her big, dark-brown eyes watched us keenly.

Of course, the shopkeeper and his wife had been prepared for our stop. Quickly they served us rice and curry in battered tin bowls. The host's wife turned to us with a questioning look, and after Chris wiggled his head in consent, she served us a meal as well. There was no cutlery. The local guests and Chris started to eat, but I hesitated for a moment.

The little girl looked at me inquiringly. She scooped up a small portion of curry with her right hand and stuffed the undefinable vegetable mush into her mouth. Her eyes rolled in delight. As a child, I always wanted to eat with my fingers and poke them into any food. But even in Sri Lanka you had to obey to certain table manners. As soon as the girl stopped eating and started to play with the rice absentmindedly, her mother reproached her with a stern look.

The shopkeeper's wife noticed my hesitation, and with a smile she placed a tin spoon beside my plate. The little girl observed my European eating habits with amazement.

Our food was only lukewarm, but heat developed rapidly in my mouth due to the spices. When I had too much of the hot vegetable, I immediately started to cough.

In addition to the rice and the curry, we were also served chapati, a kind of flat bread made of whole wheat flour. After I had taken the side-dish, the cute little girl stopped eating. Her eyes darkened. Also, all the other guests were staring at me.

"Have I made a mistake?" I asked Chris, slightly irritated.

"You took the chapati with your left hand," he informed me. The Sri Lankans take food to their mouths with their right hand only. For them, the left hand is impure. They use it for other purposes."

Still, I continued to look at him in confusion.

"Haven't you noticed that in Sri Lankan toilets, the tap for cleaning your hand is on the left side? You'll find toilet paper only in tourist hotels, being a special luxury," Chris explained to me, grinning widely.

I put down my spoon and immediately took up the bread with my right hand. Now the girl looked satisfied and continued eating.

The local people ate their meals in a hurry. I had eaten only half of my dish when the driver got up. Immediately, the passengers followed him outside, including Maggie, Chris and me. All of us mounted the bus quickly.

At the end of the coastal road, we took a turn towards interior Sri Lanka. Leaving the seaside, the landscape was changing. Closer to the ocean, we had passed green coconut palm trees, but by now only dry shrubs were growing from the arid ground. The sun was beating down on our bus, showing no mercy. Inside, the heat was getting unbearable. I was as unable to move an inch in the overcrowded vehicle.

Chris stood a little apart from me. Behind me, a local man stood very close to my back. I admit, there was not much space for anyone, but the Sri Lankan pressed himself closer to me than necessary. I tried to move away, but after the next bend, I felt his body move close to me. He was gazing out the window with innocent looking eyes. Suddenly, Chris noticed I was feeling uncomfortable.

"Don't you dare come near my wife!" he suddenly yelled in a threatening voice. The passengers looked shocked. Chris was much taller than the local men. The fair-haired German stared at the guy with furious eyes. Those, who understood the words, now threw reproachful glances at their compatriot. He looked frightened at being caught and moved away from me abruptly. Ashamed, he hid the front of his sarong behind his bag. Of course, Chris had taken advantage of his knowledge that in Sri Lanka it is morally disapproved of to touch another man's wife.

"Sorry, Madam," a Sri Lankan man in Western clothing addressed me in almost perfect English. "I feel ashamed for this man."

He got up and politely offered his seat to me. The man who had insulted me felt the disdain of our fellow passengers. He left the bus at the following stop.

Finally, we came to Tissamaharama. The town was crowded with many pilgrims taking part in the Pāda Yātra, a sacred foot pilgrimage in Sri Lanka. Tens of thousands make all or part of the arduous journey on foot from Jaffna in the north to Kataragama in the south. Busses decorated with flower garlands and green twigs departed town every five minutes. We squeezed ourselves into one of them.

Trucks stuffed with many people struggled in the traffic. They were painted in many colors elaborately decorated. To us, they looked like circus wagons. Hundreds of pilgrims had decided to make the journey to Kataragama on foot, including, families with children, mostly dressed in orange, and women carrying baskets of flowers and fruit on their heads. Buddhist monks, also in orange gowns, walked with them, and many of the monks had opened their black umbrellas to protect their shaved heads from the scorching sun. Muslims participated as well, dressed in white and with little caps on their heads. And, of course, there were the sadhus, those strange Hindu ascetics, revered as holy men.

Mostly the sadhus wore close to nothing and walked barefoot. One of them, an old man, wore only a cord with a rag around his skinny hips. The rag had been pulled through between his thighs and fixed to the cord in front and behind. The man's skinny, dark torso had been smeared with white ashes. His matted hair was long enough to touch his waist. Another sadhu traversed the length of the pilgrimage on his knees, with only a few rags wrapped around his knees. This penance was his way of showing his remorse for having done wrong in the past. Other pilgrims showed him respect by putting together their palms and moving their closed hands to their foreheads. Some touched his feet in veneration.

Our bus moved along slowly. We passed a young man carrying a heavy wooden yoke on his shoulders; he had to balance it continuously.

At last we had arrived at Kataragama. The square in front of the temple grounds hosted a fair. At many tables, vendors sold sacred offerings consisting of colorful flower garlands, lotus blossoms, tropical fruit and various sweets, which they had brought along in baskets. Food huts made of wood and palm leaves served snacks. People skilled in palmistry tried to lure customers. Drummers and flute-players enlivened the square.

At the entrance to the temple area we took off our shoes and stepped barefoot through a huge gate onto the sacred grounds.

The sour smell of fermented coconut milk hovered about the temple grounds. Believers were smashing coconuts in a depression in the ground to bring pieces to the temple's sacrifice area.

In front of a Hindu temple, an old Sadhu sat on the parched ground, his legs folded in the lotus position. His long white hair was gathered in a big clotted ball on top of his head.

A look at his face shocked me. His open mouth, ringed by a likewise white and straggly beard and mustache, looked like a gap. His tongue protruded horizontally from his mouth. He had driven iron darts through both of his cheeks as well as through his tongue, keeping the dry flesh in the aforementioned position. His eyes were wide open and bloodshot, and his gaze was empty.

"Many Hindus will keep their promises they give in times of suffering and need," Chris told me.

Maggie couldn't tear herself away from the old sadhu who stared at her, motionless. His eyes seemed to look right through her. But soon she was distracted by a young man slowly and carefully approaching the temple. He was murmuring mantras. His head was shaven and his torso naked. He had driven small iron hooks into the flesh of his breast, and red cords were fixed to those hooks. On every cord a lemon was dangling, at least twenty of them in sum. The scene was surreal.

We passed temples where the faithful put down their offerings: Hindus at their colorful and richly crafted temples, and Buddhists at a snow-white, dome-shaped dagoba.

Finally, we arrived at a field where thousands of pilgrims had gathered. Men threw themselves on the ground in ecstasy and rolled in the dust. Others sat motionless and in meditation in the dirt, their legs crossed in lotus position.

Several big wooden structures had been erected on the square. We had seen them from afar. As we came closer, we saw a young man suspended horizontally, about six or seven feet above the ground, his face pointing toward the ground. His only coverage was a red loincloth. The man's torso shined with sweat in the seething sun. His ankles were slung in cords decorated with freshly cut, green twigs. Near his shoulder blades, iron hooks had been driven through the skin of his back. Those hooks carried the penitent's whole weight, his skin stretched away from his flesh. No blood was visible, and his face showed no pain. A boy gave the atoning man some water to drink and dried his sweaty forehead. A long row of pilgrims passed by the penitent. He blessed each of them by painting a dot of ashes on their foreheads. By now I had an urgent wish to leave this scene and digest the experience. This man's deeply felt mortification had been quite different than anything I'd seen in any television documentary. Chris and I took a walk to the nearby river. We would meet Maggie in the evening.

Along the riverside, believers were taking their baths. They went into the water no farther than to their hips and poured water over their heads and shoulders. Some of the pilgrims lay on the dry grass of adjacent meadow. Families took a nap with their children in the shade of a few trees. Chris and I listened to the rhythmical beats of drums and high-pitched whistles from across the river. Over there, men were dancing themselves into a trance until the break of dusk. Dancing ecstatically and accompanied by the musicians, they moved toward the temple grounds.

After the sun had set, the temple area started to glow with colorful light arrangements. Spots and little lightbulbs had been fixed to the white walls. Torches dimly illuminated the wooden constructions from which the penitents still hung by their iron hooks. Oil-lamps shed a little light on the paths. Little bulbs in many colors decorated the bare branches of a dead tree, giving an illusion of frozen fireworks against the night sky.

Meanwhile, many people had come to stand alongside the path, where the procession's celebratory highlight was supposed to take place. The first few torch bearers appeared, followed by graceful young female dancers dressed in saris rich with golden embroidery. Men in fabulous costumes walked on long stilts. Drummers constantly beat hypnotic rhythms. Half-naked men with frightening masks whirled around them.

Finally, elephants entered the scene – mighty animals adorned with colorful brocade covers. Their heads had been wrapped in masks of fine fabric, which also covered their huge ears and their trunks. Holes had been cut out for their eyes, which made the animals look spooky. The elephants were led by their guards, the mahouts, who held long sticks. At the end of the elephant procession, the biggest and most splendid animal appeared through the temple gates. This elephant's cover was regally embroidered with golden threads; countless small lightbulbs shined from it. From far away, we watched the big animal come closer, beaming impressively. On its back, we discovered a car battery, disclosing the secret of its energy source.

By the time we left the procession, the full moon was high in the sky, yet the penitents were still hung from their wooden bars. Other pilgrims surrounded them, sweeping burning torches across their bodies. The firelight reflected in their dark eyes. I could smell burnt hair, but not one of the men showed any burns.

Stunned, I followed Chris back to the river. Only the pale moonlight lit the arid meadow was. Everywhere, exhausted people were sleeping on the dry grass. We placed ourselves beneath a tree. Only for a moment did I give any thought to poisonous snakes or scorpions. The Sri Lankans seemed not to waste any time on such worries.

This was a different Sri Lanka - far away from the milling tourist crowds. Nearby, a family had settled down. The children cuddled to their mother's sari, asleep. From far being still could hear the night reverberated with hypnotic drumbeats. I fell into a restless dream in which horribly grimacing faces haunted me.

Early morning sunbeams woke me, and happily my nightmare had disappeared. Pilgrims were bathing in the glinting waters of the Menik Ganga. Chris went into the water in his sarong. He dived under the surface with loud snorts, and when he surfaced, he poured the cool water over his head and shoulders, shaking his fair hair. On the shore, a few young local girls were watching Chris, shamefully laughing and whispering. It seems that in every culture despite various religions and different upbringing, teenagers behave much the same.

We met Maggie late in the morning. She had made a new acquaintance, a huge guy with tanned skin and muscular body. Maggie had decided to stay another night in Kataragama. For me, it was time to move on.

"I'm sure you will never forget your stay in Arugam Bay," Chris told me when we parted. "Please give my regards to Sooriya and his brothers."

Chris would have liked to come along so much, but his visa for Sri Lanka had almost expired.

"A week from now I will take a flight back to India," he said. "I will spend Christmas in Goa, for sure. But there is lots of time until then. Perhaps we will meet there?"

*

The local passengers looked at me with interest when I got onto the bus heading for Arugam Bay. I was the only tourist taking a bus toward eastern Sri Lanka. I tried to ignore their enquiring glances.

Dead tired from all the new impressions in Kataragama, I looked out of the windows, emptyheaded. An elephant was pulling a log across the street. Light and pink spots dotted his grey trunk. His skin bore sores from the heavy work he had to do. His guide urged him on impatiently, hitting his legs with a club, showing no pity. The processions in Kataragama were over. This was everyday life for the majestic giants.

I had planned to buy new provisions for myself the next bus stop. A little boy spotted me and offered peanuts wrapped in newspaper. I bought one packet and gave him a banknote. Awkwardly, the little guy rummaged about in his pockets until suddenly the driver started our bus again. Like a snake, the kid disappeared in the crowd, keeping my change. Chris had been so right when he told me that I had a lot yet to learn. Listlessly, I nibbled at the peanuts.

Inside the bus, it was unbearably warm. Even the wind coming in from the open windows provided no relief. The dirty dust from the road forced its way into the vehicle and covered my skin and lips with a brown-yellow layer. I was thirsty, and all I possessed were salty nuts.

The inside of our bus looked like a marketplace. Passengers carried all kinds of food, goods and animals. In the front, bananas and a huge sack of coconuts had been deposited. Beside me, a woman held a chicken on her lap. She stroked the hen incessantly to calm it down. I was thirsty and my mouth parched.

The stench of sweat and overripe fruit intensified the oppressive, muggy air in our bus. My glance fell on a man sitting in the front. He stared at me incessantly with a deeply stern expression. Suddenly he got up and seemingly came aggressively toward me. In his hands he held a machete, making me truly afraid. I was looking around for help, but the other passengers didn't move, waiting to see what would happen. Maybe the man is a Tamil! I thought in panic. We had entered Tamil territory by now. Mr. Sirisena had warned me.

Without saying a word, the man came to a halt beside my seat. I didn't dare to look at him, but only saw the big knife in his hand. Slowly he raised his arm and swung back. I closed my eyes and then heard a dull thud. Only when I opened my eyes again did I notice the coconut he held. He opened it skillfully with the machete and gave it to me as a gift. Greatly relieved I accepted it gratefully and drank its lukewarm juice. Never have I been more refreshed by anything. The oily fluid gave me back my spirits.

The man with the machete was still standing beside me. I took a few rupees from my pocket to pay him, but he refused. I was amazed. But he pointed toward my luggage, and he imitated smoking with two fingers. Now I got it. He had seen my cigarettes in my bag. I gave him my pack to take some out.

He thanked me politely and took all cigarettes to share them generously with other passengers. Shortly after, the men were smoking with relish and smiled friendly at me - and, of course, the air inside became worse than before.

Now an old woman dared to offer me her goods. In front of her she had placed some clay bowls, each covered with newspaper. She handed me one of those bowls, holding her forefingers to her head imitating horns.

"Curd, curd," she said to me.

"Yoghurt from water buffalo, with honey, very, very good," the man beside her explained.

My provisions had come to me finally. The buffalo yoghurt tasted excellent, and for dessert the old woman gave me bananas as a gift.

Meanwhile, the bus had to take increasing efforts to get ahead on the bumpy road. We passed a water reservoir. On its banks a swarm of pink flamingos rested. Some herons rose toward the sky. The hot air flickered in the midday sun. Occasionally, our driver had to stop at a crossing. Hardly any villages were around.

It was late afternoon when we came to a small place that we were told was the end of the road. I had hardly stepped out of the bus when a boy addressed me.

"Hotel, Madam?"

I declined and asked him for a connection to the East Coast.

"Tomorrow morning," the boy replied and repeated his previous question unperturbed: "Hotel, Madam?"

Another bus driver confirmed that the last bus for the East Coast had left already. So, I had no choice but to spend the night in the only hotel in this place.

It seemed an exaggeration to call this simple building a hotel. Of course, its owner was quite aware that I had no alternative, and he charged me for the shabby room accordingly.

Totally exhausted, I dropped on the bed. I had in mind to go to sleep early, so as not to miss the morning bus. After I had covered myself with the thin blanket, I noticed a small elevation underneath. A dark shadow started to move. In a shock, I threw back the blanket. There in front of me sat a big fat spider with long and hairy legs.

With a leap I jumped out of my bed. Since my arrival in Sri Lanka, one of my biggest fears had been to encounter spiders like this one. I couldn't help but recall Brigitte's horror tales of dangerous tarantulas. I was not capable of killing this fleshy monster!

Would its poison be strong enough to kill me? Possibly the spider was totally harmless. Maybe this creature was just as afraid of me as I was of it. But this I doubted.

Slowly I retreated toward the door and opened it. Outside, nobody was to be seen. At that moment, the hairy representative of Arachnida began to move. It descended from the bed pole and disappeared in the darkness under my bed. I could not find a stick or broom with which to chase it out of its hiding place. Unnerved, I pushed the heavy bed through the room, which caused a hell of a noise.

I had discovered the spider again, and it seemed to be scrutinizing me as well. With all the courage I could summon, I grabbed a towel and tried to sweep it out of my room. But the beast held on to the cloth, took an elegant flight over my head, and made a safe landing back on my soft mattress. Quickly the crawler sought shelter under my blanket. I saw its shadow again. It did not move. Driven to despair, I grabbed the blanket and threw it and the spider out into the back yard. With my foot, I slammed the door shut and locked it, just in case my hairy friend tried to reenter.

Bathed in sweat, I scanned every inch inside. Although no more spiders or insects revealed themselves, I could not sleep. After this night, there was no doubt that back in Germany I was no longer going to be scared of simple, harmless house spiders. Never ever!

After sunrise, I immediately checked out of my hotel, although the manager tried to assure me that there was enough time left for breakfast. Shaking his head, he watched me leave, holding my blanket in his hands.

I entered a little tea-shop right beside the bus stop. The owner was sitting at the only table inside, obviously bored. Immediately he dusted the table and offered me a seat. I took tea and rotis, a kind of flat bread, and never took my eyes off the bus stop.

No way would I spend another night in this awful place! Of course, the hotel owner had been right. It took another two hours before the bus showed up.

Thank God I could continue my trip! We drove through an arid region. Shrubs with big thorns were skirted either side of the road. Sometimes I saw crowds of flying foxes hanging head down from the few knotty trees. These bats looked quite spooky.

In this region, there were no villages or towns. The road was in very poor condition, and the bus moved at walking speed. Our driver seemed to have doubts in his faith for Buddha, and he drove very carefully to save his vehicle's axles. I was sure we were near our destination by now, but the ride stretched on endlessly. Only few passengers were left. They clung to the seat backs in front of them as our bus crept across potholes and deep furrows. At times our bus got into quite a dangerous slant.

At last we arrived at a city called Pottuvil. Its streets were dusty. Pedestrians stepped aside to let us pass. Children welcomed us and waved gayly. The only creature unimpressed by our bus was a skinny cow. It lay on the street and refused to move. The cow, being holy to Hindi believers, did not even lift its head when the bus stopped right in front of it.

"This is terminus," the driver said to me, after he noticed that I was hesitating to leave my seat. Where was the ocean? Had we really reached the East Coast?

This place consisted of only a few neglected houses and half broken shacks. At first sight, there appeared to be no hotel to go to. A single sign in front of a tea-shop advertised "Cool Drinks," which gave me hope that occasionally a tourist might drop by. Not really knowing what to do with my luggage, I looked around and noticed a motorbike approaching me. The cyclist yelled something at me, but over the noise of his engine, I hardly understood what he was trying to tell me.

"Arugam Bay?" he practically screamed at me. I gave a nod and climbed on his motorbike, which seemed risky. While I clung to him and to my luggage, he steered the smoking vehicle out of the village.

We drove along a stretched dam and crossed a narrow bridge. Wild buffalos dozed in the shallow water. They lifted their heads drowsily as we passed them on our roaring machine. Finally, we came to a village. My first impression was of dreariness and desertion. Shacks made of palm-tree leaves bordered the village main street. A few huts stood together in little clusters. I spotted hand-painted signs indicating that several of the huts were for rent. They had names such as "Blue Oceanic Inn" and "Little Hilton." Between the huts I could make out the ocean – a peaceful bay framed by palm trees, exactly as Chris had described Arugam Bay to me.

Chapter 2

Our motorbike came to a halt in front on one of the few stone buildings in Arugam Bay. "Surfer's Lodge," read a sign above the entrance. My chauffeur announced my arrival with a loud toot on the horn, and a man dressed in pure white, wearing a small white cap, approached me. He gave the driver a few rupees and took my luggage.

The man introduced himself to me as Mustafa. He led me to a room at the backside of the hotel. It didn't look very inviting. Mold covered the walls and the toilet gave off a horrible stink. As soon as I opened the window, a swarm of flies flew in. Outside, the stench was even harder to bear than inside. Obviously, the backyard was also the hotel dump. I saw a big fat rat rummaging through food remains amid bottles and cardboard boxes. I wouldn't stay here for long, I decided, and went out to the terrace, where the restaurant was. At least here the air was better.

A bunch of tourists were sitting around a big table. Those tanned and muscular men looked like models from a sports magazine. Hardly had I sat down at a free table when one of the musclemen came over and, with an Australian accent, mumbled something like: "Good waves, today."

I nodded.

"Do you need a board?"

"No thanks, I don't surf," I replied.

The sporty guy looked at me in disbelief. I could practically see the question in his face: "What the hell is she doing here then?"

It made me remember another time, when in the Swiss Alps a man had looked at me the same way when I confessed that I was not interested in skiing.

"I'm coming from Germany," I added, almost apologetically. By now the Australian had lost his last bit of interest in me.

As the guys from the neighbouring table were being served dinner, an unappetizing smell filled our restaurant. Since my arrival in Sri Lanka, I hadn't eaten any meat, though I hadn't missed it. My previous hosts, Anura and Mr. Sirisena, were Sinhalese and Buddhists. You could eat fish from their kitchens, but no meat. In this restaurant, Mustafa was the chef, and he was a Muslim. Today the menu showed beef curry. But the stuff on the surfers' plates didn't look very appealing. I refused the smelly dish and retreated to my room. After last night's events, I craved sleep. My room was so damp, however, that I couldn't rest. In addition, loud music blared from the restaurant, yet even hammering beat was drowned out by an even louder hum from the electric generator located right outside, just beneath my window.

At daybreak, I gladly left my stuffy bedroom. The sight of the idyllic bay, surrounded by beautiful palm trees, made me forget the bothers of last night. The turquoise ocean glittered in the morning sun.

Away from the shore, in the far distance, waves were breaking. I could perceive surfers. Nearby, fishermen pulled their nets onto the beach while chanting their traditional rhythms. Right then and there, they sorted and cut up the catch, and the unavoidable stray dogs greedily fell upon the remains. The locals paid no attention to the few tourists.

In complete harmony with myself, I strolled along the shore. No beach boy came running after me, or any touts trying to sell me something. All I heard were the waves and, in far distance, the chanting of the fishermen.

Suddenly I had the feeling that somebody had been calling my name. Amazed, I turned around and saw a young woman running toward me and waving frantically.

A colorful cloth wrapped around her hips. She wore a necklace made of shells. Shells had also been plaited into her hair. Only when she came closer did I recognize Kerstin, who I had met at the hotel in Akuralla, at the beginning of my Sri Lanka trip. The young Swiss woman had changed her look quite a bit.

Now I also noticed a young man following her. His appearance was quite strange – he was more than six feet tall and so skinny that his ribs protruded. The man approached us with elastic strides and a light swing of his hips, quite in contrast to his lanky figure. He too wore a cloth around his hips this one printed with big colorful flowers. Silver rings adorned his arms and fingers, some of them with big precious stones. His fair and curly hair grew thinly in front but fell long and soft from the back of his head. On his chin I noticed a miserable little goatee. But his shiny blue eyes and an agreeable smile showing teeth and gums most impressed me.

Kerstin was very glad to find me here. A few weeks had passed since we had met in Anura's hotel.

"This is Adrian," she introduced the guy at her side. "We met in Hikkaduwa." She smiled just as widely as her new boyfriend. We had begun to stroll along the beach, and Kerstin told me what had happened after I had left Akuralla.

"My sister Brigitte finally found her destination – she is the village nurse now. In the beginning, she treated a little girl's wounds. Soon, news spread about the white nurse with the big medicine bag. Locals cannot afford to visit a doctor, so now she is busy treating the villagers' big and small ailments.

"For pills and ointments, they pay with little gifts, fresh fruit or dried fish. Sometimes they invite Brigitte for supper, which she cannot refuse.

"Her food habits have changed quite a bit," Kerstin said with a grin. "She feels really good and has even gained a little weight. At the moment, she cannot imagine leaving Akuralla ever."

We decided to continue our discussion during dinner and to meet at the cabanas; Kerstin and Adrian had rented one of the palm-leaf huts.

Shortly after sunset, I headed to the restaurant. At the entrance a sign read: Sooriya's Beach Hut. So, this was the place Chris had been raving about!

The food area consisted of a half-open room beneath a palm leaf roof surrounded by a low wall. This allowed a view of the luscious vegetation around us. Flickering oil lamps on our tables dimly illuminated the space. Here there was quiet; we weren't forced to listen to a noisy generator. The restaurant served visitors had rice and curry. All ate with their right hands. I saw no cutlery anywhere.

The kitchen in the rear of the restaurant was separated from the tables by a low wall. A Sri Lankan man with a wild mane, his upper body naked, stood at an open fireplace. His long, curly black hair fell to his shoulders and it stuck out in all directions. A beard covered half his face. He seemed very skilled with the pans and vegetables. Clearly, he savored the food he was preparing. In the glow of the fire, his well-nourished belly shined with sweat.

A moment later, Kerstin and her friend came in and we sat at one of the tables.

"Rice and curry?" Adrian asked, beaming at us. "Ram is cooking my favorite dish today. Actually, his correct name is Ramana Kumar."

Kerstin and I nodded.

"I will look after the chai," Adrian added, disappearing into the kitchen to boil some Ceylon tea. He acted quite at home here and chatted easily with the cook. The two seemed to know each other well.

Soon Adrian brought us our chai, the strong, sweetened black tea infused with boiled milk and smelling of exotic spices.

Meanwhile, Kerstin talked about Akuralla.

"Petra moved out shortly after you left," she said. "And Brigitte is not going to be carried away from Akuralla. She is thriving on being needed as a nurse even during her vacation."

Just then, a young man came to our table to serve our dinner. The resemblance between him and the cook was obvious.

The younger man had a friendly face, and his eyes cast roguish glances. His smile revealed snow-white teeth. The upper front teeth were standing apart with a little gap, so that his speech had a slight lisp to it.

"Three special curries of the house," he smiled. "Ladyfingers and drumsticks."

Never had I seen the strange, longish vegetable called murunga used in making what he called "drumstick curry."

Kerstin mixed the rice and curries with her right hand. I did the same, as I didn't want to be the only person asking for cutlery. The dishes were excellent!

"This place is run by Tamil brothers," Adrian told me as we relished our meal. "I have been coming here for years, and I enjoy its very special and wonderful atmosphere. The brothers are exceptional people."

Truly their appearance was unusual. I had seen such long-haired men only among the sadhus in Kataragama. Of course, a lot of hippie travelers grew long hair. This was, after all, the nineteen eighties. But most Sri Lankans wore their hair short.

After we had finished supper, Shiva, the younger brother, brought in small bowls filled with water. These we used to clean our hands. Somebody had turned on a cassette recorder which softly played Willie Nelson's "On the road again."

Now another local man came in. He wore a white cloth with a modest border around his hips. His forehead and upper body were painted with white ashes. His dark brown curls reached down to his shoulders.

"Namaste, Sooriya," Adrian greeted him, as the man passed our table.

The man placed one palm to the other and bowed his head, giving his regards.

For a moment his eyes sunk into mine so deeply that a shiver crept across my back.

"You are very welcome," he addressed me.

Then, he turned and headed towards the kitchen.

"That was Sooriya, the eldest brother," Adrian said. "In fact, his name is Sooriya Kumar, which means Son of the Sun," he added.

I was observed how the Tamil said a few words to his brother, our cook, then quickly left the kitchen and disappeared in the darkness. For tonight, the last sight of him was his white cloth.

Kerstin and I agreed to meet for breakfast in the restaurant next morning. She wanted to show me Sooriya's Beach Hut and her cabana in daylight. Afterward, we would go to the beach, as we had done before in Akuralla.

With my flashlight in hand, I walked back to my hotel. The bawling Australians could be heard from afar, celebrating something or other. Numerous empty beer bottles cluttered the tables.

Not inclined to party with them, I headed to my room to go to bed. Meanwhile, a bat had moved into my bathroom. It dangled head-down from the shower nozzles. I definitely had to move to a new accommodation!

The air in there was unbearably warm and humid. From the adjacent restaurant, loud hard-rock music forced its way in. Yet I found myself returning to the man who had made such a deep impression on me, and who at the same time had so perturbed me.

The next morning, Kerstin, Adrian and I had a good long breakfast at Sooriya's Beach Hut. Shiva spoiled us with a delicious fruit salad made of papayas, mangos and bananas. He also infected us with his carefree delight. Shiva joked incessantly with Kerstin and me. The day began in perfect joy.

After breakfast, Kerstin and Adrian led me to the square on the backside of our restaurant. It turned out to be a little paradise covered with luscious green vegetation. From the street, it stretched further inland. Trees afforded us shade, and flowers thrived. I noticed a few stone huts, one of which was decorated with portraits of the Hindu deities, Shiva and Ganesha.

"Sooriya painted them," Adrian said. "He is very gifted. The Shiva-Ganesh house is not for rent. Sooriya is living in it, but he is spending almost every night in his hammock outside."

Beyond that were scattered a few palm-leaf huts, Kerstin and her friend resided in one of these cabanas. Inside, on the sandy floor, stood two plank beds, plus a wooden bench on which the two had piled their luggage.

"This is to protect our stuff from being eaten by termites," Adrian said.

Their cabana had no windows, but compared to my hotel room, the air inside it was surprisingly fresh. The wind could move through the palm leaves unobstructed. The cabana had no actual door, but rather a wood frame woven with leaves and branches that fit in the entrance opening, affording privacy.

This secluded place felt so calm and pleasant. I liked it much more than my hotel, but I was afraid to live in a cabana like this all by myself. I needed a door with a lock, or else I couldn't sleep.

A hut named Hanuman Cottage had been built near the restaurant. It bore an image of Hanuman, the monkey god. Appropriately, a whole gang of monkeys was playing on its roof. Inside was a library with numerous books in many languages.

"Being ballast, those books were left behind by guests when they had to move on. Even tourists from outside the guest house bring books here. They all know that Ram loves literature and opens his library to everybody."

Also inside Hanuman Cottage were a variety of instruments, including a guitar and some drums. "Everybody may take them and play," Adrian said. "We've had fantastic sessions in here."

After our sightseeing, Adrian said goodbye. He wanted to ride his bicycle to Pottuvil in order to change money at the bank. Kerstin and I went to the beach. She seemed a little sad.

"Adrian will leave in a few days," she told me. "His visa for Sri Lanka has expired. He will travel to India and later to Thailand. I would like so much to go with him, but my time in Asia is limited. Soon I will have to return to Switzerland and go back to work. O, I would like to quit my job and join Adrian!"

"How is it possible for so many people to drop out of their routine at home?" I wondered. "Their money must be used up after a while, I would assume."

"Adrian is dealing silver jewelry and precious stones," Kerstin said. "In Sri Lanka, he has bought sapphires, and cat's eye moonstones. His friend in Berlin has an Asian boutique. He will meet him in India for delivery."

Although Kerstin wanted to spend as much time as possible with Adrian during their last common days, she was pleased to have caught up with me again. Kerstin, who had not been spending much time outside her Swiss mountain idyll, had entered a whole new world opened to her by Adrian. I could appreciate her feelings very well, because I was also young and inexperienced. We both were being overrun by one new impression after another in Asia.

From then on I encountered Sooriya quite often, and my prior insecurity in his presence soon vanished. Sometimes he joined us at our table. He had a gripping way of narrating.

On his premises, Sooriya was treated with great respect by all travelers. Some had known him for years and returned at more-or-less regular intervals. But, although there was an aura about him, Sooriya was no Guru standing aloof. Asia harbored quite a few of that kind, followed by seekers from the West hoping to find their illusion of peace, or whatever. Sometimes, Sooriya was deeply serious, and the next second he was quite amusing – and even fresh at times. I couldn't nail him down. Sometimes I had the impression I was having a conversation with an erudite European, then suddenly the equally erudite Hindu was taking to me, taking me along on a journey into Asian ways of thinking. But he conveyed no mission and never tried to indoctrinate me or convert me.

The day of Adrian's departure had come. Kerstin escorted him to his bus, which was leaving from Pottuvil. Tears showed in her eyes as she returned to our beach. She wanted to be alone, and then she went for a long walk along the shore. I could see her in the distance as she passed the bend of the bay, which is where the little tea-shop called Surfer's Spot took care of the Australian guys' surfboards. Behind this place, the beaches were deserted and lonely.

When I met Kerstin again the next day, she looked very tired.

"I always felt safe in the cabana with Adrian around," Kerstin said.

But now, being alone, she was afraid of the dark and the animal noises outside the thin walls. She had been sleepless most of the night.

I had had enough of my dirty, muggy room at Surfer's Lodge, so we agreed I would move into Kerstin's cabana. This suited me perfectly, as I was spending most of my time at Sooriya's Beach Hut anyhow.

*

Kerstin made room for my luggage in our little palm-leaf hut. First, I had to get acquainted with the habits in Sooriya's Beach Hut. In this place, we had neither electricity nor tap water. One well served as our source of bathing water, and another close to the kitchen provide potable water. We retrieved it from deep down with a bucket. Flat stones paved the ground all around the well. Banana trees bordered this pavement. With constant watering, the plants grew magnificently and, conveniently, they protected the airy "bathroom" from outside eyes.

"Please take care that no soap gets rinsed into the well," Kerstin instructed me. "You would spoil the water."

In the far rear of the square, there was a little house with a floor toilet. As there was no seat, the user had to squat down. And there was no water flush tank. Water for flushing had to be brought along from the well.

Beneath a huge Bougainvillea bush, a tiny hut had been built, too low for a person to stand upright in. Oil lamps and vases with fresh flowers adorned the façade.

"This is Sooriya's little temple," Kerstin remarked as we passed it.

During nighttime, there was no light in the rear of the space. Only a few oil lamps near the temple shone dimly.

The sun set shortly after 6 o'clock p.m. Dark night came almost immediately after, so I always had to have my flashlight ready. The brothers took great care that no strangers from outside entered the restaurant's backyard. Every night, Ram went to sleep on the wooden bench near the entrance, and Lingam, a boy helping in the kitchen, went to sleep inside the restaurant.

Lingam could neither hear nor speak. The brothers were taking care of him. In Sri Lanka, handicapped people almost have no chance to get a job and lead a normal, independent life. Lingam was treated like a family member, although getting along with him turned out to be difficult sometimes.

He could get quite nasty and loud. When something displeased him, he would screech dreadfully. With unceasing patience, the brothers would soothe him. They accepted no critical remarks from their restaurant's guests.

Our cabana was located not far away from the Shiva-Ganesh House, where Sooriya would sleep in his hammock outside. At night I felt safe because he was nearby.

In Sooriya's Beach Hut, each of the five brothers had their special tasks. Ram's empire was the kitchen, where he defended his scepter. His outstanding dishes were famous throughout Arugam Bay, and the restaurant was well visited every day.

Sooriya, the eldest of the brothers, had various functions. One of his jobs was to sweep the sandy paths, and this he did lovingly, as if nothing else in the world had more meaning.

One day I observed him from our cabana. He used a rake and a broom to clear the path of twigs, thorns and leaves. Despite the midday sun burning down, he seemed in no hurry to finish this hot, dusty work. The equanimity of his even movements struck me as I watched him. Tirelessly, he swept his broom across the sand. This was no work to him; it was definitely some kind of meditation. Deeply sunk in his movements, he didn't even notice people walking past him. Only after the last thorn and the smallest leaf had been swept aside, and the rake had left regular grooves in the sand, did Sooriya consider his work to be complete. He didn't mind when his guests came back from the beach and destroyed the tidy surface of the path, or when his brother Ram pulled a sack with coconuts across it. Sooriya's composure deeply impressed me.

Shiva's job was to buy food and other necessary things, and to assist in the restaurant. The brothers were vegetarians, and Ram created tasteful dishes in great variety. Another brother, Jothi, had built a little shop where he sold essential items to tourists. Arugam Bay had no real store then. If you wanted to buy something special, you had to drive to Pottuvil. Jothi also served as gardener, taking care of all the plants at Sooriya's Beach Hut.

The youngest brother's name was Sri Theva, and he was about seventeen years old. He had moved to Arugam Bay only recently. Before that, he had been living with his mother in the town of Mannar in the north of the island. He had just finished High School. For him it was a big adventure to meet travelers from different nations. This curly-haired guy was especially charming and unobtrusive. He always stayed in the background and showed respect to his elder brothers.

Sri was eager to learn. He and I liked to have long conversations. Being in my early twenties and European, I should have been the more experienced one, but Sri surprised me over and over again with his inner composure, his friendliness, and a kind of wise naivety you would probably never find with German teenagers.

One morning I met Sri by chance on the beach. He was taking a bath in the ocean, happily splashing about in the shallow waves near the shore.

"Come, Sri," I shouted. "Let's have a proper swim!"

"I want to stay here, where I can touch the ground with my feet," he replied. "I cannot swim."

"You are living by the beach and haven't learned to swim?"

"Why should we swim?" Sri asked. "The fishermen cannot either. They have their boats to put to sea. The men keep saying that our feet are made for walking. If we were supposed to swim, we would have fins."

Indeed, I hardly ever saw locals swim in the ocean except for a few boys who hung around with the tourists for the most part of the day. Some of these boys tried to surf, emulating the Australians.

"Nobody has ever imagined going for a swim until those tourists arrived," Sri continued. "The same with lying in the sun to get fried. We don't need to; we are tanned by nature," Sri grinned.

Having said all there was to say, he left the water. His soaked Lungi, as the Tamils call their hip cloth, was wrapped around his legs, resembling swim shorts.

I found myself a quiet spot in the sand to fry a little, as Sri put it. Except for a few other tourists, the beach was almost empty.

Far off, a local man was walking along the shore. Actually, walking does not quite describe it correctly. The old man was jumping and dancing across the sand. He was spinning round and spreading his arms towards the sun, as if he wanted to embrace it. Cautiously, he turned towards the waves getting lost in the sand. But he did not allow the spray to touch his feet. The strange old chap kept running away from every small wave, as if in fear of the water.

Nobody was paying any attention to his odd behavior. He bowed to every single tourist and greeted them effusively. The people said hello as well, and then took no further notice of him.

Suddenly the old man, who wore only a rag around his hips, turned directly toward me. He came to a halt right in front of my beach towel and began to study me. His thin white hair and his long beard fluttered wildly in the hot wind. From his furrowed face, wide-awake, dark eyes flashed impishly at me.

The man's head tilted to one side and his smile bared almost toothless gums. Only a few ruined teeth were left. However, his body seemed to belong to someone else. His posture was very upright, and his almost black skin stretched tightly on his skinny frame.

He sat down in front of me and effortlessly crossed his legs in a lotus position. Although he was smiling at me incessantly, he obviously did not want to do any trade. Yet I felt very uneasy, being stared at like this.

He noticed my notepad beside my beach towel. I almost never missed taking it along. Since I had been a young girl, I had written down everything that seemed to be of some relevance to me. This was my way of coping with my daily experiences.

But in this particular case, being here in Sri Lanka, it was essential to note down my thoughts – even if I made other people smile now and then.

A colorful ball-point pen was fixed to my notepad at all times. The pen's numerous neon colors seemed to have roused the old man's interest. I handed it over, and he looked at it from all angles. A moment later he grabbed my pad. He moved away a little and began to draw, lying on his belly.

After a while he returned pad and pen to me. The sheet showed small figures done in simple lines, just in the way little children do it. One figure had raised its arm, holding something. Another little man lay on the shore close to the waves and seemed to be asleep. I tried to tell the old man that he could keep my pen, but he refused, raising both hands with feigned indignation.

He showed his gratitude with a bow and moved on. Some distance away, he sank on his knees and started to build a sand castle.

I returned to Sooriya's Beach Hut where I met Kerstin at the entrance, having a conversation with Sooriya. I told them about my encounter with the strange old man on the beach.

"That was Swami," Kerstin laughed. "He is a bit crazy, but completely harmless."

"You can trust him," Sooriya added. "Swami has the wisdom that only children have."

Just as I prepared to go to our cabana, I spotted an elderly, hunchback woman on the side of the road. She didn't enter our yard but stood looking at Sooriya without uttering a word. Her wrinkled face carried a sad expression.

Right away Sooriya left Kerstin and me and went to the kitchen. He came back with a bowl of rice and dhal curry for the old woman. She folded her small shaky hands and moved them toward her forehead several times to show her gratitude.

Then she looked up at me. She was little more four-and-a-half feet tall. She gave me a penetrating stare and looked deep into my eyes.

Her dry and wrinkled hand stroked my arm. Without thinking, I withdrew from her. She croaked something in Tamil, addressing Sooriya.

He wiggled his head in consent and his answer made the woman chuckle. She sat down by the road and started eating.

"What did she say?" I asked Sooriya.

"She told me that you have good eyes. They reveal that you are true in feeling and acting, but your way of thinking feels wrong to her."

"And what did you answer her?"

"That you have come from Europe. Wrong thinking, you might call it distrust, is a wide-spread disease in Europe."

"This woman is Tamil and very old by now," Sooriya told Kerstin and me as he escorted us to our cabana. "Some time ago her husband has died. She has neither children nor any other living relatives. Nobody is taking care of her. In Arugam Bay, only few Tamils are left who can assist her. If we don't give her food, she will die."

Sooriya stopped for a moment as we reached our hut.

"The old woman says we will have rain soon," he turned his eyes to the sky. "As soon as the monsoon season starts here on the Eastern Coast, our guests will depart and travel to the Western Coast, where the sunny season prevails."

I looked up as well. The sky was blue and cloudless. A soft wind was blowing. I saw nothing to indicate a change in weather.

Kerstin and I spent most of our evenings in the restaurant. But sometimes she liked to visit people she had met with Adrian outside our place.

One night she left, and I felt bored in the restaurant. Sooriya had already lain down in his hammock. I went back to my cabana and tried to read a little in the dim light of an oil lamp.

Suddenly someone hit hard against our cabana, shaking it thoroughly. The door flung open and Kerstin stumbled inside.

Her hair was ruffled, and she clutched her torn lungi. She stared at me wide-eyed and let herself drop on her plank bed.

"Those nails – take those nails from my bed," she screamed hysterically, wildly brushing some sand from her bedsheet.

"What happened, Kerstin?" I got up and tried to calm her.

"His face! Suddenly he looked like a wolf! He grabbed me, and I couldn't move! But I ran and ran! And there were the dogs! I didn't find the path home anymore."

Now Sooriya was standing in the door.

"Tell him to get lost!" Kerstin screeched completely out of her mind. "Don't dare touch me! Adrian will repay you for this, as soon as he will be back."

Sooriya checked Kerstin's eyes, before he turned to me. "Tell her to stay away from drugs."

Slowly Kerstin relaxed. She lay on her bed and stared at the ceiling, spellbound, as if she was seeing a movie. I had no idea what was going on in her mind. But she stayed calm, and I asked no more questions.

Next morning Kerstin felt sick and looked very pale. I brought her some chai from the kitchen. At noon she got up and packed her belongings. All she wanted was to leave and go to her sister in Akuralla, or better, return to Germany. Kerstin didn't tell me what happened the night before. When we separated, she only said: "Take care of some of the tourists here. You cannot trust all of them. This was no local who did this to me."

Kerstin took the evening bus towards the west coast. And I was alone in my cabana now. But inside the brothers' place, I was safe. And near Sooriya, in particular, I felt completely at ease.

*

The small temple on the yard meant very much to Sooriya. One day, he took me along to show it to me, and we entered the low and dim interior. A strong scent of flowers and incense sticks hit me. Images of Lord Shiva hung on the walls. However, what really amazed me was a little Buddha figurine placed beside a picture of the Hindu god. Above the figures, the picture of an Islamic mosque was fastened to the wall, side-by-side with a crucified Jesus. Never had I seen a temple harboring the symbols of the various religions in such a peaceful union.

"In here everybody can find the god he or she is seeking," Sooriya said. "And if someone does not seek a god, he shall find peace in his heart."

After I had sat down on the floor, I noticed a wooden chest containing many items: yellowed postcards, letters, photographs, a hair clip, jewelry, shells, and money in numerous currencies. I assumed these to be souvenirs left behind by former guests.

Sooriya placed himself on the stone tiles beside me. For a while we sat in silence; he in meditation in a lotus position, and me lost in thought, on bent knees. The atmosphere in this unspectacular little temple touched me in an odd way. Sooriya did not notice me leaving. His eyes were closed, and he seemed detached from the world.

Back in the restaurant, I was able to find my way back from my floating state. I badly wanted to touch firm ground again. The cassette recorder was softly playing songs from the nineteen seventies. A few tourists were chatting about the best prices for accommodations on the west coast and current prices for marijuana.

After I finished my chai, I left the restaurant. Meanwhile, Sooriya had returned from his temple, and some of his local friends had arrived for a visit. The three men were having a lively discussion. One of them was an old man with a long and snow-white beard. His clothes were white too, and by his little cap I knew that he was a Muslim. The other visitor was Suba, a Sinhalese friend.

Here in Arugam Bay, whose local name was Ulla, different ethnic groups and religions lived side by side.

Adrian had told me that the Tamils, who are Hindus, and the Buddhist Sinhalese had begun to shun each other since the riots had started to shake the country. In Sooriya's Beach Hut, things were different. The brothers welcomed friends from all religious groups in the area.

The men's conversation seemingly was about politics. I heard them talk about the rebel Tamil Tigers. Their faces looked worried.

Liberation Tigers of Tamil Eelam, LTTE in short, was the name of the separatist organization fighting for the Tamils' independence in the North and East of Sri Lanka. As I passed the men talking, Sooriya's glance indicated I had best not interfere. It was uncommon for women to participate in men's conversations. I became aware of how little access I had to any information about the current political situation. In Arugam Bay, you couldn't even buy newspapers in English. The three men were still debating long after it had gotten dark.

Sometimes, when I wanted to swim in the mornings Sooriya came along to the beach. Just like his brothers, he could not swim. He stepped into the water only as far as he was able to stand safely. I always took an extended swim towards the sea, being watched by Sooriya. Sometimes, while I was having fun in the water, I made teasing comments and tempted him to go further. We had lots of fun on these morning excursions to the ocean.

One day, Sooriya said unexpectedly: "Teach me to swim. I want to learn it."

He was a little embarrassed whenever I made him lie on my arms, as one does with little children, as he tried moving like a swimmer. We often burst out laughing. The local boys always watching us giggled too.

Sooriya learned fast, and soon our morning swim was part of our day. Those were happy, carefree times. Sooriya made jokes and was in high spirits. Fishermen watched us with suspicious eyes.

In the village, hostilities toward Sooriya and his brothers were increasing. The more radio stations broadcast the news about assassinations by the Tamil minority, the more people in Arugam Bay were shunning their Tamil neighbors. The atmosphere within the village on this beautiful bay had been poisoned.

Sooriya was meeting with local friends at his place more often now. They would hold heated discussions about the political situation. On occasion, Sooriya's eyes had a furious flash to them, a trait I hadn't perceived before. Often in the evenings, the brothers gathered around the radio to hear the news. Alas, I didn't understand their mother tongue.

One afternoon, Sooriya returned from an errand in the village, in a bad temper. All he said was that someone had made disparaging remarks about us after seeing us swim. He refused to say any more about it and retreated to his temple.

I spent the evening in the restaurant, with Barbara. She lived in a cabana at the far end of our yard. This Canadian woman had a pale, nearly-transparent complexion. She wore the same clothes every day: tight, tiger-print leggings and a washed-out, violet batik shirt. Her short hair was dyed a loud orange and was always well-tended. Every morning she treated it with sugar water as a setting lotion, to stiffen it for her punk style.

At first, I wondered why she never changed her clothes. Then someone told me that her luggage had been stolen in Colombo. All she had left were the clothes she was wearing and her passport, always hanging around her neck, Barbara was waiting for a money transfer from Canada. The brothers had known her for a long time and offered to let her live in a cabana and eat in the restaurant for free until her money arrived from home.

Ronaldo from Italy had rented the cabana next to Barbara's. During daylight we never caught a glimpse of him, either in our yard or on the beach. Ronaldo was busy building his own house on the outskirts of Arugam Bay village. He and a Sinhalese friend labored all day long. The Italian spent the bigger part of the year in Sri Lanka. In between he flew home to work seasonal jobs. Then he had enough money for a few more months in Sri Lanka. Some time ago he had decided to build a second residence in Arugam Bay.

The following morning, Sooriya didn't join me for a swim. The sun was shining brightly, but I didn't feel very happy in the water by myself. Back on the beach, a local man addressed me. His English was bad, and I hardly could make out what he was saying. He whispered something like: "You like men with dark skin? Take me; I'm better than the Tamil."

Feeling angry, I returned to Sooriya's Beach Hut, yearning for an extensive shower. My towel, hanging in the entrance to the shower, showed that I didn't want to be disturbed. The locals didn't take off their lungis for taking a shower. Unlike Europeans, they are not used to having privacy. I undressed and poured many buckets of cool water over me.

Sooriya, meanwhile, was sitting in front of his small temple.

"We will have rain soon," he said as I came from my shower. "Will you leave as well, if the monsoon starts?"

I didn't want to go away at all. Rain wouldn't be a reason for me to leave Arugam Bay. But another problem cropped up. My three months' visa was soon going to expire. Then, by law, I had to leave Sri Lanka - at least for a while. In Dodanduwa, Chris had told me that I could apply for a new visa after a four week's stay in India.

Sooriya had been right. By the next day, huge rainclouds were gathering. At first, only a few big drops splashed onto the dry earth, but then the rain poured down in a big flood. In no time, our back yard was a lake.

The well-tended garden turned into a muddy puddle. For the time being, the arid ground was too hard-packed to be able to absorb such huge amounts of precipitation.

I ran through the warm rain to my cabana in order to save my luggage. I picked it from the sandy ground and threw it on my plank bed. The palm-leaf roof no longer provided protection. Thin streams began to meander through my cabana.

Soon the rain ceased. As quickly as the clouds had appeared, they vanished. Once again, the sun burned down from a bright-blue sky. The earth was steaming, and the air became unbearably muggy. The moldy stink I had inhaled on my arrival in Sri Lanka was back again.

My towels and bedsheet were completely soaked. Even the clothes in my backpack felt damp. I took everything outside to dry in y the sun. Ram and Shiva busied themselves cleaning up the kitchen and restaurant; a lot of water had to be swept outside. Sooriya repaired my roof provisionally, and then turned to look after his temple and other guests.

The sun dried my belongings, but in the evening the rain came back. The humidity was almost too much for me; I felt worn out. No tourists occupied the restaurant. The brothers worked hard to weatherproof everything around the kitchen and the restaurant.

That night, I went to my cabana early. The rain was not as strong as it had been before noon. The repaired roof resisted leaks. However, I couldn't fall asleep. Even if I stayed still, I kept sweating profusely. I found no rest, constantly turning from left to right and back.

Suddenly, a piercing scream made me start. I jumped up to take a look outside. The rain splashed my face and I could see absolutely nothing in the darkness. Again, I heard a woman's bloodcurdling scream. Ram ran past my hut. I joined him and together we raced across the slippery, muddy yard. The yells had come from Barbara's cabana. Sooriya was there already and tried to calm down the completely hysterical Canadian. Repeatedly she shrieked: "A rat! There's a rat in my cabana!"

Barbara was soaking wet and shivering. Her hair was plastered on her head. She pressed one hand against her temple and yelled over and over: "A rat! It bit me!"

We escorted Barbara to the restaurant. Sooriya investigated the hut, but found nothing. Only in the restaurant, in the light of an oil lamp, could we see the bare spot on her head. The rat had eaten a big tuft of her orange hair, which she had iced with sugar. No way would she return to her cabana! She was too afraid. I offered to let her sleep on the vacant plank bed in my hut. Gradually, she calmed down. Sooriya came along as we walked to my cabana.

"I am outside, in case something unusual should occur," he said. Barbara felt relieved, but was exhausted by all the excitement. She lay down on the bed and soon fell asleep. The rain continued raging.

From now on we had rain almost every day. Mostly, the days broke with bright sunshine, but at around noon, big clouds would gather, followed by a furiously pattering rain. This weather forced us to sit idly in our cabanas or in the restaurant.

More and more tourists departed. Barbara had to stay on, as her money transfer from Canada still hadn't arrived.

Soon, it would be my turn to travel to Colombo in order to apply for my visa for India, and buy a ticket. Honestly, though, I did not want to leave Arugam Bay or Sooriya at all.

*

Sooriya and I got closer in these days, and during rainy hours he began to tell me about his eventful life.

He had been born in a little village near Mannar in the North of Sri Lanka. Sooriya's parents were Tamils and devout Hindus.

"We have to be very grateful to parents for giving birth and life to us," Sooriya said. "We descend from our parents, not from God or the Creator,"

All through his childhood, Sooriya's parents had taught him to share everything with others, even if one didn't possess much. They embraced the principle of Karma, meaning that every action is followed by a reaction. This consequence doesn't necessarily have to occur in the present life; it can manifest in a future life. The cycle of reincarnation was a firm part of their faith.

"The soul chooses your mother and your father according to the Karma," Sooriya believed.

His purpose was not to convince me of his beliefs. He only wanted to give me some insight into his ways of thinking, which had been unknown to me until then.

Sooriya's ancestors were an old Ceylonese family, from which many yogis and sadhus originated, holy men living as ascetics. His father farmed vegetables and rice and was quite an educated man. As a child, he attended a British colonial school. Sooriya's mother, too, came out of a highly respected family. Her father had published numerous books in Ceylon, as Sri Lanka was formerly called. Young Sooriya had seen the books at his grandfather's home.

Of course, Sooriya's family was also very engaged in the boy's education. As a child, he had to walk several miles to a Christian school. He had neither paper nor a slate to write on.

"With our fingers, we wrote in the sand on the ground," he remembered with a smile. "In this way, I learned my first alphabet."

Not every child was able to attend a school in Ceylon, which became the Democratic Socialist Republic of Sri

Lanka in 1972. Traditional values and family knowledge were highly important foundations for the children's education and upbringing.

Sometimes Sooriya surprised me with statements that were difficult for a European girl to comprehend.

"For many generations our family has been having a special connection to birds," he said to my surprise. "The blackbirds are talking to me, too."

I stopped short, but Sooriya continued as if this was the most natural thing in the world.

"Before we sat down for a meal, the birds had to be fed first," he reminisced. "The crows cannot tell you when they are hungry. They cry. My parents have taught me to share, not only with humans, but also with the animals. The ants also got their share from my mother. Whoever came to our home, he or she received food and drink."

Whether it was Hindu sadhus stopping by on their travels, or Buddhist monks passing through in their orange robes, or a Christian priest visiting the village, all were welcome.

"We are all one," Sooriya said. "My father liked the company and was interested in the soul – the atma. Soul cannot be destroyed by fire, wind, or water, nor by anything else. It's immortal. My body will die. The soul leaves the body and persists forever."

When Sooriya was a little boy, he saw a lot of unusual people. One day a man had arrived in Sooriya's far-off village in the arid North. He was dressed as an ascetic. The man wore his hair long, and his skin was white. He had come from a faraway country called Germany. He was seeking new experiences and learning in Asia. The locals called him the "German Swami."

"I wondered why such people came to our country, and what brought him to our house. My father could speak English quite well, better than me then. I was curious about this German Swami's way of thinking. A lot of

71

people in our region had never seen a white-skinned man before, and they came to have a look at him. He became a good friend of our family. When my younger brother was born, German Swami gave him the name Ramana Kumar. It was him also, who fed Ram his first rice."

Sooriya's family was much respected. His grandfather and his father were leaders in the village. People came to ask for their advice when problems arose. Both knew much about the healing powers of herbs and other plants, and they gave medicine to the people. Sooriya was expected to take up this position later in his life. The family also was taking care of a very old and important temple nearby. Many sadhus visited this holy site on their pilgrimages.

"Two cobras guarded the entrance," Sooriya recalled.

His father was always prepared the puja, a religious rite, and Sooriya came along.

"He hoped I would take care of it in the next generation."

The father wanted to pass on all his knowledge to his eldest son, who was supposed to succeed him.

"I learned farming. My father took me to the jungle. I saw yogis living under trees. Sometimes I was afraid of what I saw. One yogi was leaving his body. It is difficult to explain it to you."

As Sooriya grew up, he met many different people at his father's house, which was always open to foreigners.

"My father opened my eyes to tolerance. Never was he judging. He looked straight into people's hearts."

But Sooriya didn't want to spend his life in the way his father did.

"The world was changing," he reflected. "I was young, about seventeen years old, and I wanted to see new things and make my own experiences."

German Swami had opened the young man's mind to a world he had been ignorant of. His curiosity and keen wish to learn had woken.

His interest in farming – growing vegetables and rice – had not been very strong at that time, Sooriya recalled.

It was a little rebellion in opposition his father's wish, which of course is part of being young. The third son, Jothi, enjoyed learning everything about plants and farming. It became his passion.

In the nineteen sixties, the first hippies showed up in the area. They came on ferries from India, and some of them arrived in Sooriya's village in Northern Sri Lanka. Their long hair, white skin, and completely different way of living fascinated the young Tamil, who had hardly ventured further than the outskirts of his village.

Sooriya became friends with one European traveler. Together they crossed the mountains in Central Sri Lanka, heading toward the Southwest. For the first time in his life, he saw the foggy rainforest in high altitude, wild waterfalls, and vast tea plantations, where the famous Ceylon Tea has its origin. Until then he had never known the feeling of cold. To afford a train ticket – or traveling at all – had been impossible before.

"Everything was new and immensely fascinating to me," he recalled.

The mostly arid region at home was in deep contrast to the vegetation on the other side of the island. For the first time, he saw coconut trees bent by the wind from the ocean, the juicy and luscious green jungle, and the beautiful sandy beaches. He -was introduced to the travelers' scene.

"Hippies in Hikkaduwa," was a headline in a Colombo newspaper, Sooriya recalled.

"I was traveling with them to many beautiful places in a van."

The young man inhaled everything he could learn from the hippies about the Western countries they had come from. For the first time, he fell in love and had a girlfriend. Touching girls or having sex before marriage was strictly forbidden at home.

"She came from Germany, like you," Sooriya smiled. "Despite the fact that I have seen so many nationalities there, I always felt strangely attracted by the Germans. They had long conversations and discussions with me that went deeper than the surface. The German girl and I developed a familiarity I had never felt in any relationship with women before. Of course, I didn't only talk with this beautiful girl."

He grinned, eyes shining. "She knew a lot about free, uninhibited love in Europe in the nineteen sixties. I was seventeen and knew nothing."

Sooriya threw me an impish look. For a moment, he was quiet, his thoughts returning to this exciting and beautiful time in his youth. At last he got up and went to fetch us some tea.

I would like to have heard more about those beginnings of the hippie era, when I was a child, too young to experience the culture. Clearly this was a bursting open by youth all over the Western world, never to be repeated again. In Germany, I had heard about the Woodstock festival and about the Beatles traveling to India. Even Sooriya in his small village, bound by ancient traditions, had been touched by this new age, which influenced him for life.

The evening with Mr. Sirisena in Dodanduwa came to mind, when he told us how the arrival of the hippies in Hikkaduwa had influenced the local culture and old traditions.

Sooriya interrupted my thoughts when he returned with two cups of steaming chai. He sat down on our bast mat again. The euphoria from before had vanished from his face.

Disturbing thoughts seemed to torture him. We sipped our tea in silence. Dusk was breaking.

"What happened next isn't a nice story," he said. "While I was having fun on the west coast, happy and living from one day to the next, my father was killed. I learned this from a newspaper. He was a well-known man and had great influence on many people. They had murdered him."

I saw a never-ending sadness in his eyes.

"The last time I saw my father; I had an argument with him and left him with a bad feeling."

Sooriya's family had tried to get hold of him, but they couldn't discover where he was staying. And even if they had known, they wouldn't have been able to contact him, as nobody in close vicinity had a telephone then. Only when he spotted the newspaper article did he realize what happened. He headed home immediately.

"I was not with my family when it happened," he said with remorse. "I left against my family's wish, because looking for adventure and fun seemed more important to me."

I saw in his eyes that the memory was still hard for him to bear.

"My father's forehead was bandaged. They had shot him in the head in front of my mother. According to tradition, I had to burn the fire three times, being the eldest son. The tradition said that I was to shave my head before. But my mother and sisters said no. They didn't want to see me like this."

As tradition demanded, he stayed until the body was completely burnt.

"Then you walk away and never look back," Sooriya said with incredible sadness in his eyes.

"Only now did I truly realize that my father was dead," Sooriya reflected. "When I left the site, I couldn't feel my own body anymore. The soul will never die," he believed. "It cannot be destroyed and only at the moment of death will it leave the body to go somewhere else."

It was two miles from the funeral site to his home. Sooriya could hear his mother and sisters crying as he arrived. The girls were still so young.

Sooriya found consolation in his belief that his father had gathered a lot of good Karma during his life. Even if he was prevented from harvesting the consequences in this life, his deeds would bear fruit as soon as he entered the cycle of rebirth.

"Everyone is responsible for their own Karma," Sooriya emphasized. "Christians believe you will enter Heaven if you have been leading – or trying to lead – a decent life. With us Hindus, things are not that simple. One single life is not enough to gain salvation, as you can never live without accumulating guilt in some way."

Sooriya was convinced that men who envied his father's influence had betrayed him, leading to his violent death. He went to court over the murder, but failed to find justice, encountering a wall of lies and corruption. The police had been bought off, and documents had been faked, he was sure. Only Sooriya's strong faith helped him to cope with the unbelievable.

"Those murderers sealed their Karmas by themselves," he consoled himself during his desperate search for justice.

"Sri Lanka is governed by a system of corruption," he said emphatically, his eyes full of fury. "Only if you have money can you can take part in their game."

The ground where his father had fallen after being shot was soaked in blood

"It was my blood. I'm descended from my father's blood," Sooriya said.

He erected a stone wall between his parents' house and the murder site. Never again did he want his family to have a look beyond that wall.

Sooriya's father had never saved any money. He owned some land, but there was no cash to pay for even the cremation.

"We had friends in our village who helped us," Sooriya said. "Among them was Suba's father. This Sinhalese man owned a bakery in our neighborhood, and he was a close friend of my father. When I was a boy, I gave him a hand baking bread."

Not many Sinhalese lived in the north at that time.

"After my father's death, Suba's father provided us with bread. You never forget a man who has given you bread. All my life, I have never had any problems dealing with Tamils or Sinhalese. This has never changed."

"People with a good heart are connected to you, no matter what nationality or religion they might have. I love them all - our hearts will decide."

Sooriya's mother had always worn colored saris, but from now on she dressed in white, which is the Hindu color for mourning.

"My father had many friends and supporters in the village," Sooriya told me. "They came to my mother's house."

She didn't want to see them.

"My husband is dead and gone," she said. "You can't bring him back. All we want is peace. I don't want any of you to come to this house again."

To Sooriya, she said: "My son, you want to see the world. Don't get stuck in this village."

Afterwards, she didn't say a single word for a long time.

Meanwhile we had finished our tea. Night had fallen, and Sooriya said goodnight. He wanted to visit his temple. Soon afterwards, he lit the oil lamps inside the simple edifice.

That evening I was not in the mood to join the other travelers in the restaurant. I was stirred too much by Sooriya's tales. Sometimes I felt so unsure I should think about all this. In Germany I was used to sharing my feelings with my friends. Alone in my cabana, I began to write down my impressions and feelings, as if I were telling them to a good companion. I felt compelled to make sense of it all, and so I scribbled until late that night.

A few days later I was heading for Colombo to book my flight to India. At one time, the legendary Christmas parties in Goa had seemed a desirable destination, but now everything seemed a little less important. Granted a choice, I would have preferred to stay in Sri Lanka with Sooriya. By now, a very special connection had developed between us.

Chapter 3

"Midnight-Express" – that's what people called that rusty, red bus. It started shortly before dusk in Pottuvil at the East Coast, rode across the island during nighttime, and arrived in the capital on the west coast in the morning. "Express," of course, was an exaggeration, as the bus needed more than ten hours for approximately 200 miles at the most. Nevertheless, this was the fastest way to get to Colombo.

I took with me only a small bag containing clothes for a few days, money and my passport. My travelers' cheques and my return ticket to Germany were deposited in the "safe" at Sooriya's Beach Hut. This safe was a simple old cupboard, secured only by a chain and a padlock. But there my valuables were protected - not because this wooden case was unbreakable, but because Ram or Lingam were guarding it all day and all night. Nobody would get near the "safe" who was not authorized to do so.

The locals watched me with interest, as I was climbed aboard their midnight express. Obviously, they were surprised to see a young female tourist traveling alone. On top of that, mostly men filled the bus; fortunately, an old, hunchbacked woman had taken a seat in the rear of the bus. She smiled at me and offered me a seat beside her. At the same time, she held her hand over her mouth, trying to hide her bad teeth.

Shortly after we had departed, it grew dark. Only a dim light in the bus revealed other passengers trying to rest on wooden benches. Some had lain down on the floor. Others tried to go to sleep while sitting, but this was difficult owing to the bad condition of the roads.

The old woman beside me began to unfold her food provisions, which consisted of a rice dish wrapped in banana leaves. Friendly, she offered one of the small green packets to me. I was not hungry, but the old woman was so appealing that I couldn't refuse. I nodded gratefully, and she smiled, content. The dish tasted very hot, but the woman had the opinion that one special spice was missing. Before I had the opportunity to refuse, she sprinkled some powder on my dish. Fortunately, it was not chilies - there were enough of those already, according to my burning throat.

Having finished her meal, she cleaned her small, trembling hands with a cloth drenched with lemon juice, and she invited me to do the same. She fell asleep after pulling part of her sari over her wrinkled face. Her head kept bumping against the window every time we hit a pothole, but this did not disturb her sleep at all.

I felt that soon I would fall into a deep, leaden sleep. Everyone in the bus had quieted down. My eyes drooped. Each time I nodded off, my head fell to my chest.

At around midnight, our bus stopped in a village in almost complete darkness. The only light came from a tea shop in a battered hut. Several passengers got out to relieve themselves behind low shrubbery. The whole place was stunk awfully, like a sewer. Some of the passengers tried to get into the shop to have some tea. I was too tired to get up; my hands tried to support my head with the help of the seat rest in front of me. I couldn't sleep in such a position, but so long as the bus was parked, I found a little rest.

I dropped into a strange state between sleeping and waking. Incoherent dreams mingled with passengers' voices and the monotonous hum of the motor. Had we got on the road again? I felt paralyzed, unable to move or open my eyes. But since I was able to hold on to the seat in front, I wouldn't slip off the seat on curves. Coldness crept inside the bus through open windows. Had we reached the mountains? I had lost all feeling of time.

I had no idea how long I had been dreaming when suddenly the bus exploded in loud uproar. Voices were talking all at once. The passengers were trying to get outside in a hurry. Also, the friendly old woman sitting beside me was trying to get past me and left the bus almost in panic, so it seemed. I could not make out what was going on. Then I looked out the window and in the pale light I made out Colombo's bus station.

Had I really been asleep for such a long time? I was very confused and tried to stagger to the exit. Now I noticed that my bag was gone! Extremely upset, I tried to find my belongings. I looked on, between, and under the seats, without success. Finally, I realized that the old woman had deceived me. She had gotten too far ahead of me and I would never get hold of her. Many of the passengers gave me reproachful looks as I tried to squeeze past them to get outside.

That powder, it flashed through my mind! What had she strewn on my food? I was dizzy and everything around me was spinning. Finally, I made it to the bus exit, but the old woman had disappeared in the crowd.

I had arrived at Colombo's bus station - having no clothes, no passport, and without a single dollar or rupee in my pockets.

*

Although it was only five o'clock in the morning, the terminal was very busy already. People were crouching on the roadside, waiting for their various busses. Some of them were lying on the dusty ground, deeply asleep with their heads put down on their bags. Porters offered their services. Kitchens on wheels sold hot tea and little dishes - if you had money. The food smelled so tempting, but now I was among those who couldn't afford it.

A woman in a dirty cotton sari reached out for me. She was hiding her face beneath her gown. Her hand was bandaged with rags. A few yards ahead a little boy was approaching me. He was seated on a wooden board with little wheels attached underneath. The child's legs had been amputated above his knees. Both stumps were wrapped in pieces of cloth. His eyes were begging me to help him, but I couldn't do anything for him.

In Arugam Bay, where I had deposited my traveler's cheques in Sooriya's cupboard, nobody had a telephone. And I had no bus ticket back. It was impossible to ask any Sri Lankan for money. Who would give a tourist a single rupee? The towns were populated with more than enough local humans in need.

Between people on their way to work and those waiting for a bus or begging, soldiers with guns on their shoulders were patrolling. Everybody who had to pass them tried to avoid eye contact. I, too, tried to be invisible to them. After all, I had no passport and consequently was unable to produce a visa. I had no other idea but to look for the German Embassy. Maybe they would be able to help me.

I asked a tuk-tuk driver how to get to the embassy. I hadn't even finished talking when he jumped out of his roaring carriage and asked me to get in. However, after he found out I had no money, he left without telling me which way to go. After I wandered around aimlessly for some time, I came to a big hotel. A porter with a purple vest stood in front of it. For one moment, he hesitated. In my dusty clothes, I didn't look like the sort of profitable guest the hotel was used to. At last he opened the door.

Quite tired, I crossed the marble floor toward the reception desk.

"Can I do something for you?" the young Sri Lankan receptionist asked me. Her English was nearly without an accent. She added a slow "Madam?"

"Would you show me the way to the German Embassy, please?"

"All embassies are in Cinnamon Gardens, a suburb," the woman informed me. "I suggest, you take a taxi there."

"Do you possibly have a city map and show me, how I can get there?" I asked the polite young receptionist.

She took a map from a drawer: "Two rupees, please."

"I'm very sorry, but I don't have those two rupees," I informed her. "Everything I had with me has been stolen."

"I feel very sorry for you, Madam," the receptionist answered, and put the map back into the drawer.

I was ready to give up and turned to leave the hotel, when I heard her call: "Wait a moment." The friendly Sri Lankan pushed a sheet in my direction, showing all the districts of Colombo.

"This is for our guests only," she whispered, looking around cautiously, in case one of the superior clerks might be nearby. She marked the way to the embassy with her pencil. "Good luck, Madam."

Having my personal map now, I left the hotel and tried to find my way through the maze of so many streets. I passed numerous magnificent colonial buildings with soldiers patrolling in front of them, crossed wide boulevards crowded with countless cars, and left behind central Colombo. Finally, I reached the slums outside the city. Shacks made of cardboard boxes, wood, tin, and cloth predominated. In front, women prepared modest meals. My stomach was grumbling, although nothing around this area smelled appetizing in any way. Swarms of flies buzzed around countless heaps of garbage. I tried to fight off the insects, but the little children by the roadsides had given up long ago. The creatures crawled all over their arms and faces.

After a seemingly endless march, the city image changed again. The streets became wider, the houses larger, and the surroundings cleaner. I was approaching Cinnamon Gardens, a residential area. The embassy had to be near now.

From a distance, I spotted two female tourists with backpacks. They turned onto a side street. I ran after them. Possibly they had a few rupees for me for something to drink. My mouth was dry. But I was too slow – they disappeared into a small hotel. "Traveler's Nest," read the nameplate outside.

Meanwhile it had become noon, and the sun was scorching. I passed a court where children were playing at a well. They were splashing and pouring water over their heads happily. For a moment, I considered walking inside and getting myself some water. Shortly afterwards, I discovered what I had been searching for. A placard on a wall let me know that, at last, I had arrived at my destination.

The Germany embassy was situated in a villa within a green garden surrounded by a high fence. I felt sure I would find help there, and that soon I'd be able to eat, drink, shower and sleep in a hotel room. In no time at all, this beautiful image was destroyed. The wrought-iron gate was locked. Then I saw the plate beside the entrance. In German it said: "Closed today due to All Saints' Day."

I couldn't believe what I was reading. They had closed the embassy in Colombo because of a Christian holiday celebrated in Germany? I started to sweat and tried to think logically. Where could I spend the night without any money? First, I had to find something to drink, as I was feeling dizzier every minute. Thus, I went back to the court where the children were playing at the well. When I entered the place, the children backed up, afraid of me. I headed for the well and the children watched with amazement as I grabbed the bucket and gulped down as much water as I could. I said thank you and left the court and a few rather dumbfounded kids.

My following task was to find a room for the night. I walked back to the hotel the two tourists had vanished in. Before I dared to enter, I disentangled my hair and tried to get the dust out of my clothes. Then I took a deep breath and stepped into the hotel.

"I would like to have a room for tonight," I addressed the porter.

Although I was feeling sick by now, I tried to smile and appear self-assured.

"Where is your luggage?" the receptionist asked suspiciously.

"I left my luggage in my hotel in Negombo," I lied. "I will have to settle personal matters at the German Embassy tomorrow. Unfortunately, they have closed their offices today."

Thank God, that I had heard of the tourist place called Negombo not far from Colombo.

"Fill in your name and the number of your passport in this form," the porter asked.

"My passport is still at the embassy," I replied for a lame excuse. "I will pick it up tomorrow."

The man seemed to buy this explanation. He passed a key across his desk without asking any further questions.

Relieved, I entered my room. This was a middle-class hotel at best, but to me it was luxurious. My bed was soft, and the sheets were pink and clean. A fan hummed on the ceiling, and there was a bathroom with blue tiles. On the sink, I found perfumed soap and fresh towels.

Because I was a proper guest now, I could order food and drink without any further problems. Everything was added to my bill.

First thing in the morning, I headed for the embassy, after I had enjoyed a good night's sleep followed by a nourishing breakfast. Today the iron gate was open, and I entered the building. A Sri Lankan welcomed me in perfect German, but he listened to my misery quite bored.

"I can issue a provisory passport for you. It suffices for you to return to Germany," he suggested.

"But I don't want to fly back to Germany," I replied. "I intend to travel to India."

"This will hardly be possible without a valid passport," the man said in return.

After a long discussion he finally agreed to provide me with a new passport.

"This will take some time, of course. The passport will be applied for in Germany. This will take approximately four to six weeks."

"I've got plenty of time."

"I thought so," the Sri Lankan concluded. "And most probably you will be disinclined to prolong your stay in Sri Lanka a little."

He issued a provisory passport for me.

"Tell me the name, address and telephone number of your hotel. I will give notice, as soon as your new passport has arrived at our embassy."

"We have no telephone there," I let him know. "At the moment I am living in a little village on the East Coast."

The man showed some feeling for the first time. He looked at me horrified and dropped his pen.

"Haven't you listened to any news at all? There have been more bombings. A state of emergency has been declared in all the north and east. This is Tamil area, young Lady. You cannot return to the Eastern shore. We have a civil war there!"

"But I must go back. My traveler's cheques are there and my ticket back home."

"I have to advise you against it," the Sri Lankan warned me again. "The political situation is tense. Military personnel are being sent to the north and east of our country. This is no holiday site any longer. If you must travel there against my advice to collect your belongings, please leave as soon as possible. We cannot guarantee your safety."

Reluctantly, the man gave me some rupees to cover my hotel bill and my bus ticket to Arugam Bay.

"Too many young people come to our Embassy in order to get money for a lot of strange reasons," he grumbled. "They tell us all kinds of odd stories."

I paid for my room, and had enough money left over to take the bus downtown and even to have a meal. The "Midnight Express" would leave for Arugam Bay later in the evening. True, I had lost my belongings by theft, but at the same time I had been given the longed-for opportunity to extend my stay in Sri Lanka.

Close to the bus terminal, I found a restaurant frequented by many local people. Here, I was sure, I would be served an inexpensive and good meal.

The dining room resembled a hall, instead of being the cozy place I had expected. Long rows of tables were occupied by hungry Sri Lankans, hastily gulping down their dishes. As soon as they had emptied their plates, they left their seats and made room for further guests. Only a few women had come to the lunch hall. When I entered, several men looked up, amazed; I was the only tourist in there. A variety of dishes had been placed on a sideboard, and I decided on two very appetizing flatbreads with fillings of hot vegetables. They tasted delicious.

"Those are the best rotis in town," a man addressed me. He was sitting on the opposite side of our table. He smiled. "Will you stay in Colombo for longer? I could show you our city."

"No," I replied. "I'll leave today."

The people beside us had finished their meals and got up. The local guy took advantage of the time before further guests sat down. He bent across the table and whispered: "We can go to a hotel. For two hours. I have money."

Before I could give him the appropriate answer, we heard a deafening explosion from the street. Pieces of wood flew by the lunch-hall entrance, and windows were bursting everywhere outside. We heard squealing tyres and vehicles crash.

Inside, the chaos was indescribable. People were shrieking. Plates fell to the floor and broke. Tables and benches were knocked over. Guests in a panic were pushing toward the exit. I tried to reach the door as well, but was pushed aside; I stumbled and fell. Feet trampled across my back. Desperately, I tried to stand up again, but among all those fleeing people I had no chance. The only thing I could do was to protect my head with my arms.

Then there was another explosion. Fragments of stone fell from the ceiling. A young man, who had tried to step over me, was hit and paused to hold his hand to a bleeding wound on his head. At last I had my chance to stand up. Smoke forced its way into the lunch hall. I had only one thought: get out of here!

Outside on the street, there was pure devastation. Hurt people lay on the pavement, bleeding. Rubble covered the ground everywhere. The wall of a shop beside the restaurant showed a big hole. People were running from one side of the street to the other. Cars and busses had crashed. Soldiers with guns ready hurried toward the shop building. I ran in the opposite direction, following the fleeing people.

Suddenly I noticed a tourist standing in a doorway, paralyzed. She was older than me, about forty, I guessed.

Her summer dress was torn and black with soot. She held on to her bag desperately.

"Come on, get away from here," I called in English. But the woman couldn't move. Pale, and with her eyes wide open, she stared in the direction from which the black smoke was rising.

Then we heard a third explosion. Fire blazed from the windows of the shop building and from the entrance of the lunch hall.

Without thinking I grabbed the tourist's arm and dragged her with me through the tangle of people, past abandoned bicycles and hooting cars, which were caught in a big jam.

"My suitcase," the woman stammered in German, but she was following me obediently through the narrow alleys of a bazaar, until we were out of reach of the fire and smoke.

Finally, we paused to take a breath. Apparently, she was coming to her senses again.

"We have to get out of Colombo," I implored her.

"My suitcase is at the bus terminal. I already bought my ticket," the tourist replied. She was still very confused and in shock.

"You can't return to the terminal. Surely no busses will leave Colombo today. Perhaps we can catch a train."

In fact, we were quite close to the railway station. But of course, we were not the only ones who wanted to leave the city by train after today's bombing. From all sides, people flooded toward the station - travelers, commuters, and others who wanted only one thing: to get out.

We hurried to the first train we were able to get through to. Its engine had a label saying "Kandy." As we had expected, all the compartments were crowded up to their ceilings, and many people had made their home on the wagon roofs. We ran from door to door, but nowhere could we find a little space for us. At last, two men pulled us up and into the train. We girls were still standing in the open door, with the two brave guys on the running board, when the horn hooted and the train started to move.

Only after we reached the suburbs did the tangle become less severe. A few stations further on, enough passengers had left the train that we were able to find a seat in one of the compartments.

Ingrid, my new companion, obviously hadn't overcome her shock yet. She kept talking endlessly.

"This is not the way I had imagined my trip to Sri Lanka," she chattered. "My eldest son was here last year, and he was very happy on this island. And I'm almost killed in a bombing shortly after I arrive! If you hadn't taken me with you, I'd probably still be standing there. My husband and my sons didn't have any faith in me, getting along on my own, anyway. If they could see me now!"

She tried to brush the soot off her dress.

"I've been reading everything I could get hold of about this country's history and culture," she babbled on. "It might have been more intelligent to study the politics."

Ingrid kept looking out the window. The steam engine had a hard time puffing up the steep slope. Rice terraces were stretched along soft, rounded hills. Bridges spanned picturesque canyons. Luscious vegetation in many shades of green surrounded us. All this seemed to have a soothing effect on my companion.

"I'm not interested in all those beaches and hotels, you know," she spoke more calmly now. "I intended to visit the temples, the ancient towns – and see scenery like this, of course."

Ingrid continued to narrate the life stories of her husband and her three grownup sons. I could hardly bear to listen, though. The oppressive heat crept through my whole body and into my head. I felt nauseous and knew I would throw up. Sweating all over, I squeezed past the other passengers. After I had climbed over bags and people on the floor, I finally reached the toilet door. The stink inside was almost too much for me. Exhausted, I sat down on the floor outside the toilet, closed my eyes and tried to breathe steadily.

After a while I heard Ingrid's concerned voice beside me. "What's wrong with you, girl?" she inquired of me. "Why don't you return to our compartment? Can I do anything for you?"

"The water, the water in Colombo," I muttered weakly. "I shouldn't have drunk the water from the well."

Then I fainted.

*

By the time we had arrived at a former dynasty's city, Kandy, I had recovered enough that at least I was able to get up. Ingrid supported me in every respect, and didn't leave me unguarded for one second. She got us a taxi.

"I have to move on to the East Coast," I told her weakly.

"No way," she contradicted me firmly. "For starters, we will take a room. You can't continue your trip in this state."

"But I've no money for a hotel," I tried to explain to her. "All my cash has been stolen."

"Don't you worry about money at the moment," she calmed me down. "You are ill, and you have to stay in bed."

She was right, of course. I was so dizzy that I was having difficulties standing on my feet. Without any further protest, I took a seat in our taxi.

"Please take us to a hotel near the Temple of the Tooth," my companion asked of the taxi driver.

His face expressed confusion. He didn't know what we were saying. Ingrid took her travel guide from her bag and read aloud: Sri Dalada Maligawa."

The taxi driver shifted into first gear and got started.

"I've been reading a lot about this famous temple in Kandy," Ingrid declared. It is said that one of Buddha's teeth is being kept there for a relic."

Our driver stopped in front of a hotel, from which the magnificently illuminated temple could be seen. The receptionist sized us up. Ingrid's dress was rather wrecked, and I hadn't changed my clothes since I left Arugam Bay. He seemed bothered by the fact that we had no luggage. Only after Ingrid showed him her passport and paid in advance did he give us our key. From me, he asked nothing.

"Have a nice stay, you and your daughter," he wished us both.

In our hotel room I dropped on the bed. Every part of my body ached, and I was dead tired. Ingrid set out for a pharmacy to get some medication for me. She ordered a hotel boy to look after me and bring me some tea. As soon as she had left our room, I fell into a restless sleep disturbed by wild dreams.

Suddenly I was back in Germany. All my friends were busy with their jobs. I wanted to tell them about Sri Lanka, but they couldn't understand me. They pretended I wasn't there at all.

Only my mother noticed me for a second: "You have to learn a profession," she advised. "You need something to do, to have a duty, a purpose."

So, I became a nurse at our hometown hospital. Yet all the patients were dark-skinned. It was my duty to dress their wounds. I had to bandage a little girl's boils and the wounds of a woman with leprosy. She had lost her fingers and toes. And I took care of a boy's stumps, whose legs had been torn off in an explosion. From an adjoining room, an old woman called for me. "My husband has died," she wailed. "Nobody will look after me, so I have to die."

I was wondering where to apply the bandage. But I couldn't help her. I became aware of the fact that I was a lousy nurse. Looking down at myself, I noticed that my hands were in bandages. I no longer had any feeling in my fingers, and I couldn't move my hands. The hospital had become unbearably hot. Probably somebody had turned up the central heating too much.

"Madam," I heard a voice call me. I was running around between countless ill or hurt people lying on stretchers who were trying to grab me with their searching hands. But I couldn't find the patient who was calling for me.

"Tea, Madam," the voice was closer now.

Gradually, I could feel my fingers again. I felt great relief when my hands were able to move. But, at the same time, the pain returned to my body. Dazed, I opened my eyes. The ill and hurt vanished. The hotel boy was standing beside my bed, holding a cup of tea in his hands.

Ingrid returned in the evening. She had bought new clothes in Kandy, and had a completely new look. Instead of her pale summer dress, she now wore loose cotton slacks with drawstrings around waist and ankles. Local seamstresses manufactured this kind of clothing especially for tourists. I never saw a Sri Lankan woman wear those slacks.

As Ingrid's suitcase had been left behind in Colombo, she had bought herself a backpack.

"My suitcase would have been a bother anyway," she remarked. "Now I'm a genuine backpacker. My sons wouldn't believe their eyes."

The following day, I felt a little better and decided to go on to the East Coast. Ingrid, who had planned a visit at the Botanical Gardens in the outskirts of Kandy, wanted to see me to the train station.

"You should have stayed a few days longer to recover properly," she said with a sorrowful goodbye.

"It's only a few hours to the coast. I can take that," I replied optimistically. But as soon as the train got started, it became clear that I had overestimated my condition. Again, I started to sweat, and dizziness as well as nausea returned. I thanked God I had found an empty seat.

We rode through a mountainous region, our steam engine bravely climbing uphill. Along an almost endless chain of gentle hills, one tea plantation followed. Tea processing factories had been erected in the middle of the luscious green scenery and every once in a while, we'd see a small temple. The women plucking tea buds looked like many colorful beads strewn all over the green terraces. The women wore big baskets on their backs, held in position by ribbons around their foreheads.

The higher our train climbed, the more fog was hovered above the landscape. As on my trip to Colombo a few days ago, we crossed over canyons by way of wooden bridges, and passed waterfalls plunging from rock faces. It was cold outside, but the windows in the compartments couldn't be shut. The other passengers pulled jackets and blankets from their bags, but I still had nothing else to put on and was freezing. We were approaching Nuwara Eliya, a place more than 6,000 feet above sea level. I had heard before of the "city above the clouds." People boarding the train at the station outside town wore thick woolen caps and wrapped themselves in blankets. Some of them wore old coats or jackets, which to me looked quite funny over their sarongs. Most people wore plastic and elastic sandals – common footwear throughout Sri Lanka.

I sat on a wooden bench in the crowded train, squeezed to the wall of the compartment and unable to maneuver.

The woman beside me unpacked her lunch. Again, I felt sick. Probably I should have stayed another day in Kandy. But that opportunity had been wasted, and somehow I had to hold out till we arrived at the coast.

Haputale was the terminus for our train. From here, I had to take the bus to the East Coast. A friendly local man offered to show me the way to the bus station.

"You have to hurry," he urged me. "The bus will leave in a minute."

As fast as I could, I followed him. He ushered me to the right bus and helped me in. A woman made her child sit on her lap and let me sit next to her by the window. Exhausted, I leaned my head against the cool glass. The bus would need several hours to make the journey. I had safely stowed my provisional passport on my body. Now I could fall asleep unworried because I had nothing left that could be stolen.

When we approached the coast, rain came gushing down, partially flooding the road.

Over and over again, the wheels of our bus sank deeply into the mud. The rain was so dense that we could hardly see what was going on outside. In the evening, we finally arrived at Pottuvil. The town seemed deserted. Not a soul stirred on the streets, not even a dog. Only when we came closer to the station did I see two figures leaning against wall under a ledge in order to find shelter from the rain. After the bus had come to a halt, the two guys left their shelter and came running in our direction. Only now did I realize they were wearing uniforms and bearing guns over their shoulders. They inspected every passenger leaving the bus and rummaged through all their belongings. A big basket with fruit they simply threw on the pavement. I was still inside the bus, waiting for my turn, shaking by fever and cramps. I was hoped urgently that they would accept my provisional passport. Most probably they had never seen such an official form.

Meanwhile, the sultry air inside the motionless bus had reached unbearable levels. When I came to the exit, the soldier scrutinized me for a moment. Then he waved his hand for me to go on. I was so relieved!

None of the motor bikers, usually waiting for tourist customers, were to be seen at the bus terminal. Through the rain, I crossed the bridge and walked along the dam to Arugam Bay. It had grown dark by now - no lights anywhere. The rain seemed to have devoured the village. Only raindrops and the wild surf of the ocean were audible. A final short distance separated me from the secure grounds of Sooriya's Beach Hut. I walked close to the roadside in order not to miss the entrance.

I only wanted to find a dry place and be with Sooriya, lie down and sleep for ages.

Chapter 4

Soaked to my skin and exhausted I stumbled through the entrance of Sooriya's Beach Hut and toward the restaurant. It was empty except for Lingam, who was busy washing dishes in the kitchen. He looked at me as if I was a ghost. I was dizzy and clung to the doorframe. No strength left, I sank to the floor. As I fainted, Lingam yelled hysterically for help.

When at last I opened my eyes, Sooriya was bending over me. He stroked my wet hair. I was in good hands.

Sooriya took me to the Shiva-Ganesh House. It was robust and its roof more water-proof than my cabana's.

In here I found a soft mattress to lie on. I had been looking forward to seeing Sooriya again, and was eager to tell him, what had happened to me in the meantime. But this had to wait – I fell into a deep sleep.

When I awoke, Sooriya was kneeling beside me, putting a cool wet cloth on my forehead. He gave me a bitter fluid to drink. I took his hand and felt reassured, then fell back asleep.

"You have to drink something," I heard Sooriya's voice and opened my eyes. He held a cup of tea. My arms and legs were leaden.

"You have been sleeping for two days," Sooriya said as he was helped me to straighten up. My whole body ached awfully, and I still had a high temperature.

"Tomorrow the doctor will come here," I heard him say before I went back to sleep.

When next I awoke, a stout local man was bending down to me. Through a haze, I could perceive his dark round face and his white shirt. The doctor spoke with Sooriya and handed him a little envelope containing a powdery substance. After the doctor said his goodbye, Sooriya made me swallow the medicine – or whatever you might call it.

A little later I felt as if I were wrapped in soft fog. My body seemed to float. A pleasant feeling of equanimity took hold of me and made me relax. I was gliding into a state between dream and reality. Sometimes I opened my eyes during daylight and saw Sooriya looking after me. When I woke up at night, there was always a lit oil-lamp beside my bed. Sooriya was sleeping in his hammock in front of the little house. Often, I could hear the rain patter on the palm-leaf roof and this kind man was always around to take care of me.

Gradually my fever went down, and I stayed awake for longer periods. Only now did I start to inspect my surroundings more closely. The pedestal of the Shiva-Ganesh-House was built of bricks, but everything else was woven with palm leaves. Small images of Hindu gods adorned the walls. Sooriya had brought my luggage in here.

"This place is drier and more comfortable than the cabana," he said. He continued to bring food and tea to me until I had recovered.

Meanwhile most tourists had left the place. Barbara was still waiting for her money from home. But despite the monsoon, a couple from Germany had arrived.

"I've known Tom for many years," Sooriya told me. "When he was a student, he would come here once a year and stay for a few weeks. Nowadays he has a good job in Germany. But whenever he is in Sri Lanka, he comes to us for a short visit."

When I was again able to eat meals in the restaurant, I got acquainted with Tom and his girlfriend Moni.

The couple reported that by now the German foreign affairs office was recommending its citizens not travel to Sri Lanka. Almost daily, the German media were reporting on the civil war.

I thought of my mother. Surely she was worried about me. She had been right about the beginning civil war.

Tomorrow, I would write her a letter. I had intended to call her from Colombo, since there are no phones in Pottuvil and Arugam Bay, but of course that plan fell through.

Tom wasn't really a nice person. Most of the time, he sat around in the restaurant in a lousy mood. It wasn't possible to go for a swim in the rainy season since the ocean was much too churned up. Big, torn-off branches and seaweed washed ashore. Water gushed across the beach again and again, so that a small lagoon developed on the sand.

Tom's friend, Moni, wouldn't let him spoil her holiday. Mostly, the pretty black-haired girl hung around with Ronaldo. Everyone could see that she was getting along very well with the charming Italian. Likely he was the main reason for Tom's irritation.

Since Moni arrived, Ronaldo spent less and less time building his house. Instead, he hung around with her constantly. Ronaldo's project delighted her, and she advised her new friend about interior design.

For some time, Tom watched them with annoyance. But after she had been gone a whole day, not appearing for lunch and returning only late noon with ruffled hair, Tom had had enough. They had a loud argument.

"We are leaving today," Tom declared with determination. "We'll return to the west coast."

"O, but I like it here," Moni retorted. "I don't have in mind to leave so soon."

"You will come with me! I won't let you stay here on your own."

"Don't worry, I won't be alone," Moni replied saucily. "If you're so keen on leaving, I won't keep you. I'm perfectly able to look after myself."

For a moment Tom stared at his girlfriend, stunned.

"You can do, whatever you want," he had made his decision. Tom turned around and hurried to his cabana for his luggage. He returned a few minutes later, however.

"God damn it, my money is gone!" he was raging. "Somebody has stolen my money bag."

He took a few threatening steps toward Moni.

"You slut!" he yelled. "Isn't it enough that you let this Italian drop-out bang you, do you want to get hold of my money, as well? Has he run out of his own cash for his bloody house?"

Before Tom could hit her, Ram and Sooriya were at hand. The cook placed himself between Tom and Moni, and Sooriya tried to calm down the furious guy. But Tom didn't want to be appeased.

"Maybe you simply lost your money bag," Barbara interjected.

Now Tom was even more enraged, and he began to accuse everyone in the place, even Barbara and me.

"You two were robbed yourselves. I'm sure you want to be refunded at my expense," he said stridently.

"This is becoming absurd," Barbara replied, but to be on the safe side, she moved back two steps.

Tom didn't even stop at accusing the brothers.

"Perhaps you have taken my money?" he turned to Ram. "We are having monsoon season, and you don't have any guests anymore. Surely you need some cash, right?"

We saw that Ram and Sooriya were very hurt by this insult. We all agreed that Tom and the two brothers should search every cabana on the place, as well as the kitchen and the restaurant. But Tom's moneybag had disappeared.

The fighting had taken place near the entrance to the place, and it seemed someone had heard our heated discussion from outside.

News spreads fast in the village. If a local had been the victim, nobody would've shown any interest. But it was very bad for the village's reputation as a tourist paradise if a visitor was robbed. In no time, Pottuvil's soldiers came to the place. We could see their hostility against the Tamil brothers. Sooriya's reaction was calm and apparently relaxed, but there was an eerie flash to his eyes. He was sensible enough to avoid looking at the soldiers. I knew how much he hated to be humiliated and accused innocently.

After the soldiers searched the place, they took Sooriya and Ram to the police station in town. Tom left that same evening, and Moni moved to Ronaldo's almost-finished house at the village's outskirts.

Jothi, Shiva and Sri were very worried about their elder brothers. Immediately after the incident, they consulted Suba. Perhaps their Sinhalese friend had an idea about what was best to be done. They discussed the situation in the kitchen.

"They have no reason to keep my brothers," I heard Shiva's desperate voice. "Sooriya and Ram haven't done anything wrong."

"I know that," Suba agreed. "But those people will take advantage of any occasion to charge them. For them, this theft came in handy."

"Suba, what has become of our village?" Shiva asked sadly. "We've always lived together in peace – the Sinhalese, the Tamils, and the Muslims. Why should we be enemies suddenly?"

"I don't know, my friend. But one thing I can tell you for sure: public opinion here has turned against you. It is said that the government will send more soldiers soon, and that this is because of the Tamils living here. As soon as this area has been taken by the Army, no tourists will visit Arugam Bay any longer. You can imagine what this means to the people in the village. They want all Tamils to get lost. Many families have already left. Maybe you should go away for a while, too. Go to your mother and sisters in Mannar before it is too late. It is dangerous for you to stay here."

In the evening, Ram returned from Pottuvil, but his brother was being kept at the police station.

"Sooriya is still being questioned," Ram reported. "They want him to confess to the theft, although they know that he is innocent."

This was a very sad night for us. In the restaurant, we waited for Sooriya to be released and come back. Every motion outside made us jump. No one wanted to eat anything.

"Of course, you cannot understand our troubles," Ram said to me, interrupting the depressing silence. "And you don't know how fast something terrible can happen to a person in Sri Lanka."

Of course, I knew what he was alluding to, but Ram had no idea that Sooriya had been telling me so much about his family.

"I know what happened to your father," I interjected.

Ram was puzzled: "Usually Sooriya doesn't talk about it."

"Well, okay then," he continued after a while. "In this case, I guess, you know that in this country things are different at times. The chief of Pottuvil's police knows about the murder of our father. They have been watching us since we moved here. Before the civil war, we were in no danger. But now everything has changed. Hatred can flare up within seconds. Armed soldiers are everywhere. I don't fear for me and my younger brothers. It's Sooriya they are after. He's got our father's charisma. His presence is a thorn in their sides."

My fear for Sooriya was increasing. What was happening to him at the police station in Pottuvil? Ram tried to calm me down.

"As long as we have foreigners staying at our place, they won't harm him. They don't want to pull tourists into our affairs. Foreign governments are not supposed to know what's really going on in this country."

Sooriya returned from Pottuvil in the morning. He hadn't slept and looked very depressed.

"Apparently they suspect me of associating with the LTTE, and that I'm an informant here in the east for the Tamil Tigers from the north," he reported.

The lost money bag had just been a lame excuse.

"They warned me not do anything wrong from now on. Also, I was advised to keep inconspicuous and not to leave the place at any time."

For a moment, he seemed weak and resigned. However, on his way to the small temple, we observed him regain his upright posture and his uncompromising will. His former energy was unbroken.

*

Sooriya felt awful about being a prisoner on his own premises. From his father's history, he knew about the despotism of Sri Lanka's police. His special aura, and the fact that his place was always well visited, aroused envy and resentment.

By now, only a few late tourists came for dinner. The holiday season was over. Sooriya didn't talk much. Mostly, after finishing dinner he retreated to the back yard. He would glance at me discreetly to follow him. After some time, I also said good night. It was risky to be seen together too often. Only Ram was aware of our game, but he made no comment.

One evening, when I was telling Sooriya that I had to leave for India soon, he took up his tale about his previous life.

"After my father was murdered, I simply wasn't capable of staying in my home town," he began. "As the eldest son, I should have been his heir, but I was too young and not ready to succeed my father. I was no help to my family, not even to myself."

At that time Sooriya had decided to set out for India.

"It was like an escape, not feeling my body," he said. "My mother insisted on giving me her last money."

It wasn't very much though. Sooriya took the ferry from northern Sri Lanka to southern India along "Adam's Bridge," a chain of sandbanks, coral reefs, and small islands, about 20 miles in length.

Without a rupee, he arrived in Madras (today's Chennai).

"There was so much poverty," Sooriya remembered. "Dead bodies lay in the streets. Children searched for food like dogs, me as well. A mother with children, having almost nothing to eat themselves, gave me a chapati. This touched me very much."

Sooriya was still mourning his father and felt guilty because he had let his family down during those difficult times.

For the beginning he stayed overnight in a church. Later he got acquainted with a Dutchman with whom he would travel through India and visit many places. They had no money for a train, so they traveled on foot.

"I have walked through India for hundreds of miles in order to find forgiveness for the man who killed my father."

Sooriya met sadhus and yogis on his long trip. On their footpath, those ascetics never stayed at the same place for more than two or three days. They used to sleep under trees.

"They were like flowing rivers. In the jungle I have experienced a strong spiritual connection between them and me. Even a sadhu lady from Sri Lanka stayed with them. She wore her hair in long dreadlocks, and was a very magic person."

"How old was she?" I wanted to know.

"Nobody knew her age," he replied. "Maybe eighty, perhaps ninety. Whenever I sat near her, she took all my pain away from me. She seemed to know everything about me, although I hadn't told her anything. And she helped me to go through my grief to the other side."

He didn't believe in meeting someone accidentally: "People you are supposed to meet during your life, you will meet," he was convinced.

For me, this was a completely unfamiliar world. I would never be able to tell such stories to even my best friends without being declared nuts. But for the moment, Germany was more distant than ever to me. In Sri Lanka, I belonged to a minority raised in a different religion.

Sooriya had also met Maharishi Mahesh Yogi in India, the holy man who inspired the Beatles.

"Many Europeans at that time were looking for spiritual knowledge and wisdom," Sooriya said. Some of them were misguided by profiteers who only wanted to make money with this movement.

"Sometimes I was a student, other times I was a servant," Sooriya said.

He learned to cook with simple ingredients. Knowledgeable men taught him yoga and meditation and helped him forget his grief for a while.

He spent much time at Hindu temples, learning skills in "Sacred Copper Art," the art of working with copper, crafting beautiful objects and images to adorn temples.

Sooriya told me how hard he had been working for little money.

"I did not feel the hot sun, or the wind, or the pain when I had to walk on stones barefooted."

In northern India he got to know "Puri-Baba," an old man who burned dead bodies and strewed the ashes into the Ganges. "Mother Ganga," as he called the famous river, was sacred to him.

"The river will always find its path," Sooriya said. "My life is like this river."

Sooriya's journey lasted for five years before he came to the Himalayan village where he lived with a sadhu who invited him home to his small and simple hut.

"He taught me everything about fire, which is my element."

One day the sadhu gave him his blessing.

"At that moment my heart broke," Sooriya recalled. "I was crying, and all my pain and all my bitterness fell from me. I was able now to decide in favor of love instead of hatred. If I don't heal myself, I can't live with people."

His sadhu-friend revealed to him that his life would be a new one if his heart opened to love, forgiveness and understanding. While Sooriya was reminiscing, I became aware how touched he was by the memory of this turning point in his life.

He had wanted to stay in the region, but his friend said to him: "You cannot be a sadhu. Many people are waiting for you to bring light to them, Sooriya Kumar. Your life will become a good one, and you will do good to your fellow beings."

The sadhu blessed him with sacred ashes, and Sooriya set out for his new life.

"I was making the first steps on my life's journey, as it was intended for me," he concluded for the night.

*

Barbara and I were the only guests on the property now. Day in, day out, the Canadian had been waiting for her money transfer from home – without success. Moreover, I would soon receive my new passport from the German

Embassy. Then I would have to leave Sri Lanka. The restaurants and lodgings in Arugam Bay were deserted – the tourists had gone.

Occasionally, when I bought something in Jothi's little shop, I met Fred, who could speak German. He had been living in Arugam Bay for a long time. Fred hardly ever visited a restaurant. He was married to a local woman, and they lived off the tourist scene. From time to time I enjoyed talking to someone in my mother tongue. One day he told me how he had ended up here.

"In the beginning of the 1970s, I heard about a beautiful place called Arugam Bay – parties, surfing, smoking pot," Fred was grinning. "In 1975, I was a young British soldier who had been deployed at U-Tapao in Thailand, one of Asia's biggest airports. The last six months of the war in Vietnam were lying ahead of us. Almost all the B-52 long-range bombers were lifting off from U-Tapao. England was playing no official role in this war, but a British freighter had been captured, most probably by the Vietcong. It was our job to settle this."

This slender, fair-haired man seemed unsentimental as he spoke.

"Finally, in 1977, I had a long vacation," Fred continued. "I sat on my motorbike – a nice BMW R 69 S – and was off to India!"

From there he had taken the ferry to Talaimannar in northern Sri Lanka.

"Sri Lanka means 'Beautiful Land', but I didn't like it very much," Fred said. "I had seen far more interesting countries before."

Fred had an extraordinary history: "My genetic father was a diplomat from Douglas on the Isle of Man."

His father had met Fred's mother, a Dutch woman, in Hong Kong. Their son had been born there.

"I have two birth certificates, one from Hong Kong, and one issued in Germany," he said.

His genetic father had been married to someone other than his mother, Fred explained. In Berlin, his mother met a German man who married her and adopted young Fred.

"The birth certificates had been forged so that my diplomat father's honour could be preserved," Fred knew.

His mother died when the boy was four years old. A few years later, the German man who had adopted Fred lost his life as well.

"From the time I was ten years old, I have lived in various countries and mostly on my own - in Africa, Uganda, Kenya, and Tanzania - and later on in Brazil. But this is a long story..."

Fred let his past be and turned back to the present - how he had settled down right here, of all places.

"After I crossed the bridge into Arugam Bay, something clicked in my head! This place is something very special."

He took a big gulp from his bottle.

"I parked the bike opposite Sooriya's Beach Hut. Lousy waves during that time of the year. No parties in sight. But then I saw this attractive Sri Lankan girl standing on the other side of the road. I had to get her into my bed - normal procedure, if you were an ex-soldier with a 1970s feeling. But this was not as easy as I had thought; I had to marry her first.

"Ok, so we got married within a fortnight. Since then, I'm stuck here," he said drily.

He didn't really make a sad impression on me.

"My wife was born into an honored Tamil family with roots in Colombo and Jaffna. She was in Arugam Bay only for a holiday at the time we met. We thought it wise not to advertise our marriage or show ourselves together in public; it wasn't a bad idea, really, if you look at the situation nowadays. Several members of my wife's family have been killed since in this insane civil war— murdered by formerly nice, but now very envious, neighbors. The international news media isn't well informed, and neither are the tourists. We know the names of those murderers, but they don't have to fear a trial. This, too, is Sri Lanka – Silly Lanka – a country like no other."

Fred said goodbye to go home to his wife, who was pregnant. Before he left, he gave me a piece of advice: "Rumor is spreading that you're not only a tourist for Sooriya. Whatever you both are doing, keep it hidden behind the hedges of Beach Hut, or even better in your cabana. You mean more danger for Sooriya. I know what I'm talking about."

It was raining every day. Sunshine in the morning was followed by massive rainstorms at noon. Big drops came down and within a few minutes made a big muddy puddle of our place. The ocean was raging and huge waves were pounding the shore.

Barbara and I had become something like friends. To while away the time, we had begun to play carrom, a popular board game in Sri Lanka. Being inside restaurant was preferable to the violent monsoon outside.

Sometimes I sat on the low wall to the backyard, from which I had a good view of the garden. The rainy days here were not as grey as in Germany. Nature seemed to explode with greenery. The sunbeams shining through this sea of leaves were reflected by millions of raindrops. Strong, colorful blossoms somehow withstood the patter of the monsoon rain. It was quite an event to see the vegetation and ground drink greedily after the dry season. Only a few days ago, all the plants had looked brown and dead. Now countless young, juicy green shoots sprouted from their buds.

Sooriya and I spent long afternoons together during the wet season. But Barbara became increasingly depressed by the rain. She missed the entertaining evenings in the restaurant, where interesting travelers from many nations had met. Whenever the rain tapered away, she set off for Pottuvil.

One day she returned from the town beaming with joy. Finally, her money had been transferred to a bank in Colombo. She intended to leave next morning.

Barbara promised us she'd be back from the capital within three days. Upon her return, she intended to pay for the long period Sooriya had let her live and eat at the place. The brothers needed the money urgently.

She put her passport into the "safe." Barbara had almost no luggage left after having been robbed, and she was very happy that at last she'd be able to buy new clothes in Colombo with the money from her transfer. I had lent her a little money for the bus to the capital, and in return she promised to inquire about my passport at the German Embassy.

Barbara hadn't returned after the three days. We had been relying on her. Then I noticed that cash was missing from my bag. After a week without any news from her, we decided to open the cotton bag she had put in the safe. It was filled with paper scraps. Now we knew: she'd never intended to pay for the accommodation and food. We also assumed that it was her who had stolen Tom's money bag. Clearly, we would never hear from Barbara again.

The shameless way she had betrayed Sooriya and his brothers left me speechless. They had gone out of their way to help her.

"It's only money," Sooriya calmed me, surprised at my anger. "Money will come and go. I'm only sad that we've lost a friend."

Sooriya hadn't left the property since his problems with the soldiers from Pottuvil. He seemed unsatisfied and depressed. My friend so hated being restricted!

Suba took on the task of buying the necessary things now in Arugam Bay and in town. But even the Sinhalese experienced disapproval and hostility by now. He was being shunned in the village; nobody liked to talk to him any longer. People advised him to stay away from the Tamil brothers.

The men at our place listened to the radio much of their time. In Colombo, the bombings were increasing. More and more Tamils had been forced to retreat to the north. The eastern territories, where Tamils and Sinhalese still lived side by side, were being occupied by the Sri Lankan army.

Meanwhile, the restaurant shut to tourists. I was the last tourist there and took my meals in the kitchen, together with the brothers and Suba. Many of the groceries we guests had been used to were no longer available. But I had long since adjusted to local food.

In the meantime, the rain showers were lessening some; then, in no time at all, the sun turned the place into an open-air sauna.

One morning, I returned from the well where I had rinsed my musty smelling clothes. I had only a few hours to get them dry in the sun. Sooriya had just finished his morning yoga and meditation in his small temple.

"Today is a special day," he called from afar. "Something exceptional will happen. It is on its way here."

"Have you received a message?" I replied, happy about his optimistic mood.

"News, yes, but not by the means you are imagining. I just know that someone or something will come to us today. There will be a change."

"How can you know?" I insisted. He was making me curious.

"The blackbirds told me."

I glanced at Sooriya, examining him. You never knew if he was serious or making fun. But he looked very assured. I recalled his family's special attachment to crows. I couldn't imagine anything concrete, and my European way of judging was considerably hampering me.

"I have to tell Ram immediately," he exclaimed, and without any further explanation, Sooriya walked past me and toward the kitchen, where his brother was preparing breakfast.

I followed him quickly. The brothers were speaking in Tamil, but their faces showed that they believed him.

Sooriya dressed himself in his finest white lungi and retreated to his temple. Ram and Shiva waited in the restaurant. They had no doubts about their eldest brother's premonition. Even I was waiting, although I had difficulty believing in blackbirds predicting anything.

Every time someone walked by the entrance to the place, Shiva jumped up in expectation. Nothing happened. At noon, it started to rain as usual, and we were still holding out in the restaurant.

All of a sudden, a bicycle turned into the Beach Hut entrance. The soaked postman from town handed Ram a letter addressed to Sooriya. Ram ran back to the dry restaurant, and Shiva raced to the temple to fetch his elder brother.

Sooriya had painted ashes on his forehead and his chest. By the time he arrived at the restaurant, the markings had been smeared by the rain. As Sooriya took the envelope, I was able to read the sender's name. The letter had been sent from the USA. He examined the envelope from every angle.

"Don't you want to open it?" I asked.

He smiled at my impatience:

"This letter has been on a long journey before it arrived here. No harm will be done if we wait a little longer," he replied with calm composure. Sooriya then returned to the temple, to read the letter there.

Ram waited calmly and patiently; Shiva paced up and down the restaurant, and I was bursting with anticipation.

At last, Sooriya returned and told his brothers, in Tamil, what the letter said. I could read from her faces, that they had received good news. Finally, Sooriya was so nice as to tell me, as well.

"Some time ago," he began, "some American students were staying here. They were taking part in a project nearby, studying traditional agriculture in Sri Lanka. For recreation, they liked to visit Arugam Bay to swim and surf and party with the tourists. I gave them a bit of the herbal wisdom that sadhus passed on to me during my stay in India. Especially, Peter became a very close friend to me. I haven't heard from them for a long time. In this letter from Peter, he writes that he and his fellow students have been reading about the civil war in Sri Lanka, and that they are worried. The daily news in the USA is publishing horrible pictures. At their university, the students have been collecting money, and they want me to come live in America until the civil war is over. One of their fathers has some influence, and he would arrange everything for me."

Sooriya fell silent for a moment. "This is a tempting offer, you know, and I feel very grateful that the students haven't forgotten me. But I can't leave my brothers behind."

Ram and Shiva protested violently.

"They won't harm me and our younger brothers," Ram said turning to me. "The villagers are after Sooriya. I feel afraid for him. Talk to him, perhaps he'll listen to you."

"Nobody can come to a decision except me," Sooriya threw in. "I have to think about this. Tomorrow morning, I shall walk to Crocodile Rock. This magic site will help me find the right answer."

Then Sooriya turned to me: "I want you to come along and meet with this special place."

"Crocodile Rock?" I was wondering at the strange name. "Is it shaped like a crocodile?"

"No," Sooriya replied. "It belongs to the crocodiles."

*

It was still dark when we set out. Sooriya preferred not to be seen by the villagers. It was very well possible that soldiers were on patrol on the beach.

"Crocodile Rock is a secluded place." he said. "We have to be very careful that nobody follows us there."

The moon bathed the ocean in a fluid silver glow as we snuck along the beach below palm trees in the cover of night. A few dogs tried to follow us, but Sooriya made them go away, whispering a single command.

However, I couldn't get rid of the feeling that we still were being tracked. I turned around and thought that I saw a dark shape. Sooriya turned as well, but then went on hastily.

"Somebody is hunting us," I tried to make Sooriya aware.

"That's ok," he assured me." "He is a friend."

Soon we passed the little tea-shop at the end of the bay, where the Australians had deposited their boards. Everything was lying in silence. The local beach boy, who guarded the surfboards, was soundly asleep.

Only after we had rounded the bend past the tea-shop did we leave the sheltering palm trees. As we could no longer be seen from the village, we proceeded along the shore in the moonlight. The surf broke loudly, drowning out any other noise. In the darkness, nothing could be seen except a few yards of beach right in front of us, and the black border ahead where the jungle began.

I was relieved when morning dawned. Again, I turned around, and now I clearly saw the man who was still following us from some distance.

Slowly, he strolled through the sand, swinging a stick in one hand. Seemingly uninterested in us, he sat down and scribbled something with his stick. After a few minutes he jumped up again and ran toward us.

"Swami!" Sooriya called him, but the sound of the surf swallowed his words. Now I recognized the crazy old man I met before on my morning swims. He was swirling in our direction and singing loudly in a contest with the gushing sea. Sooriya said something to him in Tamil. The flipped-out old guy came to me, bowed deeply, and moved his folded hands to his forehead.

"This means he wants to say sorry, because he has frightened you," Sooriya explained.

Swami sat down again and took a beatific look at the ocean. The sun was rising above the horizon now, and the waves turned a beautiful orange.

We stayed fascinated, but Sooriya urged me to go on. Swami remained seated and said hello to this gorgeous daybreak. A little later, he jumped up to follow us again, always keeping the same distance between him and us.

At bright daylight the landscape had lost its threatening impression. Ahead of us stretched a long, wide beach. No humans or huts occupied the space between here and the thick, dense jungle. Many birds performed a very noisy concert. A gang of screeching monkeys played in the tree tops.

The temperature had been quite agreeable until now, but the higher the sun rose, the more the heat bothered me. Sooriya seemed unaffected. He traversed the hot sand at a steady pace. He always walked like this. I had trouble keeping up with him. My skin started to burn, and I felt exhausted.

"I need a break," I gasped eventually. My feet seemed to be made of lead.

Sooriya took a cloth from his bag. He dipped it into the sea and wrapped it around my head like a turban. In addition, he wet his spare lungi and covered my shoulders with it.

"We have to go on," he urged me again. "The midday sun will burn your skin and you'll look like a lobster."

"Like a lobster?" I looked at my reddening arms.

"We villagers call tourists, who have been roasting in the sun too long, lobsters," Sooriya admitted with a grin. He, of course, was protected from the sun by his dark skin.

Meanwhile, Swami had disappeared. My first thought was that he had given up his pursuit. But, suddenly, the white-haired old man emerged from the jungle. In his hands he held two coconuts, in which he opened holes with a pointed stone.

With a theatrical bow, he handed us the shells. Gratefully, we relished the lukewarm juice. Strengthened, I was able to continue our trip.

At last we could make out Crocodile Rock from afar - massive black metamorphic rock sloping gently upward out of the sand. I was so glad when we arrived at our destination. But Sooriya wanted to walk farther.

"Another rock will follow, with a cave in it," he said. "Some say it belongs to Crocodile Rock, others call it Elephant Rock. It doesn't really matter. In this area we have both crocodiles and elephants. In Sri Lanka, sometimes names are not so important."

Soon I saw the black colossus looming at the edge of the Indian Ocean. At the foot of the rock, a lake glittered in the sun, surrounded by lush greenery. A narrow strip of sand separated the lake's calm, clear water from the ocean surf.

A swim in a fresh water lake! That is exactly the right thing to lift my spirits, I thought. I wanted to run to the lake's edge and jump in, but immediately Sooriya grabbed my arm.

"Don't get too close," he warned me. "Crocodiles are living there."

Shocked, I came to a halt. Swami, however, was not afraid at all. Singing a song, he skipped to the lakeshore and filled empty coconut shells with the fresh water. Within a moment, flat crocodile snouts emerged from below the surface. They approached Swami, who continued to busy himself with the shells, still completely relaxed. Shortly before the reptiles could snap at him, the very agile old man jumped on the lowest boulder of Elephant Rock and climbed up to us, balancing a filled shell in one hand.

Coming from the direction of Arugam Bay, the rock was accessible only by way of the sandy strip that separated the lake from the sea. The rock itself was steep and slippery. Just below the top, we found the cave, where we settled down. Inside it was cool and shady. A soft breeze blew from the ocean, and we relished the grand view across the beach, the sea, and the jungle treetops. Our idyll would have been perfect, but for the crocodiles, which were hiding under the vegetation reaching into the lake. They frightened me.

"Crocodiles don't climb on rocks," Sooriya soothed me, having noticed my worried glance.

When Swami felt sure that the beasts had retreated far enough, he climbed down to refill our shells. He moved in no hurry. Obviously, he knew exactly how much time it would take the crocodiles to cross the lake from its shady shore to the foot of our rock. Once more, the sleek animals were too late.

Sooriya had taken along tea leaves. An old metal pot had been deposited in a crevice. As soon as Swami brought up water, he climbed down again and ran into the jungle to fetch wood for a fire.

The tea that Sooriya boiled on our fireplace tasted sweet and salty at the same time. But a few gulps of it livened me up, and all the pains of our long walk were forgotten.

We sat on a ledge outside the cave and watched Swami having fun teasing the crocodiles. Then, in the blink of an eye, he left us.

In the afternoon, Swami returned. He brought with him leaves and fruit from the jungle. With rice from Beach Hut and with Swami's dark green leaves, Sooriya prepared a tasty dish on our fireplace. The ingredients were very healthy, he emphasized. This was a common dish in poor families. During his stay in India, Sooriya learned to cook nourishing meals with simple ingredients.

After our little dinner, Swami said goodbye. He folded his hands, bowed his head, and gaily twinkled at me before climbing down. Once again, he couldn't resist washing his face by the lakeside until the crocodiles had almost reached the spot where he was splashing about. The crazy old guy danced along the beach, singing. I watched him until the distance had swallowed him.

Sooriya and I spent the night in the cave. A fierce thunderstorm had come up. Violent lightning above the ocean repeatedly illuminated the darkness for a few seconds. I wasn't listening to animal noises from the jungle or to the stirred-up ocean. I had even forgotten about the crocodiles gliding through the dark water in the lake below. This night on the Rock belonged to Sooriya and me, and no one and nothing else existed except us.

When I woke up the following morning, he was sitting on the ledge outside, deep in meditation. The storm had calmed and the waves had smoothed down. I watched Sooriya from our bed. His legs were crossed in the lotus position, and his hands rested on his knees, relaxed. He had closed his eyes, and the breeze played with his dark brown curls. Sooriya seemed to feel my eyes on him. He looked at me and smiled: "Tea is ready. You have been sleeping for many hours."

Swami appeared on the beach. In his hands he held avocados and wild mangos from the jungle. Sooriya took the fruit gratefully but insisted on Swami keeping some for himself before he retreated.

Silently, I watched Sooriya cut the fruit into appetizing pieces. Fully absorbed in the act, he demonstrated his respect for the food. We had been so close last night, and now his mind had moved on to someplace else.

Was he struggling to decide whether or not to go to America? How would Sooriya get along in the Western world? I knew him only in his Asian environment, in a tropical climate, dressed only in his lungi and always barefoot. I was unable to imagine him in a Western suit, wearing shoes and possibly a warm jacket. Had he ever seen snow or skyscrapers or highways? In Arugam Bay, there wasn't a single television set where you might get a tiny idea about foreign countries and cultures.

Lost in thought, Sooriya looked toward the ocean, the sand, and the magnificent landscape, seemingly without seeing them. A herd of elephants had appeared and taken a few steps out of the jungle. They were so peaceful. Being in no hurry, they leisurely trotted alongside their youngsters. Was it in my imagination, or had I in fact heard crows cawing? The sound gave me a chill up my spine. Sooriya fixed his calm eyes to mine.

"You mustn't be afraid," he said and smiled. "Not of the black birds and not for me."

Then he began to tell me about another part of his life, about which I had no idea. Sometimes I had asked myself where he acquired his urbane self-confidence. It was this quality that set him apart from all the other locals I had met. How could this Sri Lankan in his beginning thirties have accumulated such a profound knowledge and global understanding? Never had I felt misunderstood by him, although I was an European, a foreigner. To me, Sooriya was so familiar, and at the same time a mystery.

*

"From India, after I left my sadhu, I didn't return to Sri Lanka," he began his tale. "I wanted to see Europe. I had come across so many travelers from that continent. The sadhu from the foothills of the Himalayas had sent me on this trip."

Sooriya had almost no money when he set out from India toward Europe in the beginning of the 1970s. His path led him through Pakistan and across the Khyber Pass to Afghanistan.

"At that time Afghanistan was one of the most beautiful Muslim countries," he said. "They were wonderful people. They offered me food. I couldn't accept meat, though, because I'm a vegetarian. All I needed simply came to me."

Sometimes he earned enough money to take a train, but mostly he hitchhiked.

"Many trucks were taking this rout," he recalled, "and also numerous travelers with their VW vans or simple trailers."

Sooriya wasn't hitchhiking the way we do in Europe, thumb up. Often, he decided to stay in a village or a town for a few days. Friendly travelers offered to take him along in their cars for some distance. His journey took him all the way through Iran.

"I was very interested in the nomads' lives," he told me. "Riding on their camels, they looked like shadows in the desert. This impression molded me. We all are nomads on our lives' journeys. The body is only the vehicle or the camel, and it carries you from one place to another."

After he reached Turkey, he became fascinated with the mosques and the prayers being sung by the muezzins. He had been very moved, even if he wasn't allowed to join their prayers. His next stop was Istanbul.

"Right opposite the Blue Mosque there was the Pudding-Shop, where travelers from many European countries met – mostly French, German or Swiss. It didn't matter to them which color or nationality you were. Most noticeable was the fact that the Europeans who were still on their way to India were very different from those who had just returned from there. The latter had learned meditation, yoga, and new music. Many of them carried their instruments with them for many thousand miles. New impressions had changed the young men and women. And for me, this was the best time in my life. We were like a family."

From Istanbul, Sooriya set out for Europe. He hitchhiked through Bulgaria and arrived in the former Yugoslavia.

"This was Tito's era," Sooriya informed me. "They were having extremely difficult times in Yugoslavia then."

For a whole month, Sooriya spent every night in the train station of the city of Belgrade. In the early mornings, he had to leave as soon as the cleaners showed up. Sooriya had arrived in Europe.

I assumed that his sad facial expression showed disappointment and the loss of his dreams. But, as if he was able to read my thoughts, he continued:

"I had come without any expectations at all. Only rigid points of view can be disappointed."

Sooriya hitchhiked to Dubrovnik, located at the Mediterranean Sea, followed by Split.

"Although the Yugoslavians were having such hard times, I was meeting with so much honesty and friendliness. From India I had been used to theft, but in Yugoslavia I was having many good experiences."

He fell quiet for a moment, smiling to himself.

"They invited me to dinner – and they were having a drink, that was unknown to me."

I was surprised to hear him add: "Schnapps." I didn't know this German word was common in English.

For the young Hindu, unused to any liquor at all, drinking the local Slivovitz obviously was a very good new experience.

Sooriya would sleep on the beach or sometimes climbed across a wall to spend a night in a school building. One time the police arrested him and put him in jail for a night.

"On this plank bed I had my first good night in weeks," he said, taking a positive point of view. The policemen didn't speak any English, and my Yugoslavian consisted of about three words. Next day, they returned my passport to me and let me go."

Sooriya left Yugoslavia and went on to Austria.

"In Vienna I met two young women. They were very interested in India and asked me if I was skilled in palmistry. I knew a bit about it, I told them. I was very surprised when my visions obviously were right. Blackbirds were sitting around us everywhere."

In Vienna, Sooriya had a wonderful time. He met and befriended many young people.

"After a while I decided to hitchhike to Rome. I stood at a roadside for a whole day, but nobody wanted to take me along. A Catholic priest, who had been watching me for quite a while, approached me. With a gesture of his hand, he stopped passing cars. The drivers would come to a halt, and he inquired of all of them where they were heading. One family was on their way to Florence and invited me to come with them. So, I took a seat in their car."

In Florence, the architecture and churches greatly impressed Sooriya. What he had learned about "Sacred

Temple Art" in India had its equivalent in the local art, but in a different way. Being a Hindu, he didn't think in isolated religious categories. He gave no preference to Buddhist temples, Muslim mosques or Christian churches. Being from Sri Lanka, it was a gift for Sooriya, to be able to see so many beautiful things. And, as always, he firmly believed he was walking a predetermined path.

His journey led him from Florence to Rome where Sooriya visited the Vatican and St. Peter's Cathedral with its impressive dome.

At the "Spanish Stairs," tourists from many nations met. Some of them had been in Asia as well. They took great interest in Sooriya. His whole appearance seemed exotic to them. In the seventies, not many travelers from completely different cultures showed up in European capitals.

"Those young people were wide open and curious of what I might be telling them. And they were very eager to help me," Sooriya remembered.

Soon they were chatting about this and that, and sometimes his new acquaintances invited him home to stay overnight. He stayed in Rome for a while to explore the ancient city with all its history. Sooriya was fascinated by its famous architecture. But he was eager to continue his journey through Europe. Wandering along the coast, he visited Pisa, Genoa and Milan. A kind Australian man surprised him by giving him 50 dollars, so that he was able to get to Switzerland.

"The coldness was biting," Sooriya recalled. "I had no warm clothes, not even a sleeping bag. But what a beautiful landscape! Everything was so different from elsewhere." For a moment, he tried to find the right words to describe his impression. "So clean and orderly," he added at last.

Maria, a Swiss woman he had met on one of his trips, had given him her address. He should visit her whenever he came to her home country, she had said to him.

Irresolute, he stood in front of the huge premises, located at a lake. Sooriya hadn't thought that Maria's family was so wealthy. But, finally, he rang the bell. A domestic servant opened the door.

"Their language sounded very strange to me with its guttural pronunciation, when I heard Swiss German for the first time."

The villa was luxuriously furnished with marble tiles and valuable furniture. These unusual surroundings intimidated him a little, but he received a heartfelt welcome.

"I had my own room with a modern bathroom. Never had I seen one like this before." He grinned to recall such a funny occasion.

"I intended to freshen up, but the countless little flacons and tubes confused me, and I couldn't find out which one was for brushing my teeth. I wasn't able to read the labels."

Without giving it any further thought, Sooriya decided on something with a fine scent to it. However, as soon as he had started to brush, an unbelievable amount of foam filled his mouth, and he couldn't get it to stop foaming.

"Up to today, I have never found out what it was," Sooriya chuckled.

During his childhood he hadn't known toothbrushes. In Sri Lanka and India, people broke little branches from the neem tree to clean their teeth. These contain antibiotic substances, and Sooriya's snow-white teeth showed that it works.

Sooriya declined to lie down in the big elegant bed. He was accustomed to sleeping on the floor. He took only his pillow down and cautiously wrapped it in his clothes, in order not to soil it. On the carpet, he spread his bedsheet. The chambermaid looked a little startled when she asked him to come downstairs for dinner.

"Plates had been placed on the table in front of me, flanked by at least four or five different knives and forks."

On his trips, Sooriya had been afraid on only a few occasions. But this situation made him sweat with embarrassment. He had never eaten with cutlery.

"Finally, I grabbed a knife at random, tried to cut something on my plate - and my food went flying through the air and across the festively set table."

Sooriya burst out laughing at the memory.

"The domestic help cut my food into little bites, as if I was a child."

His hosts didn't disapprove of his clumsiness. They relished their meat dishes, and the vegetarian from Sri Lanka was enjoyed exquisitely prepared vegetables.

"Although the Swiss family was so kind to me, I didn't want to stay for long. This was too much of everything for my taste. I had to get out of there. The family insisted on giving me money for my further journey. Oh, this was very much money, for someone like me."

With the cash, it was possible for Sooriya to take a train to Zurich via Luzern. Near Zurich lived acquaintances he had met in India. They picked him up at the station with their VW camper.

"For them I was a guru," he said. "I was preparing Indian dishes for them and their friends while I was staying at their place. We talked for hours every night, while some of them were making music. I felt very much at home with my Zurich hosts."

Among the young people who had made long trips, it was a common habit to exchange addresses. Because Sooriya wanted to get on to Germany, his Zurich friends gave him an address in a little town near Munich.

"Actually, I would have left the place sooner, but there was this nice girl called Ilse..."

Sooriya was smiling at his memory of her.

"We listened to music from Cat Stevens or Simon and Garfunkel. This was a beautiful time."

In Germany he felt so good that he decided to stay longer. Sooriya started taking German lessons at the Goethe Institute in Munich. He stuck with it for six months.

When he told me about it, I was very surprised. He had always spoken to me in English. I wasn't aware he could speak German. He gave me a few samples of my language. His accent was so funny! But soon he returned to English, which was much easier for him. From now on, our conversations got more detailed and easier. Whenever I lacked an English word, I would say it in German, and Sooriya could understand me right away.

In Munich he liked to visit the "Englischer Garten," a large park designed in English tradition, mirroring nature. There he met African musicians, among many other people. One day, a German addressed him. His appearance was quite wild, especially his long beard. The man invited Sooriya for dinner in a restaurant and turned out to be well-educated, a scholar with a doctorate.

"When he said goodbye to me, he gave me about two hundred German marks and his address. I was to call him at any time, whenever I might have a problem."

Sooriya finished his German lessons at Goethe Institute after six months. Meanwhile he became rather good at my language.

"You get along much easier in a foreign country if you know the language of its people," he emphasized.

Nonetheless, he wanted to get away from the little town outside Munich. Sooriya was a restless man then. In his words: a river must flow. Nothing will stop the flow designated for the river.

A photographer from Amsterdam, who had been very interested in India, had given Sooriya his address. So Sooriya traveled to the Netherlands, where he spent three months.

Once more, he was drawn to Germany, and he decided to visit Bernd. Bernd's parents were living on a big farm in Lower Saxony, a German province, and Sooriya enjoyed helping them, especially with the animals. As a vegetarian, he had to get used to all the meat around him and in many dishes. He enjoyed vegetables and developed a love of the farm's cheese.

The farmers offered him training in dairy farming, and he agreed. Sooriya passed his final examinations in dairy farming after two and a half years.

He had written letters to his family in Sri Lanka, and his brother Ram decided to visit, taking the overland route.

"We were having such a great and carefree time," Sooriya enthused.

Traveling with Ram through Germany, they got to know Hans. He was living in a commune. Its members were living in an old "Fachwerkhaus" (a half-timbered house built in the traditional style of framework) in the countryside.

"Hans Baba," Sooriya called him. Baba is a very respectful Hindi affix to a name, meaning father or teacher. Hans was the only European he ever called Baba. People, who are supposed to meet, will meet, he firmly believed.

"He had a big heart, and he was doing what in his opinion had to be done," Sooriya said. "The people living in this commune, one of the early ones in the area, had come from many nations. The Molbergen-House was well known in the scene. Ram and I stayed with them for a while, leaving and returning from time to time. Hans Baba's house was open to everybody. In the 1960s, Hans was one of the first Germans traveling to India and Sri Lanka by land, with a little car, a Renault 4. You could feel the Asian influence on him."

Whenever Ram and Sooriya visited Hans, they would cook for the whole commune. Their Asian food was very popular in the Molbergen-House. And, of course, everyone was very interested in Sooriya's knowledge of yoga and meditation.

"I was exotic to them. At that time, not many people from Sri Lanka or India were visiting Germany. The young generation's interest in my culture was big in the 1970s. Young people wanted to break up obsolete structures, to give and take tolerance, to learn and teach. Europe was modernizing, and I was only a small grain of sand in this big dune. But a dune is made of millions of grains."

Sooriya went on to Denmark, where he lived in the Free City of Christiania, an autonomous municipal area in the capital Copenhagen, tolerated by the state of Denmark.

Hippies and illegal house occupants had settled down in Christiania in the beginning 1970s, being the alternative scene of Copenhagen.

"This was a period of complete upheaval in Europe and a revolution against the parents' obsolete values and habits," Sooriya said. "A young guy told me that his father owned factories in 120 countries. The son didn't want his money, nor to succeed him; he just wanted to be left alone by him."

Via Sweden, Sooriya reached freezing Lapland and Finland.

The Finnish villagers he encountered had never seen a dark-skinned man like him before.

"Go away, gipsy man, it's too cold for you," Sooriya recalled hearing. "He is looking like someone from a tropical country, with the sun shining all day long."

Sooriya grinned, for in this very moment big Sri Lankan rain clouds were clustering.

"I've met so many interesting people on my trips. Sometimes I get the impression I know more about Germany than most locals, because I've been hitchhiking from south to north and from west to east. It felt like a second home country to me. I've found many friends there, and we keep in touch. Many of them have visited me at the Beach Hut, since I own our place in Arugam Bay. It has always been a place for meeting friends, and they call me Sooriya Baba."

He visited Europe eight times, overland from Asia, sometimes accompanied by Ram, until he felt he wanted to settle down in wonderful Arugam Bay. Unfortunately, now he had to leave it involuntarily because of politics.

"This belongs to my Karma, too, and to my predetermined future," Sooriya was sure.

Despite the difficult circumstances in his country, he seemed calm and optimistic.

"I'm not afraid of a life in America," he stated finally. "But I fear for my family. Shall I leave them on their own once more? Shall I follow my river?"

The next day Sooriya had come to a decision.

"I'll accept my friends' offer and go to America, until Sri Lanka has returned to normal. From there, I'll able to help my family in a better way. In Arugam Bay I'll stay a prisoner with no opportunity to act in any way. I haven't been looking for this development. This has come to me, and it is confronting me with a new situation. I'm so grateful to my American friends for helping me."

It wasn't so certain that he could get out of his country during the current political situation. Tamils were not being allowed to leave Sri Lanka.

"If I'm successful, I'll try to earn some money in USA and send it to my family. This is the best I can do. This is a big chance for a Tamil guy."

But Sooriya worried about his family.

"My brothers should leave Arugam Bay as well," Sooriya agonized. "They have to fight their ways through to the north and to Mannar, where our mother and sisters are living. I'll ask Suba to take care of the place until we're able to return. He is a Sinhalese; he won't be exposed to any hostilities after we are gone. Not many tourists will come to our place after the monsoon season, anyhow. All those soldiers – who would want to spend his holidays in a country having a civil war?"

At around noon, the rain returned. We were still sitting in the cave below the rock's top. The pouring rain was like a liquid curtain drawn in front of our cave's exit. Nonetheless, we had to leave in the afternoon.

It made no sense to protect ourselves from the flood. Within a few minutes we were soaked to the skin. The ocean was so wild; we were unable to hear each other. So, we walked along the shore in silence.

Swami had been gone since morning. Only when we were approaching Arugam Bay in the evening did he show up from nowhere. We were holding out in the thicket until the sun had set. Then we set foot on the bay. In Surfers' Spot, we saw a light. Local beach boys were sitting inside.

In a snap decision, Swami ran towards the tea shop and began to dance around as if he had gone crazy. He skipped about, threw himself on the floor, and kicked his legs into the air like a baby.

Despite his bad teeth showing, his laughter was infectious and irresistible. Of course, everybody knew this strange old guy, and his behavior was okay with everybody. The young men laughed at him and invited him for a drink. Sometimes Swami puzzled me. He was a bit crazy, but this time he clearly wanted to distract the boys so that we could return to the place unseen.

"What does it mean, if people say that you're crazy," Sooriya seemed to have read my mind. "Who is normal? The soldiers? The bomb attackers? We Asians or you Europeans?"

There was no time for further philosophical contemplation. Sooriya and I were sneaking back to his place in the dark of night. Nobody seemed to have noticed our absence. Only Ram, Shiva and Sri were waiting impatiently for us, and for Sooriya's decision. They were very glad to hear what their elder brother was telling them. The only thing left to do now was to prepare Sooriya's departure.

Chapter 5

The next morning the brothers held counsel with Suba about what had to be organized. Sooriya needed a passport, and it was not easy to get one issued in the current political situation. The administrative body was in Colombo. But it was very dangerous for Sooriya to be seen in the capital. Suba had heard the latest news in the radio. Meanwhile the government had declared a state of emergency in the whole country. From sunset to sunrise nobody could stay outside in the streets.

"Today the doctor who has cured you from your illness has come to us from Colombo," Sooriya informed me at around noon. "He wants me to visit him tonight, and he has asked if you want to join us."

Of course, the curfew was also compulsory in Arugam Bay, but the doctor was living only a few huts away from us, and the street running through the village usually was neglected by the soldiers.

"I need to see him," Sooriya emphasized. "He can help me. The doctor is a man of considerable influence, and he is Sinhalese. In Colombo, he runs a private clinic. And in our village, he owns a few cabana places and restaurants. Sometimes he comes here to look after his property and to relax from Colombo. We've known each other for a very long time. I trust him."

Before the sun had set, we were off to our doctor's place. A young Sinhalese man who was taking care of the doctor's cabanas welcomed me. As for Sooriya - he didn't even look at him. But he let him enter and ushered us to a terrace bordering the beach.

The doctor welcomed us with his hands reached out. He was even bigger than I remembered him. His white shirt was almost too small for his belly. He had opened its upper buttons, and the black and curly hair emerged from the tight garment. Around his neck he wore a long and heavy golden chain.

"How good to see you, my friend," he greeted Sooriya. "And how nice that you have come along," he turned to me. "Monsoon period is a boring season. I am very pleased that the two of you are joining me tonight."

We sat down at a table on the terrace. The doctor's restaurant was abandoned and closed by now, but whenever the boss showed up from Colombo, the kitchen would open, of course, and the best dishes would be prepared."

"Glasses for me and my friends," the doctor called, and the young Sinhalese immediately returned with a bottle of Arrack.

Our host filled our glasses with the lukewarm liquor and took a big gulp.

"How are you, Sooriya? I hope everything is alright with you and your brothers, and that you can live in something near peace here, far away from our chaos in Colombo."

Both men were talking in English with each other.

"Well, to be honest ..." Sooriya began, but he didn't finish his sentence, because in this very second the Sinhalese employee was returning from the kitchen. He was dishing up the most exquisite food - lobster, big prawns, shark steaks and various vegetable curries. The Sinhalese placed the dishes in front of Sooriya very reluctantly.

We were having a fine meal, and the doctor drank a lot of Arrack, chatting about the good old days and how long he and Sooriya had known each other. He told me about the gay and careless evenings they had spent with tourists.

"Sometimes I need this, when Colombo has become too stressful for me," the doctor declared and refilled our glasses. "In Arugam Bay, I can relax, and sometimes I envy my old friend Sooriya for his quiet life."

After dinner the young Sinhalese cleared our table.

"I won't need you any longer," the doctor called to him, and the man left us to ourselves.

"Sooriya," the doctor said in a low voice. "I'm not here to talk about politics with you, but if you are in trouble around here, or if I can be of any help to you, please let me know."

"In fact, I need your help, Doc," Sooriya whispered back to him. "I've been offered the opportunity to leave Sri Lanka for a while. But I need a passport."

"What's your plan? Do you have a plan?" asked the doctor. "The authorities won't issue any passports during the curfew."

Sooriya told him of the American students who had invited him to the USA. The stout doctor had to think for a moment.

"At the immigration office, I know a man who has owed me a favour for quite some time," he said. "On Sunday I'll return to Colombo and see what I can do for you."

The topic had come to an end. The doctor took another big gulp of his Arrack and switched to more pleasant subjects.

Late that night, after the bottle had been killed at last, Sooriya and I set out to walk the few yards to Beach Hut. We were sneaking through the darkness, not daring to put on our flashlights. Everybody in the village seemed to sleep deeply.

After sunset next day, it became clear I had been drinking too much of this fine Arrack. Still a little dazed, I heard loud voices in front of my cabana. The place was crowded with soldiers who had come to take Sooriya with them.

"What are you blaming him for?" I heard Ram ask them.

"He has been violating the curfew. Last night he was observed by villagers."

I saw Sri disappear around the corner toward the exit in a hurry. He returned with the doctor just in time, before the soldiers could take Sooriya with them.

The doctor smiled nicely at the soldiers and the local chief of the police, who had showed up as well. The two Sinhalese men seemed to know each other well. The doctor talked to the police officer insistently. He smiled persuasively throughout their conversation. I didn't understand a word, but I had the impression, that the doctor was vouching for Sooriya and declaring himself guilty of the nocturnal adventure.

He raised his hand to his mouth, as if he was drinking from a glass, and swayed a little, as if drunk. Pottuvil's head police officer wiggled his head left and right and started to laugh. At last, by the doctor's efforts Sooriya was set free.

"Say thank you to the doctor," the police officer hissed at Sooriya. "This is the last time you'll get away with it so easily."

Before he and his soldiers left, he took a step toward me, threatening: "It will be better for you if you leave soon."

As long as the doctor was in Arugam Bay, Sooriya was in no danger. The villagers deeply respected the wealthy physician, and no one wanted to pick a quarrel with him. But the fact that Sooriya, of all people, was being supported by this influential Sinhalese was increasing their envy and resentment toward him.

Before he left, the doctor advised Sooriya to send a note to his helpful American friends. They were to write a letter of recommendation on the best formal university stationery. In addition, the doctor would bring his influence to bear on Colombo's officials.

"I'll do Pottuvil's chief of the police a little favour in Colombo," the doctor said to Sooriya. "That's why he'll leave you alone for a little while, because he knows that I like you, even though you're a Tamil. But beware of him."

In a few days the doctor wanted to be back in Arugam Bay.

"If you have things to do in Colombo, you can always come along with me in my Jeep," he offered me.

Before our friend left for the capital, I took a few pictures of Sooriya with my little camera. He had combed his hair to a tight knot in his neck, to look respectable. The doctor needed the photographs for Sooriya's passport.

"Knowing certain people and paying baksheesh helps you to obtain almost everything in Sri Lanka," the doctor was grinning, when he got into his jeep. Then he stepped on the gas, ignoring the clucking chickens trying to get out of his way.

Sooriya immediately started to write his letter to the American students and I took it to Pottuvil's post office, where a big surprise was waiting for me. I received the message that my new passport had arrived at the German Embassy. Now the only thing I had to do was to take the bus to Colombo. But I was so fed up with those long night trips by bus. So, I decided to accept the doc's offer to take me with him after his next stop in Arugam Bay.

*

After a few days the doc returned from Colombo with good news for us. Sooriya would receive a passport for his departure, but things were still taking a little time. This time the doc couldn't stay for long at Arugam Bay. After he had done some business here, I had to be ready to leave with him the following day.

We left on a Saturday noon. I was so glad that I didn't have to take the Midnight Express this time. The trip in the doctor's car was so comfortable, and I got to enjoy the sight of the green tea plantations and the rice farmers on their fields. The doc was fun to talk to. His English was perfect, and he was very educated and entertaining. He also seemed to be pleased to spend the trip in the company of a young European girl. By the time we arrived in Colombo, it had grown dark.

"I have to show up at a party in the Angel Club," the doc said as we drove through a suburb. "I've got to talk to business partners. Actually, only members will be admitted, but if you come with me, this will be no problem. After our meeting I'll give you a ride to a hotel."

The Sri Lankan who opened the gate to the Angel Club, was studying me as amazed as I was looking at him. He was dressed like a British butler and was behaving exactly like one. The man wore a pair of black trousers, a white bleached shirt, and a waistcoat. Around his collar he had tied a wine-red bow tie. His stylish dress code was disturbed only by Sri Lanka's beloved plastic sandals. But with his head raised and walking erect, he elegantly ushered us to the garden.

On entering the parklike estate, I felt like I was back to Europe. From speakers came disco music, and some couples were dancing to it. The guests, all of them Sri Lankans, were exclusively dressed European style; for the ladies, skirts and dresses covered their knees; for the men, white shirts and dark trousers. I was feeling quite out of place with my wrinkled cotton slacks.

Countless paper lanterns decorated the garden. Around a water basin with many illuminated fountains, guests were sitting and drinking beer and cocktails. Beside the basin, servants had arranged a buffet with selected delicacies. One servant had exclusively been ordered to chase away the flies.

The doc took me to the bar and ordered whisky for himself.

"Want one, too?" he asked me with a wink. He was visibly amused at the ladies' disgust when I accepted. Then he retreated to a table together with two other men, to discuss business.

Soon, a group of young men ended my loneliness at the bar. Obviously, they found my presence very distracting.

"Fernandez," one of the local men introduced himself to me. His skin was remarkably fair, and he wore a brown moustache.

"This is an unusual name in Sri Lanka," I remarked.

"Fernandez is a Burgher. Burghers are descendants of a Euro-Asian ethnic group, when Europeans mingled with Sri Lankan women. One of his ancestors was a Dutch sailor."

The young men were curious to hear about my experiences in Sri Lanka. When I told them that I had been staying in Arugam Bay most of my time, they were shocked.

"That's war zone," Fernandez exclaimed. "I thought that all tourists had left the East Coast by now."

But he didn't want to get involved in a political debate and changed the subject. Fernandez was an amusing entertainer. His tales about his Dutch ancestor and other legends were quite interesting.

"Many tourists tell me that Sri Lanka is a paradise," he chatted. "According to one legend, our island was indeed the original paradise. On Adam's Peak, one of our highest mountains, there is a footprint supposed to be of Adam's descent. Others believe it is Buddha's or Shiva's. Every year, thousands of pilgrims wander to this place:

Christians, Buddhists and Hindus. The legend says that Adam and Eve were expelled from Sri Lanka and driven to India."

"Once I took the ferry from Sri Lanka to India along the chain of islands of Adam's Bridge," one of Fernandez's friends threw in. "Since then, I have believed in this legend. Compared to India, Sri Lanka definitely is the paradise."

Time went by quickly, and we were later than the doc had intended. He had been consuming many drinks, which the butler was only too ready to serve. When we left the Angel Club, the doctor was rather drunk.

"A good acquaintance of mine has a small hotel nearby," he spoke thickly. "I'll give you a ride there."

He was far beyond being fit to drive, but what could I do? He staggered to his Jeep and I followed him. It was the middle of the night, and I had no clue where we were.

We kept knocking on the hotel's door for a considerable time before the sleepy owner opened it. The two Sinhalese had a talk with each other.

"There is no room left," the doctor excused himself. "I can't take you home either, because my wife would have fits if I brought a tourist along at night. It will be difficult to find a room around this time."

He made another try and handed the hotel owner some money. This was the best thing he could have done, as so often in this country. The proprietor let us come in. The three children had to move to their parents' bed, and I was accommodated in the children's bedroom. The doc staggered back to his car and drove home to his family.

The next morning, I hailed a tuk-tuk for a ride to the German Embassy. The man who showed me inside also presented to me my brand-new passport.

"Of course, your visa has long expired since," he remarked in fluent German. "You'll have to leave the country within the next few days. This, here, is our official letter of exoneration for you, as your new passport has no visa seals. You had better book your flight today."

It was Christmas time by now. I had intended to spend Christmas in India. I thought of my friend Christian's description of the famous Goa parties. But I wasn't interested in those anymore. Before I left Sri Lanka, I wanted to be with Sooriya on the Holy Night. Naturally, the Hindu brothers were not accustomed to celebrating Christmas, but they had planned a little party for Moni, Ronaldo and me.

In downtown Colombo, I found a travel agency and booked a flight to southern India, dated the 26th December, 1983. What could happen to me if I delayed my departure a little? The most important thing was to avoid any passport controls. The same evening, I took the bus back to the East Coast.

*

As I had expected, the guard at the bridge to Arugam Bay wasn't pleased to see me again. The soldier knew me by face, so he didn't want to see my passport. I showed him my air ticket to India, instead.

"I'll leave soon," I tried to make the Sinhalese understand by letting my hand glide through the air like a plane.

He didn't seem to look at the date. My finger was pointing at my destination: Trivandrum/India.

"Go," he snapped at me, jerking his head toward the bridge. He was having a few words with his partner. This soldier turned around immediately and walked away, most probably to report to the head of police that I had returned once more.

Sooriya's Beach Hut had become something like a home, now that the number of tourists had been reduced to Moni, Ronaldo and me. The kitchen was exclusively Ram's territory, but I could frequent it as often as I liked to prepare small dishes for myself. I kept a list of whatever provisions I took from the kitchen stock, such as fruit for a fresh salad or a left-over dhal curry. The hot dhal, made of lentils boiled in coconut milk, had become one of my favorite dishes. Sometimes, I bought our groceries. Then I would prepare a European dish with all the provisions I was able to find in Pottuvil. One evening, we were having vegetarian pizza, which was gladly partaken of by Ronaldo and Moni. Being a south German, I could not resist experimenting with our traditional handmade noodles called "Spaetzle". Lacking good gravy or our traditional lentil stew, which in Germany are essential to a dish of Spaetzle, I served dhal with them – which was a little unusual. But Sooriya remembered having eaten Spaetzle in southern Germany quite often. His younger brothers were very curious to watch how I scraped fine chips of fresh dough from a wooden plate into boiling water, where they turned into solid noodles, shaped like worms.

In our kitchen, a kettle with hot water hung above the fireplace from morning till night. I brewed my tea by pouring boiling water into a strainer filled with roughly cut, dried Ceylon tea leaves. In no time I had a strong dark tea, which I sweetened with thick-flowing and sugared evaporated milk from a tin. In Sooriya's Beach Hut, we had no bottled soft drinks any longer.

I had long since become accustomed to wearing a comfortable and uncomplicated lungi, although the cloth was meant to be wrapped around men. But in the "library" cabana I found a sari left behind by a female tourist. Ram's wife taught me to wrap the fabric, which measured eight yards in length, in the local technique. She and her two little children were frequenting the place more often now.

"You look very beautiful," Sooriya welcomed me when I entered the restaurant that evening. Lingam, however, burst out laughing and screeching, all the time pointing his finger at me. The wrapping was too complicated for me and would have taken too much time for everyday use. How were the local women able to do their daily tasks without losing their saris? I decided to return to my lungi and my t-shirts.

Day by day we waited for news from the American students. Finally, one morning the postman came. Sooriya had to sign a receipt, which made us conclude that the letter was important. Sooriya's air ticket to Los Angeles had arrived at last! A professor's letter of recommendation was enclosed. Sooriya was to give lectures at his university, he quoted from the letter, and his accommodation had been arranged.

However, our joy about Sooriya's departure didn't last. A few days after the arrival of the good news, I could sense a strangely tense mood between the brothers as soon as I entered the restaurant. They seemed to be having a crisis council and were debating in Tamil. I was not invited to take part. A letter was lying on the kitchen table, sent from Colombo. Ram didn't answer my questions, and Sooriya steered clear of me.

In the afternoon I joined their youngest brother, Sri, who wanted to buy a few groceries in the village.

In a hut on the outskirts of Arugam Bay, a woman sold homemade water buffalo curd, kept in clay cups. She didn't mind if her customers were Tamil or Sinhalese. Only her proceeds mattered to her.

On our way back, I told Sri, how worried I was. It was quite clear that Sooriya was having a serious problem.

"Is something wrong with his passport?" I asked him. "No, no, not with his passport," he replied.

The young Tamil I had been getting along so well with all the time hesitated to continue. Obviously, his eldest brother had told him not to talk to me about this topic.

"Before I fly to India, I have to know if everything is working out well with Sooriya's departure," I prodded him, hoping he would tell me his secret.

"The doc has written that the departure requires a cash sum of one thousand US dollars, to be shown on entry into the United States. They won't let anybody in without money. Our family cannot raise this amount. Sooriya declines to talk to you about it. Even if you had the sum, he wouldn't take it. He doesn't want you to feel obliged to help him."

Back on our place, I asked Ram to take my bag from the "safe". I retreated to my cabana and counted my traveler's cheques.

I had a little more than one thousand dollars.

In Goa, life was within your means, so I had been told. And after one month I would receive a new visa for Sri Lanka. Okay, my stay in Asia would be shorter than I had been planning, but so what? To me, my Asia trip would be just another new event in my life. But for Sooriya's future, it was essential that he leave Sri Lanka for the USA. I would never forgive myself if something happened to him during the civil war.

Sri confessed to his brother that he had spoken with me about the money. When Sooriya entered my cabana, he saw my traveler's checks still spread on the floor.

It was hard work to convince him to take the money. At last he agreed on one condition.

"I only have to show the one thousand dollars to the authorities at the entry airport," he said. "I'll return the money to you right away. As soon as I am standing on American soil, I'll get along fine."

Ram and Shiva were relieved when we informed them of this solution. On the other hand, the bank in Pottuvil

143

had to be provided with enough dollar notes by their Colombo head office. This took us another few days. My own departure to India was approaching. Christmas was right ahead.

*

Christmas Day was exceptionally warm. For a change, it didn't rain at noon. Moni and I had prepared an arrack punch for our Christmas party. There was still some time left, before the party would start in the evening. I was very melancholic. I had to leave the next day, and I was very worried about Sooriya and his brothers. We tourists were shielding them, so long as we didn't leave. Ronaldo's visa had expired as well, and Moni would take the same plane to Italy. Except for Fred, no foreign witness would be left in Arugam Bay.

I was thinking of my family in Germany. I wasn't exactly homesick, but the Holy Night and Christmas Day are special dates, where families come together, and this was my first time spending those holidays without my family. Surely, they would think of me today. I had sent them a postcard telling them that I would fly to India. Possibly my mother might be less worried, now that she knew I was leaving Sri Lanka and its civil war. Was it snowing in Germany, while I was sweating from tropical temperatures? I went outside to look for Sooriya and found him in his temple.

"Today I'm thinking a lot about my family," I said, and sat down beside him.

"As soon as I have safely arrived in the USA, my thoughts will be in Sri Lanka and with my brothers," he replied. "I'll celebrate our puja festivities every full moon with milk rice and probably with fruit different from what I have been used to in Sri Lanka. In my thoughts, I will also be with you..."

On Christmas Eve we were unable to celebrate happily. Our sorrows depressed our mood, and it was my farewell from Sri Lanka and Sooriya.

"By now there aren't many Tamils left in Arugam Bay," Suba said to the brothers. "You are in danger, and you should leave as soon as possible."

"It will take some more time, until I receive all the documents necessary for my departure," Sooriya replied. "But my brothers will set off before more soldiers arrive. I've heard that they have erected more road blocks. I'll stay here and take care of myself."

After our Christmas dinner, Sooriya and I retired to the Shiva-Ganesh house early. This was my goodbye to Sooriya. Of course, I wasn't looking forward to India. I would have preferred to see Sooriya to the airport and be sure that he got out of Sri Lanka safely.

"Don't worry too much," Sooriya tried to calm me. "Everything will turn out well."

Next day, Moni and Ronaldo came to say goodbye to me. They had decided to move back to Sooriya's Beach Hut for the last few days, until their flight to Europe. Ronaldo had a Sinhalese friend in Arugam Bay who promised to guard his house during his absence. Ronaldo wanted to be back in a few weeks.

"By then this stupid civil war will be over," he said optimistically. No one believed it.

It was so hard to say goodbye to Sooriya. I kissed him and wished him good luck, though I knew he didn't believe in luck, but in predestination.

We had no idea, if we would ever see each other again. I had in mind to stay in India for four weeks, according to the regulations, and then return to Sri Lanka with a new visa. Nobody was able to estimate how long it would take Sooriya to gather all the documents necessary for his departure for the USA, or if things worked out in his favour at all. The dollar notes had arrived at the bank just in time.

Now we were sure his U.S. entry wouldn't be denied because of lack of money. I had no idea which of my friends would still be in Arugam Bay by the time I returned from India.

With a heavy heart, I took my backpack and walked along the road toward Pottuvil. A few kids came along to the bridge, where the guard was waiting; as always, they were singing and laughing.

The soldier was standing in the shade of a tree, his gun leaning against its trunk. We knew each other. I had crossed the bridge often, this way or the other, and he had hardly ever bothered me. Now he looked at my luggage and came toward me, his gun in his hands.

"Go?" he asked, speaking bad English.

I nodded and hoped he wouldn't stop me.

"Not come back," he warned me. "Not tourists here, not good place."

His voice wasn't barking this time; he sounded more like he was advising me. I nodded my head in consent, and he let me pass across the bridge.

The bus to Colombo was almost empty. Most of the locals wanted to stay at home if they didn't have any urgent errands to run. I put my luggage on the seat beside mine and looked out my window. Just when we wanted to leave Pottuvil, we were held up by a road block. Every local passenger had to leave the bus and pass the barrier on foot. Being a tourist, I was the only person, who was allowed to stay seated.

The trip was well known to me. In a few minutes, we would see a clearing followed by many potholes. Sooriya had told me about the elephants that showed up here from time to time. I had never seen them before. But today, there they were - a herd of mighty pachyderms and their youngsters. Our driver had to slam on the brakes.

The huge animals ignored us, crossing the street at their leisure.

This time we arrived in Colombo early - before four o'clock in the morning.

Somehow, I had to spend my time in safe surroundings, until the first bus set off to the airport. It was dangerous to roam about Colombo at night.

I bought myself a railway station ticket, which was also an admission ticket to the station during nighttime. Authorities wanted to avoid having homeless persons moved in there. In addition, everyone was afraid of bombings. The station was being guarded around the clock, soldiers patrolling everywhere. I deposited my luggage in a locker and looked around for a cozy place to stay overnight.

"Ladies Waiting Room," read a sign above a door. It was well attended - ladies were lying on the floor, with children cuddling close to mothers. Some women snoozed on benches. I sat down on the floor and closed my eyes, leaning against a wall. In a few hours I'd be in India. I remembered the young Sri Lankan's words in the Angel Club that night with the doc: "Compared to India, Sri Lanka is the paradise."

Chapter 6

As soon as I had entered Colombo Airport, I had the feeling I already had left Sri Lanka. At the departure terminal, German group travelers tried to check in with the help of overworked airport personnel. For some reason their flight back to Germany was delayed. All around them laborers carried heavy suitcases. Mothers and fathers tried to calm whining children. Travel guides attempted to mollify their complaining guests.

Inside the airport building, home seemed so close. In a few hours, this group would land in a wintery Germany. The distance of my journey to Goa was a shorter one, but the journey itself would take longer. Goa was a very popular destination for travelers who wanted to feel like the hippies who had discovered the former Portuguese colony in the late 1960s. But Goa had no airport. My flight would take me to Trivandrum (today's Thiruvananthapuram) in the South of the Indian subcontinent. From there, I had to travel on by train.

Only few passengers were waiting at the counter for the short flight between Sri Lanka and India. The atmosphere was quieter at that counter compared to the bustle at the international flight counters. The local passengers waited their turn with calm composure. A female tourist approached our queue, dragging two big, heavy suitcases. She was sweating heavily, which wasn't surprising since she was wearing a pair of corduroy slacks and a frilled blouse with long sleeves.

"Flight to Trivandrum?" she addressed me in English.

"Yes, this is your counter," I answered in German, because I knew immediately from her dominant accent that she was from southern Germany.

We were the only Western tourists on board and were given seats side by side. The young Bavarian girl seemed very glad to have another German to talk to. She chatted freely about her plans in India. Her name was Heidrun, and she had left her home village in Upper Bavaria to work in an orphanage in south India. Her aunt was a nun who had been living there for years.

"My aunt Agnes has always been so impressive to me, whenever she has visited us in Germany," Heidrun told me. "She was always so very engaged and enthusiastic about India and her work there. I really admire people, who sacrifice their lives for other beings. My aunt has always been my idol."

Half an hour later we landed on Trivandrum's small airport. Heidrun's aunt was there, waiting for her niece. A short, heavy-set woman, she couldn't be missed as we saw her striding toward us in the arrival hall.

"Thank God and welcome to India, my child!" she exclaimed from afar, gesticulating broadly.

The nun had parked her pick-up truck in front of the arrival hall. I said goodbye to Heidrun, wishing her the best. I asked the Sister directions for the bus to Trivandrum's town center, where I intended to catch the train to Goa right away.

"We'll pass the station anyhow," Heidrun's aunt replied, and offered to take me there.

"Tell me about our home, child," the nun asked her niece as she steered the pickup through dense traffic. "How are your parents?"

But Heidrun wasn't as talkative now as she had been in the plane.

"Everything's all right," she replied meekly.

All these new impressions seemed to have completely overwhelmed the Bavarian village girl. Her aunt smiled at her, sympathetically.

"You will learn to love India," she assured her. "This needs time. Believe me, India is a wonderful country, and many wonderful people live here."

"I don't know," Heidrun demurred, looking out of the car, spellbound.

With risky maneuvers and hooting her horn, the nun drove the pickup to downtown Trivandrum. There was no humble reserve in her, and her stock of Bavarian curses was quite impressive.

"The locals won't understand what I'm saying, anyhow," she justified herself. "So, I'm not insulting anyone, right?"

It was fun riding with the feisty, salty-tongued nun, but nonetheless I felt relief when at last we arrived at the station unharmed.

"You have to visit the churches in Goa," Heidrun's aunt advised me. "Goa once was a Portuguese colony. It has more churches than Hindu temples. Gorgeous churches! O, how I'd like to come with you! But my children in our orphanage are waiting for me."

When I said goodbye, she held my arm for a second. "Of course, I know that you young girls won't travel to Goa because of the churches. Be careful. Stay away from drugs," were her last words to me.

The nun blessed me and waved at me, smiling, before I dived into the masses of Indians forcing their way into the station. I guess that Heidrun envied me my journey. She was quite pale, and I believe she would have preferred taking the earliest flight to Munich.

In front of the ticket booth, countless people were queueing. Asia makes you get used to waiting. A young boy was selling hot tea and lukewarm lemonade.

I was the only tourist in the station. Most probably, the young Indian men were staring at me for only one reason – it was unusual that a young white woman traveled on her own, so I thought. A few were obviously talking about me, and others threw hidden glances at me.

"Here is not for you," at last a young Indian addressed me in broken English.

"But I wish to buy a train ticket," I replied, irritated.

The air was warm and stuffy, I was tired, and I was definitely not interested in any discussions.

"Here no ticket for you," he answered, grinning widely.

Why couldn't I buy a ticket in this place? And why was this guy grinning so impertinently? Before I was able to give him an appropriate answer, he pointed to a booth a few yards away.

"There for you, Madam," he explained, still smiling.

Only now I noticed that my queue was for men only. In the neighbouring queue two Indian women, wearing colored saris, were waiting.

"Ladies-Counter," read the sign. A ticket booth for women only! This had to be a relic from British colonial times. I queued in behind the two women, and I was handed my ticket. The men obviously were satisfied now.

"This will be a long trip, Madam," the woman behind the counter informed me. "Would you like a reservation and a sleeper?"

What a luxury! I didn't know that Indian trains had sleeping compartments. So, for a few extra rupees, I booked a "sleeper."

A stream engine pulled the old train, which seemed to date from colonial times as well. The second-class compartments were hopelessly overcrowded. Many passengers sat closely packed on wooden benches, or they found a little space on the floor. Carefully, I stepped across baskets, luggage and chickens until at last I found my compartment with my seat number. But there was no "sleeper." For now, however, I was glad to have found a relatively comfortable seat. My luggage could be stored on a wooden shelf above our heads.

On the bench opposite me, four men were sitting and staring at me incessantly. I took a book from my bag, hoping that they might quit. No way. Apparently, in this part of the world it was not impolite to stare at other people. I felt very uneasy. The Indian woman sitting beside me pulled her sari over her face and fell asleep. I would have liked to hide behind a sari as well.

It was getting dark. The light was too dim for reading. I asked my fellow passengers for the sleeping car, but they didn't seem to understand me. I showed one of them my ticket.

"Sleeper," the Indian man said, wiggled his head and pointed up to the luggage shelf.

Surely, he had misunderstood what I was trying to say, I thought. Or he was making fun of me? The men were talking to each other and laughing.

Now one of them got up and stepped on his seat. From there he climbed up to the shelf.

"Sleeper," he repeated. He stretched and yawned, and shortly after he was snoring.

The wooden shelf above my head wasn't for my luggage; it was my sleeper! Now I realized why all the locals had placed their belongings below the benches.

To climb up to my shelf wasn't as easy as one might think. In vain, I looked for something like a ladder. At last, one of the men helped me up, while the rest of them smiled, amused. I laid my head on my backpack and stretched. Up there, the train swayed like a ship in rough sea. I grabbed the iron bars bearing the shelf, afraid to fall. But a few minutes later, the constant swaying and rattling made me fall asleep after all.

*

The next day I reached Goa, the smallest of India's federal states. The towns, which our train was passing or crossing, all had a very unusual flair. Buildings built during Portuguese colonial times alternated with typically Asian ones. Mighty churches towered above the houses.

Western and Eastern styles mingled in very characteristic ways.

Goa didn't receive any package tours then. The airport was too far away. But backpackers didn't shun the strenuous journey to its gorgeous beaches. Goa was a mecca for low-budget travelers and dropouts. Especially around Christmas, they liked to come here from the cold Western countries. And those backpackers, who had already been on the move through India, gathered en masse for the legendary Christmas parties. This had not the slightest to do with traditional Indian culture, of course.

I took the bus to Chapora. Back in Dodanduwa, Chris had told me about this place. He said he wanted to spend the holidays here this year. It was the main season, and in Chapora, there were only a few little hotels which were already booked. But every local with a spare dwelling, no matter if it was a house, a hut, or just one room, would put up tourists. Mostly, the accommodation was booked for several months ahead, because many guests wanted to stay some time.

I was lucky to find a simple room on the outskirts near the river. My only furniture consisted of a bast mat lying on the bare ground, and an empty bucket for fetching water. Beside my shack, I discovered the well belonging to it. A female tourist was taking her shower. She wore a large colored cloth around her torso. She soaped her skin through the cloth.

The first thing I did was to enter a restaurant to have something to eat. At the tables inside, an international clientele had gathered. Most of the tourists were speaking English. Joints were making their rounds. Goa had its own laws – you could smoke your marijuana in public whenever you wanted.

The travelers had developed their specific fashion. Almost every male tourist wore a lungi; some also wore colorful vests from Rajasthan with little mirrors worked into the fabric. Some of them liked to wear their hair in long dreadlocks, like the Hindu sadhus. Many women dressed in long, colorful skirts and filigree Indian silver rings and necklaces. The dress code seemed to be loud and flashy – a mix of Western and Indian styles.

That night, I went to bed early. I was exhausted from the long trip from Sri Lanka to Goa. The bast mat was very uncomfortable. From outside, I could hear stray dogs barking and the black pigs grunting. Those pigs were omnipresent in Chapora's streets. They ate simply everything, including the food remains commonly thrown in the ditches – a natural waste disposal system.

I felt very alone and homesick for Sri Lanka and Sooriya at Beach Hut.

Next morning, I made my first excursion to the shore. From town, it was a short walk to Vagator Beach. Here, as well, the backpackers had installed their own morals. Most of them were bathing completely naked, although this was forbidden in India, contradicting the local moral – but they simply ignored the Indian people's habits. Thoughtless and naked, they enjoyed lying in the sand, jumping in the ocean waves, or even playing volleyball in the sand, displaying their dancing body parts.

Today was a Sunday, and for the Indian population, this was a holiday. Hordes of local men made trips to see the naked whites populating Goa's beaches. The men wore modern suits with long trousers and shirts. Dressed like this, they would walk up and down the shore, watching the naked tourists, who couldn't care less.

A woman with bright orange hair was swimming in the ocean. I watched her. Her henna hair looked familiar, and the moment she left the water, I recognized her. It was Maggie from Hikkaduwa. In fact, I had expected that she would spend the Christmas season in Goa. She had listened to Chris' raptures about it as well. Funny enough, travelers came across each other all the time, no matter how far apart their destinations had been planned. They talked on and on about their trips and exchanged insider tips and hints. Although all of them insisted on being individualists, they all gathered at certain in-places during certain seasons. Maggie recognized me as well.

"Nice to see you again," she greeted me.

I asked her if Theresa had come along.

"No, she didn't," Maggie answered. "Shortly after you left us, she took a flight back to England."

Maggie was in a hurry. She had a date in Chapora, of course.

"What do you have in mind on New Year's Eve?" she asked me. "Come and join us at our big party in Anjuna."

And so, we arranged a meeting place.

"O, before I forget it, I met Chris on Christmas," she said. "He is living at Arambol Beach."

On New Year's Eve, I met Maggie at a restaurant in Chapora. She had hired two local motor bikers to give us a ride to the party in Anjuna. The festivity was to take place in the garden of a big colonial-style villa. When I asked Maggie who had been organizing the party, she had to decline.

The closer we came, the noisier the beats of the hammering music became. Someone opened the wrought-iron gate to let us in. Our bikers threw curious glances in the direction of the garden, but only whites were admitted.

The party had been going on for quite a while. The site was crowded with travelers from all places of Goa's beach area. Joints were making their rounds from one hand to the next, and all kinds of soft and hard drugs were being dealt within the garden walls.

Floodlights illuminated palm trees and other tropical plants. Red, yellow, blue and pink spots created a surreal atmosphere. You almost forgot that the real India still existed on the other side of the tall walls. Evidently, most of the guests had switched to another kind of reality. Some sat on the grass, dreaming, while others were dancing in a trance, having lost all track of here and now.

At around midnight, everyone welcomed the New Year with liquor libations. People embraced and kissed, not knowing who was who. And now the party blasted off! Two young girls danced with their arms outstretched. One of them took a break. She sat down, her feet bloodstained, but she seemed unaware of the fact. A young guy of about eighteen stared at me with wild eyes, as if he had seen a ghost.

I didn't know what kind of drugs they were consuming. In any case, this was my first of the famous Goa parties.

Maggie had met a young Italian and had vanished. I had no idea where the hell I had stranded myself, or how I might get back to my room in Chapora. Lucky for me, outside the gate a few local motor bikers were waiting to take guests to their respective places. Morning was dawning when I arrived at my room.

The bigger part of New Year's Day I spent in bed. I felt sick and didn't want to walk to the beach. Plus I disliked going to a restaurant after the hustle and bustle of last night. But my room wasn't inviting, either. Lying on that bast mat made my bones ache. I would never feel comfortable here. I recalled that Maggie had told me Chris was living at a lonely beach in the North of Goa.

"The bay is supposed to be beautiful, with only a few huts let to tourists," she had said. "For my taste, much too boring," she added.

I decided to stay in Chapora for a few more days and purchase necessary supplies, before moving to quiet Arambol Beach.

*

Arambol Beach wasn't far from Chapora, but the trip took half a day all the same. First, I had to travel by bus, and then take a ferry across a river. There was no bridge. On the other side, I got on another bus, which finally brought me to the little fishing village in the north of Goa.

At the bus stop in Arambol Beach, a few Indian boys awaited newcomers. One boy guided me to the beach, where he showed me small stone houses for rent. There were no hotels, only a few small outdoor restaurants. I decided for an accommodation in the shade of several tall coconut palms, not far from the ocean shore. At least this time the tiny room was furnished with a real mattress.

After I had freshened up at the well, I entered one of the beach restaurants and asked the waiter for Chris.

"A German with blond hair and a tattoo on his shoulder?"

The Indian knew him. Chris sometimes came here. After all, there weren't so many restaurants on the beach. The Indian pointed at a tourist sitting in a corner by himself.

"That's Mike," the waiter introduced me to him. "He knows where the German guy is living."

Mike was tall and tanned and had a moustache. With a very American accent, he offered to take me to Chris' lodgings. They knew each other.

Chris was living in a little house at the foot of a mountain covered with palm trees all the way to the beach. The building had been painted white and was topped by a flat roof. The two rooms inside had separate entrances. Mike and Chris shared the house.

On our arrival, Chris' door was wide open. I entered the dark room. There was no window. He was asleep, and he looked frightening. I recalled our intriguing conversations on Mr. Sirisena's terrace at the beginning of my adventures. I had almost been envious of his experience and his self-assured way of life, knowing no restrictions. Without his enthusiasm for Arugam Bay, I'd never have traveled to Sri Lanka's East Coast.

Now, Chris looked really ill. He had lost considerable weight since we last met, and his cheeks were hollow. His legs were raw with inflamed sand-flea bites; probably he had been scratching. When I touched his shoulder, he opened his eyes. Chris looked at me amazed and smiled; he was very pleased to see me.

"Didn't we have a date for Christmas?" he grinned. "Where have you been hanging around?"

With some effort, he got up, and we went outside for fresh air. In front of the little house, there was an open fireplace. Chris put a kettle on it to make some tea, then rolled a joint. His hands were shaking, and he seemed nervous.

"Arugam Bay paradise," he said with dreamy eyes when I told him about Beach Hut. "I've often been thinking of you, when the political situation got worse there. After I had recommended this place to you, I was always hoping that I hadn't given you the wrong advice. Mr. Sirisena has been right about his warnings of the civil war."

I told Chris, who also knew Sooriya and his brothers, what had happened during my stay there.

"You seem changed," Chris noticed. "Where has the little naïve tourist gone? Sometimes it's beautiful to see what Asia makes out of people, but sometimes it's also frightening," he philosophized.

But soon Chris apologized and said that he had to leave because he had something important to deal with. We agreed to meet in one of the beach restaurants in the evening.

I had already ordered jumbo prawns for dinner when Chris came in.

"Hi, Andy," Chris greeted a gray-haired tourist at the neighboring table. The man showed no reaction, nor did he say a word. He just stared off into the distance.

"He is one of those who have been broken by the Asia-Virus," Chris said, continuing the conversation we had in the afternoon.

Suddenly the man called Andy left his table and looked at us confused.

"I have to get my luggage," he said to Chris. "I must go to Varanasi. There I will die. I want my dead body to be burnt; they must strew my ashes into the Ganges. Today is a good day to die."

The guy's odd behavior didn't disturb Chris in the least.

"Take a last puff? It's good stuff, Andy," Chris asked him, relaxed. "For today it's too late to drive to Varanasi. There'll be enough time for dying tomorrow."

Andy sat down again and took a few deep puffs from Chris' wooden chillum. The wrinkles in his worn face smoothed out a little. Without a further word, he left us.

"Andy, I'll add it to your bill," the Indian waiter shouted. "By the way, tomorrow is a good day for paying."

"People call him Acid-Andy," Chris told me. "They say he has consumed so much LSD that he never completely comes down. Sometimes - at lucid intervals - you can have a conversation with him. In fact, Andy is quite intelligent. But mostly his mind is reduced to its own little world."

Chris didn't stay long. He was sorry, but he didn't feel well. The inflammations on his legs' skin were hurting. I promised to bring him one of my ointments – a remnant from my Swiss friend Brigitte from Akuralla – tomorrow.

I liked Arambol Beach. It was much calmer than Chapora's beach, and there was no tourist-peeping by Indian men. So, I decided to stay a little longer.

I had planned to travel to India's Northern regions – to Rajasthan, perhaps even to Nepal. But now that my travel budget had been diminished by one thousand dollars, I had to be thrifty to get by with my remaining money during the following month, until I was allowed to return to Sri Lanka.

Next morning, I set out to Chris' little house, together with my ointment. The door was half open, and I entered the dark room. Chris was lying on his mattress, his arm still ligated, a syringe in his hand.

"Couldn't you have called or knocked somehow?" he greeted me angrily. "Please don't think that I'm a junkie. I only do it sometimes, when I don't feel good."

I didn't believe one word. I put down the ointment and left him to his dreams.

Chris and I met only on rare occasions. The inflammations on his legs' skin became worse and were growing into suppurating wounds. He had to spend almost all his time in his dark room. Chris was unable to take long walks any longer because of his aching legs. It was so sad to see him like this. But talking or trying to give good advice would have been a waste of time.

The days went by slowly. Was Sooriya still in Arugam Bay? I so hoped the preparations for his departure were successful. But on the other hand, I was longed to see him on my return to Sri Lanka.

Goa's travelers, taking drugs from dusk to dawn, were boring me. Parties, parties, and more parties – nothing else seemed to interest anybody. Everything, even if it was only the sunset, was a reason to party. As soon as the sun was hanging just above the horizon in the evening, hippie tourists would gather and start passing around joints.

"Bom Shiva, Bom Shankar," some of the white hippies called to heaven in adoration. Probably most of them didn't know what they were doing or talking about – it was cool, and it was "Indian." They were inhaling deeply, as if they might inhale godlike wisdom. The ceremonial fuss was getting on my nerves.

My stay in Goa was drawing to its close. Soon I'd be allowed to apply for a new visa for Sri Lanka. Chris had asked me to come along to a full-moon party. This was to be my goodbye beach party from Goa.

Once a month, the full-moon party was held on a small beach on the opposite side of the Arambol Mountain.

"We have to cross the cliffs," Chris said. "On the other side there is a small lagoon where the party will take place."

He couldn't wear any shoes because of his spreading wounds. He had wrapped his feet with rags. The cliffs were quite sharp-edged, as well as the rocks, which were covered with many mussels.

Waves were cooling my feet, but the saltwater was causing a lot of pain to Chris' wounds. I could see it in his face.

"The salt is disinfecting everything," he said bravely and smiled.

We had come to a small bay. A fresh-water source was feeding a small lake separated from the ocean by a wide sand bank.

Quite a few tourists had arrived already. Some of them were bathing in the sea; others were frying in the sun on the nice beach. A cassette recorder was playing the ever present 1970s music. My first impulse was to jump into the fresh water lake and have a good long swim. Chris turned to a group of tourists smoking ganja.

When it grew darker, the people on the beach became quiet. The travelers watched fascinated as the impressive sun took a dive into the ocean. The waves turned orange, then red, then a dark violet. Now the full moon was the only light on our beach, and the waves looked like a silver sheet. A few torches were lit.

Acid Andy had also come. Suddenly, he got up from the sand and walked to the shore and into the water, as if he had been hypnotized. Two hippies followed him and brought him back to the beach.

"Just have a smoke, Andy. Drown yourself tomorrow, okay?" they repeated the rescue rite, which seemed to always work.

Andy was smoking, and he was freezing. Goa nights were cold.

A young Israeli was sitting beside me in the sand. He was eighteen or nineteen at most. He was astonished at the scenery.

"I arrived in Goa two days ago," he told me. "I had the impression that Sri Lanka was quite different somehow."

I was so glad to meet somebody who could report news from the island.

"At the moment, the political situation has calmed down a bit," he said.

"Even the ferry between Sri Lanka and India has been taken up again. But you never know how long things will keep quiet."

That was good news. Perhaps the soldiers had retreated from the East Coast by now. All I could do was hope that Sooriya and his brothers were safe.

"Actually, I had in mind to travel to India with my Sri Lankan friend," the Israeli said. "But he wasn't allowed to come along. Most Sri Lankans have no possibility to leave their island."

Sooriya's only chance to leave the country against all odds was the doctor. I hoped that the doc had told the truth about his good connections.

It was late. Many hippie guests were asleep, lying in the sand. A few were still dancing, although there wasn't any music playing any longer. I decided to leave this place, but the moonlit way back across the cliffs was difficult.

So, I waited for early sunrise. The Israeli guy and I set out for Arambol Beach. Chris had curled up in the sand and was sleeping. I left without saying goodbye. The sun was amiable enough to heat the rocks. The Israeli was a real gentleman and escorted me to my room.

"You know, I'd prefer to return to Sri Lanka as well," he said, tired, when he left me. "This drug stuff in Goa is disgusting – strange subculture. Soon I'll take the ship to Bombay [today's Mumbai] and continue my journey from there to India's north."

His thoughts were the same as mine. Goa's hippie scene was so superficial, irrelevant and self-destructive. Was this the big freedom to be found in Asia?

I was looking forward to being back in Sri Lanka soon. Dead tired, I fell asleep. The last I heard was a cawing blackbird, and I started to dream of Arugam Bay.

*

For my return to Sri Lanka, I decided not to book a flight, but to take the ferry, which was running again, according to my Israeli friend. My budget had shrunk to almost zero.

To get to Rameswaram in southern India, where the ferry would cast off, I faced a long journey. This time I knew what awaited me when I booked a 'sleeper' on my train.

On Indian railways one can travel for many days and nights without lacking anything. I ordered a rice dish wrapped in banana leaves. The rice and vegetable mix looked a little strange but was very tasty.

At every station, traders entered the trains to roam our compartments and sell food and beverages to the passengers. We could buy hot tea or coffee, all kinds of fresh fruit, nuts and sweets – even cigarettes if you wanted, in a pack or just one. The Indians mostly preferred affordable thin beedies made of rolled tobacco leaves.

My journey was taking me through inner South India. This route wasn't much frequented by tourists, who usually preferred routes suggested by various travel guides. For Christmas they went to Goa, and in spring they turned to the desert state of Rajasthan before its temperatures got unbearably high. During summer, many travelers would escape from the heat to Nepal's mountainous areas.

I crossed India from the southwestern shore to the Southeast Coast, passing through many villages and towns whose names would never be printed in any travel guide.

At last I arrived in Madras, and I was completely worn out. All I desired was a shower and a real bed. At the station I had to bargain with a rickshaw driver about his price for taking me to a nearby lodge.

"Very green, very cool," the man promised.

It felt quite strange to sit on the tall rickshaw with its two big wheels, while the man pulled his vehicle quite fast through the dense traffic. His hands held the two wooden bars left and right of his body, and his feet were running all the way. The man's shirt was torn, revealing almost-black torso. He wasn't young any more, but when we arrived at the lodge, he wasn't noticeably out of breath.

The lodge had been built close to a main street and it didn't look very inviting. But after I opened the door, I saw that the rickshaw man hadn't promised too much. Lush potted plants had been placed between the tables in the restaurant area. Fans hummed from the ceiling. Before going to my room, I ordered a Masala dosa, a kind of cross pancake with a spicy potato stuffing.

How happy I was to have a shower with unceasingly running warm water! Over and over, I relished the luxurious foam and its wonderful scent. The brown soup coming from my long hair went down the drain. Clean white, soft towels awaited me.

I hadn't slept so well for a very long time. In Germany I would never have wasted a thought on what a treat such a comfortable bed might be for me. In the morning, I ordered breakfast in my room, because I wasn't ready yet to leave my cozy bed with its clean blanket and soft cushion. I prolonged my stay in Madras for a few days precisely because of this comfort.

Sooriya came to my mind. His life in Madras during the 1960s had been a totally different one. Having no money at all, he had suffered from hunger. His bed had been a church floor. Sooriya's experiences in India were widely set apart from my short tourist episode.

Back on Madras' streets Indian reality soon caught up with me. It was loud, hectic and dirty. To find out when or if a ferry would leave for Sri Lanka seemed impossible. I went to a travel agency, where I was told that the ferry momentarily wasn't running. But I had the impression the man was trying to sell me a flight ticket to Colombo.

Back at my lodge's reception desk, I was told that my ferry would leave a week from now. Did they want to keep me, being a paying guest? At dinner I heard somebody say he had arrived from Sri Lanka by ferry a few days ago. I had to travel to Rameswaram at India's southern tip on the off-chance. This was alright, as I was refreshed and well nourished. I was looking forward to Sri Lanka.

Having arrived at the little port of Rameswaram, I was told that Sri Lanka had recently suffered several terrorist attacks. Ferries could be held up at any time. Nobody knew if I might catch a ferry on the following day. I took a hotel room near the port.

At seven o'clock in the morning, I crossed the harbor in a small rowing boat. No other tourists shared the trip. Local passengers kept listening to the captain's radio.

Their worried faces showed the situation was critical. We had to wait for hours for the ferry to set off. We received permission to depart at around noon. The ferry set course for Talaimannar.

After several hours, I could make out Sri Lanka's coastline. Although everything looked peaceful, the crew as well as the passengers grew tense. Without further delay, row boats brought us to shore. Talaimannar's entry officer indicated I should leave the north as soon as possible. Further bombings had been reported.

The ferry's arrival had been too late for me to catch the train to Colombo in time. I'd have to take another one tomorrow.

*

From Sooriya's tales I knew that his mother and sisters were living in Mannar. Talaimannar, at the tip of Mannar peninsula, is connected to the main island by a road. It was only a short distance from Talaimannar harbor to Mannar. If everything had turned out well since my departure from Arugam Bay, Sooriya's brothers would be with their family by now. I decided to pay them a visit.

It wasn't easy to find their house. Mannar had almost never been visited by tourists, unless by accident, and nobody seemed to speak English. Finally, I met a man who knew the family. He was kind enough to guide me to their house on the outskirts of Mannar. A woman was sitting in front, kneading dough in a tin bowl. She lifted her head in amazement, when I approached her.

I couldn't address her in English, so I simply said the names of Sooriya and Ramana. She quickly got up and disappeared inside the house. A few minutes later Sri stepped outside.

"What are you doing in Mannar?" he shouted amazed and gave me a hearty hug, watched by his mother's skeptical look. This kind of physical contact wasn't common at all in Sri Lanka.

Sri introduced me to his mother. He explained to her who I was and that I had been living at Sooriya's Beach Hut. Suddenly she smiled and with a friendly gesture invited me to come inside. Sri bade me to sit down on a bast mat on the ground. His mother left us hurriedly.

"She wants to get Shiva and Ram," Sooriya's youngest brother said. "They are staying at my sister's house not far from here."

Relieved that the brothers were fine, I enquired after Sooriya.

"We don't know how he is doing," Sri replied, worried. "After Moni and Ronaldo left Arugam Bay, a few villagers were spreading lies about us. Suba warned us just in time, before the soldiers heard the rumors. We left Arugam Bay the same night, but Sooriya wanted to hide somewhere. He was still waiting for the doctor, who had promised to bring him his passport and departure permission from Colombo. Since then we haven't heard of him."

Ram and Shiva soon arrived. Their mother served us fresh tea. When I looked into her warmhearted eyes, I remembered Sooriya's words describing her. His mother hadn't said a word since her husband was murdered, so he had told me. Yes, she still wouldn't talk, but her eyes welcomed me in her home.

"We are very concerned," Ram began to speak. "We've received no news of our friend Suba, either. He had been staying at Beach Hut. We can't go back to find out what has happened to Sooriya. In case he has made it to America, he surely will write us a letter immediately. We are waiting for any news all day long."

I promised to let the brothers know whatever I was able to find out as soon as I arrived in Arugam Bay.

"I'll be in no danger when I travel to the East Coast," I assured them. "The soldiers won't do me any harm."

Ram insisted that I stay the night in his house, "Joy-Cottage," with his family. Tomorrow was early enough to leave.

"You can go for a swim if you like," Shiva offered. "I'll ask my sisters to accompany you."

Soon he returned with two of his sisters. They spoke no English, but Shiva had already told them where to go with me.

Outside Mannar, there was a lake. An ancient irrigation system of numerous reservoirs watered the arid but fertile soil in the north. Farmers cultivated the surrounding fields with the aid of their oxen. On either side of the path grew cactus.

In the distance we could see peacocks spreading their glamorous feather tails. On the lakeshore, I found no possibility to hide from nosy glances while I was bathing. But the sisters took care of everything. The younger one wrapped her body in a big cloth, and after she had taken off her clothes underneath it, she jumped into the water. The elder sister handed me another cloth that would serve as my swim suit. The water was wonderfully refreshing. I tried to swim with the fabric floating around me, which wasn't so easy. The elder sister waited outside the water, caring for our privacy.

Suddenly I saw Shiva running across the field. He excitedly called something to his sister. It sounded like important news. Hectically waving her arms, the young woman turned toward me, indicating I should leave the water immediately.

"You have to depart right now," Shiva shouted breathlessly as soon as he reached us. "Hurry up, or it will be too late."

"What happened?" I asked him, frightened, while I fought with the wet cloth.

"An assassin's attack. A bomb exploded on the train to Colombo. There are dead people and many hurt. The route has been closed. You understand? No trains any longer, only a few minibuses are left. If you miss them, you will never be able to leave Mannar. Please run to the bus stop right now with my sister while I fetch your luggage."

Quickly I jumped into my clothes and hurried downtown together with Shiva's sister. Most probably I was lucky that the ferry had been late. I might have been sitting in that train.

At Mannar's bus station, pure chaos had broken out. Only two minibuses sat in the parking lot, and both were hopelessly overcrowded. Shiva had already arrived with my luggage and was urging and persuading the passengers – but there seemed no way they might let me squeeze in.

"Money!" Shiva shouted. "Give me some money. Rupees, dollars, no matter what!"

Hastily I pulled a few dollars out of my bag. I hadn't changed any Sri Lankan rupees yet. Shiva thrust the money into the minibus with his outstretched arm. These tactics had the effect we had been waiting for. A girl of about sixteen years grabbed the notes, pulled me inside, and sat on her friend's lap. Shiva threw in my luggage, and instantly the minibus raced off.

My bag was lying on my knees while the two girls tried to sit in a somewhat bearable position. A long journey lay ahead.

Our minibus took the road and the dam between Mannar and the northern main island. After only a few miles on the coastal road, we had to surmount our first obstacle: a log barring our way. Soldiers with machine guns encircled our vehicle and ordered us to get out. They searched our luggage meticulously. We women were allowed back in, but all the men had to show everything they were wearing close to their bodies, which seemed

169

ridiculous if you consider that you can't hide much under a lungi.

This was a good occasion for the women to snatch the most comfortable seats, including my two girls, who counted and shared the money they had received from me by way of Shiva. The soldiers arrested two men; the other they allowed back on our bus. Thank God the soldiers paid no attention to the fact that our minibus was overcrowded.

The sun set, and our bus rode through the night. We were driving through another arid area. Hardly anyone slept. All we were hoped for was to get past the rebel zone safely.

Shortly before sunrise, we reached Colombo. The city wasn't foreign or threatening to me any longer. By now I was familiar with its streets, houses, tea-shops, scents, crowds of people, and constant traffic jams.

First off, I had to settle a few things in Colombo-Fort. This was Colombo's commercial district with banks, department stores, and the General Post Office, from where I could make long-distance calls. It took quite some time until I was put through to Germany, but finally I heard my mother's familiar voice, low and far away. She had been worried continuously since she last heard from me. Daily news in Germany constantly reported on the civil war in Sri Lanka, broadcasting horrible pictures. Mother was well informed about the political situation – much better than I.

"I'll be home soon," I tried to reassure her. But the connection collapsed.

Tired from our night trip, I sat down on the ground under the awning of a big department store. After I had wiped the sweat from my forehead, I carelessly dropped my cloth. Exhausted, I leaned back and closed my eyes. I thought of my family at home, my friends, of a bathtub with hot water and beautiful foam, my comfortable bed, fresh bread from the oven with cheese and a glass of wine...

But suddenly a tourist's unfriendly voice interrupted my dreams. The man spoke English.

"Look at that, Elisabeth. They are so disgusting, these seedy hippie girls."

I opened my weary eyes. An elegantly dressed elderly couple was standing in front of me. For one moment the wife's eyes expressed some emotion resembling pity. She laid a little money on my cloth beside me.

"You shouldn't support those drug addicts," her husband nagged. But before I could say anything, they disappeared into the store. I looked down on my clothes, surprised. The guy had just called me a "seedy hippie girl." Well, I had to admit that my clothes had suffered a bit from traveling. The colorful Goa look had given way to a dusty grey. My leather sandals from India were hand-made and very hippie-like. Sun and seawater had bleached my ruffled hair, and my skin was deeply tanned. Above all, the stings of all kinds of insects on my legs had become inflamed and purple. I noticed businessmen throwing disapproving glances at me. I was due for a shower and some clean clothes.

I decided to take a hotel room near the bus terminal and get some rest. After an extensive shower, I fell onto the comfortable bed and into a deep sleep.

It was late evening when I woke up. I had to hurry if I wanted to catch the Midnight Express to the East Coast. After a good sleep, I felt much better. Being refreshed and restored, I could easily survive another night trip in a bus. I was looking forward to Arugam Bay and became increasingly excited. Would I see Sooriya once more, or had he already arrived in the USA?

*

I caught the Midnight Express just in time. I sat down and watched the bustle outside through my window. A tourist was squeezing himself through the crowd, regardless of whom he shoved aside with his bag and big surfboard. In the end, our driver refused to let him and his voluminous luggage on board, because almost all the seats were taken, and the aisle was already stuffed with bags and baskets.

Defiantly, the surfer blocked the door with his foot and his board. He tried to intimidate the driver with his threatening voice. From his accent, I immediately recognized the surfer was from Australia. He was much taller than our bus driver, and a regular muscleman, but the short, thin driver wasn't impressed. The louder the Australian argued, the more stubborn our driver grew.

"Your board needs as much room as two men," the driver persisted. "You have to buy three tickets."

After a long debate followed by all passengers with high interest, the Australian gave in and paid the amount due. Cursing, he dragged his surfboard inside the vehicle and approached the seat beside me.

"They fleece you on every occasion possible," he complained as he sat down.

His name was Nick. His destiny was the same as mine – Arugam Bay – where he was to meet his Australian surfer buddies.

"My friends say that the waves there are the best ones," he said to me. "That's the only reason they fly to Sri Lanka every single year, as if we didn't have enough proper beaches at home! Well, I admit that Sri Lanka is quite beautiful, and a vacation is affordable. If only there weren't those dumb locals."

"When did your friends arrive there?" I inquired.

"About two weeks ago."

This news cheered me up. So, a few tourists were staying in Arugam Bay after all. This was a good sign.

Had the soldiers left the area? Had everything returned to calm and peaceful? Meanwhile, the rainy season was over in the east. A new season had come, and along with it beautiful weather that would attract many travelers.

Night had fallen. Most of the passengers cuddled in comfortable positions. Yawning, I pulled my lungi out of my bag and folded it into a cushion. I tried to sleep for a while.

In the middle of the night loud voices woke us up. Our bus had stopped. Outside, there was complete darkness. I saw nothing, but I heard a man barking orders. The passengers got up, took their luggage, and went toward the exit. A military vehicle was blocking up the way outside. With sleepy eyes, I queued up. The Australian stayed seated, bored.

"This doesn't concern us, does it?" he questioned, declining to queue up and trying to go back to sleep.

Outside, we had to line up and endure a thorough search. One soldier shined his flashlight in my face, but he didn't want to look at my luggage.

Another soldier – I'm sure he wasn't older than eighteen – went into the bus, his rifle raised. From inside we heard voices; Nick's sounded aggressive.

You stupid guy! I thought. Don't ever argue with soldiers.

Several times the young Sinhalese asked Nick to follow him outside, but the Australian stubbornly refused. The debate grew heated, and in the end the soldier was furiously yelling at Nick. But the Australian tourist was wildly determined not to give in: "Fuck you, I'm..."

His sentence broke off. All of us were holding our breath. Afraid, we stared helplessly at the bus. Then Nick appeared in the door, his arms folded behind his head. The rifle's barrel touched the back of his head.

"Go!" the young soldier yelled at Nick and kicked him off the steps. The Australian landed on his knees on the

173

road, his hands still behind his head. Nick's bag was emptied on the asphalt. He didn't move. The young soldier disappeared in the bus and returned with Nick's surfboard. With his knife, he stabbed at it many times, then threw it in the ditch. When Nick looked up, the soldier pressed the barrel of his gun to his forehead.

The situation had grown extremely tense. No sound was to be heard. Then one of the young soldier's older companions said something in a soothing voice. I only understood the word 'tourist.' It sounded like something dirty.

Nick shot a concealed glance at me. Quickly I looked down, hoping that he might do the same. Nervously, the young officer still aimed his rifle at Nick's head.

His companion put his arm around his shoulders and tried to persuade him to let go. Finally, the furious soldier relented, turned around, and returned to the military vehicle. Other soldiers ordered us to go back to our bus.

Nick was still kneeling on the road. I helped the shaky guy get up. Hastily, we picked up his belongings and got back aboard our Midnight Express. Slowly, our driver passed the military police car.

For the rest of our journey, Nick didn't say a single word. He was in shock.

Chapter 7

In Pottuvil, everything seemed to be taking its regular
course. We saw no military police on the main street
through town. Only at the bridge to Arugam Bay did we
see one soldier who was sheltering from the sun under a
tree. He hardly took notice of us.

Arugam Bay looked like a ghost town. Neither locals
nor tourists were anywhere to be seen. The cabanas on
both sides of the main street were in a lousy condition.
Apparently not many guests had returned after the
monsoon season, and nobody had repaired the cabanas,
which had been damaged by the long rain.

"What a godforsaken place," the Australian grumbled.
"Why the hell do people come here for surfing?"

I showed him where to find Surfer's Lodge. Surely his
friends were hanging around there.

But now I wasn't wasting any more time. I hurried
toward Sooriya's Beach Hut. From afar, I saw that the
sign had been removed. Loaded with many emotions
ranging from joy to fear, I entered the place.

Nobody was in the restaurant. No oil lamps sat on the
tables, or flowers arranged in loving care. Everybody
seemed gone. I grew increasingly afraid that something
bad had happened. When I entered the kitchen, I touched
the water kettle hanging above the fire place – it was hot.
I saw a used cup from which someone had recently drunk
tea. But there were almost no groceries.

My heart was racing as I snuck around to the
restaurant's backside. Nearly all the huts had been
destroyed; only a few bamboo frames were left. Yet one
cabana looked habitable. Obviously, it had been repaired
recently. Its palm leaves were fresh and green.

The place looked spooky and deserted. Cautiously, I
moved across the backyard toward Sooriya's little temple.
From outside, it seemed undamaged. Blackbirds sat on its

roof, but they flew up croaking when I came closer. I slipped inside and was very shocked at the sight of it. Everything had been destroyed and desecrated.

The Buddha statue had been stolen, all the pictures of the Hindu gods had been torn, and the Christian cross had been broken. The wooden chest, where many travelers had laid devotional objects or money and other valuables, had been looted. Only a few soaked photographs had been left behind. Feeling melancholy, I took a close look at them. They showed a happy couple being served dinner by the carefree and laughing young Shiva; a snapshot of a high-spirited Ram drinking arrack from a bottle. Those happy times were over.

My gloomy thoughts were interrupted by the well-known noise of the squeaking winch, which always announced to everyone at the place that someone was pulling up water from the well.

I took a cautious look from inside the temple. The banana plants were growing so densely, so I wasn't able to identify the person at the well.

At last I could make out a man. It wasn't Sooriya, but a man I knew quite well. I recognized Suba, the brothers' close friend. I left my hiding place. The Sinhalese was quite shocked when I emerged from the green leaves. But immediately he smiled, relieved, and joy spread all over his face.

Together we entered the kitchen through the backdoor. And while he was preparing a tasty dish from very few groceries, he told me what had happened since I had left Arugam Bay a few weeks ago.

"From the day you were gone, the soldiers have been surveying the place very closely," Suba reported. "They intended to intimidate us, walking by the entrance to Beach Hut all day long. I think, they were waiting for Moni and Ronaldo to leave. Both of them were buying groceries for us, because I myself was too afraid to go to

Pottuvil. Their ticket back to Europe had been booked already. Shortly before they left, all of us quickly made every effort to avoid any danger to the brothers.

Ram, Jothi, Shiva, and Sri were able to set off to Mannar without anyone noticing. Sooriya left the same night, unnoticed by anyone. The following day, soldiers raided the place and destroyed everything. I was helpless, but lucky that I was allowed to stay here. Of course, I will look after the place until the brothers will be back."

"Where is Sooriya? Have you heard news of him?" I asked Suba.

"Don't worry. Our friend isn't far off," he reassured me. "It is better if you don't know where he is hiding."

"But I have to see him," I begged.

"That's much too dangerous," Suba said firmly. "They would follow us. Even I won't visit him in his hideout. They are incessantly watching where I go."

Suba informed me that everything had been taken care of for Sooriya's departure for the USA. Day in and day out, Suba waited for the doc, who was to bring along the passport and the departure permission from Colombo.

"No one will stop the doctor," Suba was sure. "The Chief of Police would never dare to do this. Not every Tamil has such influential Sinhalese friends as Sooriya does."

Suba paused, reflecting. "You've known Sooriya only for a short while. He has been helping many people, without ever expecting anything in return. If he is in need, there will always be someone to help him. Most probably he isn't even aware that he has an exceptional influence on people. This will be helpful in America. I hope that the Western world won't spoil him."

Suba took the water kettle to make fresh tea. I thought about Sooriya's words, when he was telling me about his travels through Europe.

"Everything I needed has come to me," he had said. I had listened to his tales, taking everything for granted, although it wasn't usual at all at that time for a young Tamil to set off on such a journey. I had long since accepted that he was different – logic couldn't explain it.

Suba was amazed to hear that I had returned from India by ferry and had visited the brothers in Mannar. He was relieved to hear that they had made it to their mother.

"They are very worried about Sooriya," I told him. "Why haven't you given them notice?"

"I wasn't able to, although I'm aware that they are waiting for news," Suba said, justifying himself. "I've told the soldiers, that I don't know where they have gone. By sending a letter to Mannar, I'd have given them away."

Ronaldo's house at the outskirts of Arugam Bay had been confiscated by the army. The Italian's Sinhalese friend, who was taking care of it, hadn't been able to prevent the seizure. Now the beautiful house was inhabited by an officer.

"Ronaldo won't get it back," Suba said. "Officially, foreigners aren't allowed to own land in Sri Lanka. It's better not to try to do so with the help of a local."

Suba had restored the restaurant and would re-open it soon. He had been taught by Ram and had become a good cook. Beach Hut would earn a little money from new guests, which was necessary for rebuilding the cabanas. The Shiva-Ganesh house was damaged, but it was still good enough to sleep in. Suba carried my luggage inside.

"Tomorrow I'll begin to repair the roof," he promised.

The stars were shining down on me through a big hole in the roof. Fortunately, there were no monkeys. They would have jumped inside, and I was afraid of them. I was thinking of Sooriya. He loved sleeping outside with the stars above him. Animals didn't scare him.

The next day, Suba and I re-erected a heavy wooden sign saying "Sooriya's Beach Hut" at the entrance to the place. Soldiers had knocked it down and thrown it into a ditch. As Suba wasn't inclined to leave the place, I did all the grocery shopping.

He wanted to be prepared for possible guests coming to the restaurant. And he didn't allow me to pay for my accommodation in the little house.

"You've done enough for Sooriya already," he said. "Sooriya has taken your money with him. Our safe here would have been robbed by the army. Before he left, Ram gave me the order to treat you as a friend of his family, in case you returned. You may live here as long as you wish to stay."

In the afternoon, I went to the beach. I had nearly forgotten how beautiful this bay was, especially when there was no monsoon season. A few tourists were there, and at some distance from the shore, I perceived a few surfers.

Meanwhile, Suba had confided Sooriya's hiding place to me. He was only a few miles away from me and had not the faintest idea of how close I was to him. I looked along the beach to the bend, past Surfers' Point, and wanted to run to the lake with the crocodiles – where Sooriya was hiding in the cave.

At last, the doctor arrived from Colombo. Of course, somebody told him immediately that I had returned. He sent a Sinhalese boy to the place to invite me for dinner. By now, the curfew had been lifted.

Shortly after sunset, I entered the doctor's place. His boy served us exquisite fish dishes – a long-missed luxury. And, of course, we had the inevitable bottle of arrack. After dinner, the boy retreated to the kitchen, and finally we were alone.

The doc secretly slipped me an envelope under the table.

"I got all the documents Sooriya needs," he whispered. "It wasn't easy, and it took longer than I had planned. I had to talk to many people. Nobody may know that it was me who has been helping him."

Quickly, I hid the envelope in my bag.

"Sooriya has to be very careful," the doctor admonished me. "He mustn't show up in Arugam Bay or Pottuvil. Wherever you're hiding him, he has to get on the bus to Colombo somewhere else."

The doc had a few more words of advice for us.

"Sooriya mustn't disclose his Tamil identity. The best thing to do is not to say a single word. His language might betray him. Make him dress modestly, no loud colors. It would be an advantage if you accompanied him to Colombo. As you are aware, the presence of tourists always is the best insurance."

For Sooriya's arrival in Colombo, everything had been prepared.

"A friend of mine will wait for him at the bus terminal at the time agreed upon. You met Fernandez at the Angel Club, remember? He will give Sooriya a ride to the airport on his motorbike."

"Please tell Sooriya that I will miss our conversations so much," he instructed me before we parted.

Suba had waited for my return in Beach Hut's kitchen, but when I entered the restaurant, he pretended to be completely indifferent. Two women guests were sitting at a table, relishing a fruit salad. Fortunately, the plants on the property bore fruit most of the year – including the banana plant that was growing into our "bathroom," as I noticed in the morning on my way to the well. I loved the early snack. Now I waited in the kitchen for the women to pay and leave the restaurant.

Suba heaved a relieved sigh when he heard that I had with me all the documents Sooriya required.

"I'll bring them to Sooriya as soon as possible," Suba laid out his plan. "I will leave Arugam Bay after sunset and move through the thicket in the darkness. After I've hit on the beach, past surfers' spot, I'll be able run on toward Crocodile Rock unnoticed."

"No, I will go," I replied firmly. "Your absence might attract attention. What if guests want to have breakfast or dinner, and no one is attending the kitchen? Haven't you noticed the boy who's snooping about here and watching the place several times a day?

A better plan had to be made.

"To do our everyday tasks as usual will be the least conspicuous," I suggested.

"Female tourists make walks on the beach; this is familiar to the villagers. I'll do the same during the day. No one will pester me. They all are happy about every tourist who has come despite the difficult political situation," I tried to convince Suba.

I wouldn't have given him a chance anyhow. So, in the end, he consented to my obsession to meet Sooriya for the last time.

In my little beach bag, I packed a pair of trousers, a shirt and sandals, which Suba, wisely looking ahead, had bought a while ago.

"Wearing those, he will look quite average in Colombo," he said. "And moreover, he can't possibly get on a plane to America in a lungi and barefoot!"

We added a few provisions. Probably by now his food was reduced to the jungle's gifts. I was growing more nervous hourly and found no sleep that night. My impatience to meet Sooriya made me forget the danger of our operation.

*

Dressed for a day on the beach, I set out for Sooriya's hideout the following day. Suba had begun to repair the fence to the street in full view; this and his noisy hammering were enough to show anyone that he wasn't involved in anything illegal.

Fortunately, I wasn't the only tourist on the beach. Fishermen were pulling a heavy catamaran on the shore. They were much too busy to notice a lonely tourist girl strolling along the seaside. Unhindered, I passed the tea shop Surfer's Spot on the other end of the bay. There were no guests yet. The boy who had been assigned to guard the surfboards was dozing in a hammock. A few yards ahead, I would reach the place where the beach makes a bend; from this point on, I was invisible to anyone from the village.

I tried to look inconspicuous as I turned around to have a last check. The catamaran was lying in the sand, and the fishermen were sorting their catch. No one had watched me. Nevertheless, I waited a few more minutes to be sure that nobody was following me. Then I felt safe enough to move off to Crocodile Rock.

Swami came to my mind: I saw him dance and skip in the sand. And of course, I was thinking of the night in the cave with Sooriya. He had no idea that I was on my way to him. But the more the distance between the village and me increased, the more anxious I grew. The military police might have tracked him down in his hideout. The distance to the rock seemed to be longer than the first time. The sun was burning down on my head and shoulders, but I had taken along a big cloth. I dipped it into the water – this would cool my head. My skin was sufficiently protected by the deep tan I had gained during the past few months. The sea was even, as if someone had polished it – and quiet. All the animal noises from the jungle sounded threatening. Monkeys were shrieking, and I heard the trumpeting of invisible elephants. Suddenly hundreds of birds flew up, and instinctively I looked for cover. Kumana National Park with its countless wild animals wasn't far away.

How happy I would have been if Swami had been around to distract me, pulling faces and clowning about. Surely, he'd have fetched a yellow king coconut from the jungle to spoil me with its refreshing juice. My excitement was increasing, and I was walking faster. At last the big dark rock loomed ahead.

Along the edge of the jungle, I cautiously approached the little lake at the foot of the Rock. There was nobody around, except for a crocodile dozing on the sandbank that separated the lake from the ocean. This was the only place from where I could climb up to the cave. But how was I to get past the reptile? This crocodile seemed to guard the rock!

At my feet, I discovered an empty coconut shell. I picked it up and threw it against the rock. The shell fell back to the ground just beside the animal. It hurled itself on it, then seemed to lie in wait for some prey. But then the crocodile changed its mind, for suddenly it got up and disappeared into the lake.

This was my chance. I flitted across the sand and climbed up the steep, smooth rock face to the ledge below the cave. My heart was pounding when I peered into the cave. It was deserted. A few empty coconut shells lay on the ground. Someone had been here recently, because the fruit remains in the shells were still fresh and juicy.

I struggled up to the top of the ledge. Pieces of charcoal lay in the fireplace. I decided to hide in a niche and wait to see what might happen. Someone was climbing up; little stones were coming off, falling toward the lake.

Frightened, I retreated a little further inside. A man entered the cave. I was so relieved when I recognized the brown curly mane! He had lost weight but seemed fine. Sooriya went to the fireplace, a smile on his face.

Just as I was about to show myself, I heard his familiar voice: "I was hoping you would come back before I leave my country."

"How did you know I'm here?" I asked, leaving my hiding place.

"I saw your footprints in the sand," he laughed.

Slowly, he stepped toward me.

"But the prints could have been left by locals or even soldiers."

"They haven't got such small feet, and they don't wear that kind of sandal," he said, and embraced me at last.

We celebrated our reunion. Finally, I was able to surprise Sooriya with the good news – I had brought along all the necessary documents for his departure.

Being aware that we were spending our last day and night together, we intended to enjoy every second.

The following morning, I had to return to Arugam Bay, to avoid my absence attracting any unwanted attention. I tore a small piece off the envelope containing Sooriya's documents and scribbled on it my mother's address and telephone number in Germany.

We had agreed on a plan for Sooriya's departure. I was going to accompany him to Colombo. So, our final goodbye was put off one last time.

The fact that Sooriya was in good health consoled me. I hoped so much that our operation would be successful. Whatever was lying ahead in America for him, at least his life would no longer be exposed to any insidious threats. There had to be an end to this civil war and all the hatred one day. Surely, Sooriya would be able to return to Sri Lanka then. And maybe I would meet him again ...

Lost in my thoughts, I was getting over the strenuous march back to Arugam Bay. It was late afternoon when I arrived at Surfer's Spot. Sweating and thirsty, I entered the little tea shop. The surfers and a few local boys met there every night for a few bottles of beer.

"Well, well, have you been sunbathing in private?" one of the Australians turned to me. "Isn't it a bit lonely on that beach back there?"

Two young locals were giggling and whispering, as if they had a big secret.

"Yes, I know," the surfer murmured. "The white girls like to lie in the sand over there without their bikini tops. You guys watch them, right?"

As if I had been caught, I pulled an innocent face and winked at them, causing smug laughter.

"I like that girl," another muscleman butted in, amused.

It was time for me to empty my glass and get going. I walked by a few fishermen repairing their nets. I wanted them to remember the young tourist girl, and purposely bent down once or twice to pick up a few pretty shells.

Nobody had noticed my absence last night. In Beach Hut's restaurant, a few guests were already having dinner. Suba cast me a questioning look as he placed a bowl of rice and curry in front of me.

"Everything okay?" he inquired innocently. "Did you have a nice day?"

After all his guests had gone away, I informed Suba about our meeting at Crocodile Rock. Only few days were left to Sooriya's departure.

*

Many miles on foot lay ahead of Sooriya to the stop where he would catch the bus to Colombo. To begin with, he had to pass Arugam Bay and Pottuvil at a safe distance. To avoid public roads, he took a path through the jungle. At the insignificant bus stop, situated between Pottuvil and Moneragala, nobody would recognize him.

On the evening we both had agreed upon, I set out from Arugam Bay. For the last time, I walked along the main street and crossed the bridge to Pottuvil. Would I ever come back here? While I was waiting for the Midnight Express, I bought a bottle of lemonade at a booth with a label saying, "Cool Drinks." In fact, the drink was the same temperature as the air outside.

"No power, Madam," the boy said, only after he had opened my bottle. I guessed he said this to everybody. Most probably, he'd never had any cool drinks to begin with.

I hoped Sooriya had made it to his bus stop without any unforeseen incidents. His passport, the flight ticket, and the one thousand dollars were safely stowed away in a small bag tied around my neck and hidden close to my skin. In case the military police searched him in one of their raids, they mustn't find any documents or money on him, whereas I had never been searched in a bus.

The Midnight Express wasn't fully occupied, and I put my backpack on the seat beside me. In Pottuvil, as usual, a few soldiers entered the bus for an inspection. With bored faces they looked in a few bags; soon they let us continue our journey.

Meanwhile, it had grown dark. I looked around the bus and at my fellow passengers. There was nobody I knew from Arugam Bay. All these people seemed to be from Pottuvil or elsewhere. But, there was always the possibility that someone could recognize Sooriya as soon as he got on the bus.

At last, we arrived at the appointed bus stop. This wasn't a proper stop with lights around. I couldn't make out any specific person outside. I held my breath until finally Sooriya appeared in the door. He looked so unfamiliar with his Western clothing. His beard had been shaved, and he had combed and tied up his curly mane in his neck. Without saying a word, he handed the driver a banknote.

"Colombo?" asked the driver.

Sooriya wiggled his head in consent. I put my luggage on the floor, and he sat down beside me. Nobody would have recognized him tonight. Silently, he squeezed my hand.

Our trip to Colombo went on without any unusual occurrences. I felt safe. But, shortly before our arrival in Colombo, the Midnight Express was stopped by the army. All passengers had to get out.

"Passport," a soldier said, shining his flashlight in my face. I was nervous and hoped he didn't notice the sweat on my forehead. No, no, I tried to soothe myself. Sweating in a stuffy bus was nothing unusual. My own documents I had put in a separate bag attached to my belt. I handed him my passport.

"Tourist?"

I nodded.

Now it was Sooriya's turn. The soldier addressed him in Sinhalese, which Sooriya didn't understand. In order to avoid being unmasked as a Tamil, we had agreed that he would point to his mouth and ears with his hands and utter a few inarticulate sounds. He sounded like Lingam at Beach Hut.

"This man cannot hear or speak," I explained to the soldier.

"You know him?"

Again, I nodded.

"What's his name?"

Don't make a mistake now, I thought by myself. A Sinhalese man could never be called Sooriya Kumar. This name was typically Tamil.

"Suba," I answered him, for this was the only Sinhalese name I could recall.

"And? What else?"

I hesitated. I didn't know Suba's surname. Thank God, my gray-haired Sinhalese landlord from Hikkaduwa came to my mind.

"Sirisena," I burst out. "His name is Suba Sirisena."

Sooriya pretended to be absentminded. The soldier was satisfied and let us enter our bus again.

In Colombo, a new morning was dawning. At the central bus terminal, we immediately tried to immerse ourselves in the general bustle. We succeeded in getting out of the way of the patrolling military police. Now nothing unforeseen must happen.

Motor bikers were passing us. Many people were on their way to their various jobs. I saw a moped on which two grown-ups and three children had found room – along with a naked baby in a bucket! No one was wearing helmets, so it was easier for me to make out Fernandez on his bike. Sooriya had never met his chauffeur, whom the doctor had assigned to take my dear friend to the airport.

I was very anxious about the money we had with us. For Sri Lankans, a thousand dollars was an unbelievable sum. A beggar stretched his arm toward us, and Sooriya gave him his last rupees. Gratefully, the old man put his palms together and his hands touched his forehead in the typical way of greeting someone respect. Both men seemed to communicate with their eyes. The beggar wiggled his head and smiled at me in greeting. His eyes looked at me as if he knew and understood.

But there was no time to hang on to my emotions. A second later I spotted a motor biker squeezing his bike through the dense traffic. Fernandez had discovered us from far because of my light skin.

"We have to drive off immediately," the Burgher welcomed us in English. "Soldiers are rounding up the bus right over there. They will be through in a minute. We should get lost as soon as possible."

We had only a moment for an emotional goodbye. To embrace each other might have aroused attention. Imperceptibly to anyone except the three of us, I pulled the little bag from under my t-shirt and shoved it into Sooriya's hand.

"We will meet again," he said. "I'm quite sure of it; if not in this life, then in a coming one."

But as I didn't believe in future lives the way he did, I was inconsolable. Sooriya climbed on the pillion of Fernandez' bike.

"You will hear from me, I'll write to you," he promised. And the bike sped toward the airport. In this moment, I realized that my journey had come to an end.

*

Dazed and sad, I wandered through Colombo's streets. I felt exhausted from all the traveling. Now that Sooriya was gone, Sri Lanka had lost all its fascination. Even if I had money left to prolong my stay, nothing held me here anymore.

A few hot rotis from a mobile kitchen – for my body's sake – gave me enough will power to go to the General Post Office (GPO). This is the address I had given to my parents, for I never knew where and for how long I might stay at a certain location. The GPO maintained a P.O. box labeled "Mail for Foreigners" – and it was always unlocked. You could find your mail in various partitions marked with initials. Nobody sent valuables to the P.O. box – so who would steal a letter?

Sure enough, I found a letter from my mother, which made me indescribably happy. I looked at the stamp. The letter had been sent a long time ago, and obviously had been lying in the box for quite a while. I sat down on the stairs and read my mum's letter with tears running down my cheeks.

She hadn't heard from me for weeks, she wrote. The media back home had reported casualties in Sri Lanka, including among tourists. My family considered sending my brother to Sri Lanka to search for me. At least I should have told them whether I was in Sri Lanka or India, I thought, feeling remorse. My mother was virtually begging me to call her and come home.

I felt so sorry that I had caused her such a lot of worry. I had promised to write periodically, and had kept my promise, yet my family hardly ever received my letters. In India, other travelers had advised me to insist that the post officer put the stamps on my letter and cancel them as I watched. Otherwise, some clerks might throw the letter away and sell the same stamps to another customer. I had not always taken this advice.

For the first time on my journey, I felt badly homesick. Without further ado, I hurried to a travel agency and booked my flight back to Germany. My open-ended ticket had become quite creased because I always carried it around with me. If I had ever lost it ... unthinkable! I had no money left for a new one.

My plane would take off in a few days. Hikkaduwa – that was the place I had to go. I wanted to stay there during my last days in Sri Lanka. It was only a short distance from Colombo. Months ago, I had deposited my jeans, a pair of shoes, and a jacket at Mr. Sirisena's house. I'd need my warm clothes for my flight back to Germany. Around this time of the year, it was cold back home.

I knew the way to Colombo's bus terminal and its minibus stops by heart.

"Hikkaduwa! Hikkaduwa!" a cashier yelled from the minibus.

"Hikkaduwa? Hikkaduwa?" I asked, assuring myself.

For a moment the man looked puzzled, then he laughed and let me in. I even found a comfortable seat.

Three hours later we had arrived in Dodanduwa, outside Hikkaduwa, on the southwestern shore. I asked the driver to let me out. He stopped his minibus right in front of Mr. Sirisena's guesthouse. Upali, the youngest son, recognized me at once and welcomed me with a big smile. He ran to his parents' hut to tell them I had returned.

Mr. Sirisena approached me, his big belly still protruding and his walk still swaying.

This time, he told me I could choose whichever of the light blue houses I preferred. All three were unoccupied.

"Bad times," Mr. Sirisena complained. "There are only few tourists nowadays. It's the Tamils' fault. People are booking their vacation elsewhere, as long as we're having this civil war."

I was too tired to get involved in a debate with him. First, I wanted to have a good long shower. Meanwhile, Mrs. Sirisena prepared the rice-and-curry house special.

"Not very hot?" Upali asked me, grinning.

"Do it your way, please," I replied.

Upali watched me curiously as I ate. I had got used to chilies and no longer needed Upali's coconut rasps.

After a good night's sleep in a very comfortable bed, I decided to walk to Hikkaduwa next day. Everything seemed much the same, though the village looked clean and tidy. The touts were doing business as usual, bargaining with tourists for necklaces and rings. The boys recognized me and waved. No one pestered me this time.

Suddenly, I discovered a woman I knew in one of the outdoor restaurants. She was sitting at a table together with two girls and a bottle of Arrack.

"I've spent every vacation in Sri Lanka for many years," Petra was telling the girls, speaking thickly. "I know the country, all the beaches and temples, and the famous Buddha statues ..."

For a moment she seemed to recognize me, but then she continued blabbering and obviously enjoyed that the girls were listening to her, fascinated. I grew tired of all the tourist bustle and returned to Mr. Sirisena's green oasis. In my little house, while the temperature was too high to go outside, I completed my notes about my recent experiences.

Sometimes I saw Mr. Sirisena's daughter visit her family – they would meet on the terrace only after I had retreated to my house. The girl was a married woman now, but she didn't look very happy. Her head bowed, she entered the place walking a few steps behind her husband. He seemed to be about twenty years older than her.

Mr. Sirisena and his son-in-law had sat down at a table on the terrace. Mother and daughter went inside. The daughter only returned to serve tea. Her eyes had lost their curious joy.

Every sunset made me sentimental; I would think of Sooriya. How would he get along in the Western world? I envisioned him standing in the arrival hall of Los Angeles' vast airport, carrying his small cotton bag, his bare feet in sandals because he hated wearing shoes so much. What would happen if the American students didn't pick him up? The eighties in the USA were quite different from the seventies that Sooriya had known in Europe.

I knew I might see Germany with different eyes, even after such a short absence. All through my journey I felt the urge to write down everything of importance to me. Who might want to hear my story back home? Who would understand it?

On the day of my departure, Mr. Sirisena made the bus stop for me for the last time. The minibus was cram-full, but the cashier opened the co-driver's door for me. He allowed me to sit down beside a shy young Buddhist monk. The boy had been shaved bald and wore the typical saffron-colored cloth. He was eight years old at the most. For the last time I would see Hikkaduwa and Akuralla with its idyllic little hotel located beneath coconut palms.

Relaxed, I leaned back and enjoyed the ride on the coastal road passing beaches and villages along the seaside. The bus stopped at the famous Buddhist temple, as usual, and I handed the driver a banknote for the offertory. I had always been protected on all my trips in Asia, by whom or from what, I didn't know. In Colombo, I gave a beggar my last rupees before I got on another bus to the airport.

A plane from Europe had landed recently and tired holidaymakers were leaving the arrival terminal to get in their various coaches. A girl with a huge backpack was standing at the exit, unsure what to do next. She was about my age.

"Do you want to go to Colombo?" I addressed her. "The bus will leave at the stop across the street."

The girl, who had pale skin and long brown hair, smiled at me. She waved at me cheerfully before running across the parking lot to reach the bus.

"Have a good journey!" I yelled.

The bus driver started the engine just as she reached the street. She ran even faster, her backpack heavily bumping against her back. Grinning, the bus driver watched her in his rearview mirror. He always does this, I thought with a shake of my head.

Getting on my plane was like stepping into another world. The air conditioning froze me. A woman of around fifty sat down beside me; she smelled of an awful perfume and hairspray.

"It's time to go home," she turned to me. "I had expected a little more comfort. We have been paying a lot of money for two weeks' vacation in Sri Lanka. And this heat, the mosquitos and worst of all, the food! And all those pestering locals. Next year we'll spend our holidays in Europe again."

In my mind I was in Arugam Bay and with Sooriya ...

"How have your holidays been?" The disappointed tourist called me back into reality.

Blackbirds were rising beside the runway as our plane accelerated. The Boeing flew a loop above the ocean.

"Holiday fever will come and go," Marcus had said to me back in our home town. "Some people are immune to it, others will be infected. And for me – I will always long for Sri Lanka."

Chapter 8

One world I had left and the other I hadn't come back to yet -not only physically. My thoughts constantly returned to my experiences of the past months or flew ahead to my home country. How would my future be in Germany?

What a luxury it was to be served a glass of wine on the plane! The scents and smells coming from the kitchen had become so unfamiliar to me. I hadn't missed meat in Sri Lanka, either for religious or ideological reasons. If you ever visit a Colombo market and see all the meat displayed in the hot sun, you'll never want to eat it. The meat offered on the plane wasn't attractive to me either.

From a few seats behind mine came the voices of a couple talking in the familiar dialect of my home region. We started a conversation and they offered to take me along in their car towards southern Germany. The remaining distance to my hometown wasn't difficult to travel - hitchhiking in the '80s was easy for a young woman. Sooriya, I guessed, would have a hard time compared to me.

I looked forward to witnessing my mother's surprised face. At last, all her worries would be gone. But upon my arrival, I discovered the door of our house was locked. They had gone on a holiday! No one was expecting me. I took my luggage and walked to my favorite pub, where I had spent many an evening prior to my Asia journey.

"Back from a vacation? You're so tanned," the Greek pub owner welcomed me. "Haven't seen you for a long time."

Numerous patrons sat around the tables drinking wine and beer. It was somebody's birthday, and the bartender treated everyone to a round of Ouzo. It was a noisy little pub.

"Sri Lanka? Isn't that the country where people are killing each other in a civil war right now?" Somebody asked me. "You can see it on TV all day long. That's where you've been on holiday?"

For most Europeans, to arrive in Asia for the first time is a cultural shock. But to come home after months away can be a shock as well. On my journey I almost never worried about finding an accommodation for the coming night. Now, I asked myself: Where I might spend my first night back in Germany? The pub had a telephone, of course. I called my best friend, and a few minutes later she arrived to pick me up.

For many years we had been inseparable. When she asked me: "Tell me, how did you like it?" My immediate response was simply: "Sri Lanka is beautiful."

It was hard to describe everything that had happened during my stay in Sri Lanka.

Now that I was back, I had to start a new life. I had no apartment of my own, and I had quit my job for good before I set out to Asia. For the time being, I moved in with my friend.

Sooriya had promised to write me letters to my parents' address, which I had given him at Crocodile Rock. Happily, he kept his promise.

For some time, Sooriya wrote, he lived with his student friends in Los Angeles, keeping their house and cooking for all of them. Later, his friend Peter and he traveled through California. From San Francisco they went to Oregon to live for a while on a farm. From there they traveled to Montana and to the Rocky Mountains in Colorado. Sooriya was eager to see many places in America, but he always returned to Los Angeles. He met Caroline, and they moved to Honolulu, Hawaii, where her parents were living.

He fell in love with Hawaii as soon as he set his foot on the island of O'ahu. The climate, the vegetation, the ocean – all of it was so like Sri Lanka.

"Father Phil, a priest, gave me my first home," he wrote. "He provided us with food and a bed."

Caroline and Sooriya lived in an agricultural community doing biological farming. First, he planted a Bodhi tree to thank his gods. In India and Sri Lanka, the Bodhi tree is sacred. The saying goes that Buddha was enlightened beneath one. Sooriya planted many trees and taught the members of the community everything he knew about herbs. Like everyone else, he worked on the farm or cooked meals for everyone.

The last I heard of him, he and Caroline had moved into a house not far from the farm but close to the seaside. They married and she gave birth to a son. They called him Sai after the Indian spiritual leader Shirdi Sai Baba, whose small portrait Sooriya always carried with him.

*

Many years went passed during which I met a young man with whom I was shared many interests, including traveling. He hadn't been in Asia yet; he was attracted by Mexico, Guatemala, and Belize.

We moved to a little town near Cologne, where he went to university. I decided to study German language and literature and cultural anthropology. Both topics had long interested me greatly. For a long time, I considered writing a book about Sooriya and my experiences in Sri Lanka. It was just an idea.

My future husband and I journeyed to Australia and New Zealand. It was so different traveling as a couple: we acted as a unit. Consequently, we had only casual contact with local people; our conversations with them were shallow. With a camper, we made trips to the outback, and my partner climbed on the famous Ayers Rock in the desert. I had declined to make the strenuous climb up in the intense heat. I had good reason: shortly before we set off, my doctor told me I was pregnant.

It's really eerie to drive for days through an almost uninhabited area. "Next gasoline station 250 miles," read a sign. No wonder the Australians in the Outback needed the "Flying Doctors" in their small airplanes. I recalled the Australian TV series with the same name that was broadcast in Germany a few years ago.

We visited a place called Coober Pedy in the Australian desert, where residents live in caves. The extreme heat during summer - and the opal exploitation - had led to this kind of housing. "The white man's hole," the place's name was supposed to mean. In a dugout hotel - meaning dug out of a rock face - my friend asked me to be his wife.

Of course, my life changed completely the moment I became a mother. My daughter Aline and I were alone for long periods in our house on the outskirts of Cologne. My husband's job required him to travel a lot. But while it was beautiful to see our little daughter grow up, I missed having interesting discussions and adventures.

One day, while I was tidying up, I found the diaries I had kept during my time in Sri Lanka and I started reading one after another. They brought back happy and exciting memories of Sooriya, calling into being many images. What had become of him? We had stopped writing. Having married, I had a new surname, and I had long ago left my hometown in southern Germany. Whenever my little daughter was having a nap, I would let myself be absorbed by my old notes. In my mind, every time I opened one of my precious diaries I was setting off to Sri Lanka once more.

My plan to write a book started taking shape. Would Sooriya have approved of my wish to publish his story? Or his brothers? I decided to change all their names and not to mention Arugam Bay by its real name. I referred to just a little fishing village on Sri Lanka's East Coast. And I omitted many details if they turned out to be too personal.

Once again, I had come to a turning point in my life. Married life left me unhappy. Writing saved me from drowning in gray dullness. If only in my thoughts, Sooriya had returned.

My manuscript was almost complete, but it had to wait. After my husband and I separated, I was too unhappy to concentrate on it. My daughter Aline and I moved back to my hometown, where I found a job as a journalist. To write about other people and happenings was a new experience for me. But this mental distance was exactly what I needed; my heart was too sad for personal issues.

Then, around Christmas 2004, a horrible tsunami hit Asia. I watched TV every spare minute. What had happened to Sooriya's brothers? Were they okay? I surfed in the internet for news about Arugam Bay. A list was published with the names of people who had survived. Sooriya's brother Ram was among them. That was all I could find out.

Shrugging off my lethargy, I became determined to finish my manuscript. The words started pouring out of me, and I spent many nights in front of my computer.

The satisfaction and happiness that I felt at the sight of my own printed book – holding it in my hands – cannot be described in simple words.

The resonance my book caused on my homepage overwhelmed me. Fans from Germany and the surrounding German-speaking countries sent e-mails to tell me they had met Sooriya in Sri Lanka or on his travels during the 1970s. Every one of my readers seemed to know that my story took place in Arugam Bay, although I never mentioned its correct name in the book.

I discovered that Sri Lanka online platforms were discussing my book. Until then I didn't know that such internet platforms existed, where Sri Lanka fans and insiders exchanged their experiences and gave useful advice.

A couple wrote to tell me they had been guests at Sooriya's Beach Hut in the early 1980s. They had been so impressed by Sooriya that they had decided to call their first child by his name. When they had a daughter, they named her Suria. Attached I found a pretty photograph of her, now fair-haired and almost all grown up.

Another reader e-mailed a picture of Ram in Sri Lanka, holding a copy of my book. The once well-nourished Ram had grown thin. The civil war and the tsunami had left their mark on his face. People e-mailed pictures of the place, which had been destroyed by the floods. Only the front wall of the Shiva-Ganesh House was left intact. Miraculously, the paintings of Shiva and Ganesh remained unharmed.

Some of my readers said they had walked the strenuous path to Crocodile Rock, following in Sooriya's tracks. Even Ilse, whom young Sooriya had met in Germany, emailed to let me know she had kept all his letters from the nineteen seventies. So many people from Germany, Austria and Switzerland had never forgotten him.

In 1984, when Sooriya left Sri Lanka during the civil war, we all hoped the conflict would end soon. Twenty-five years later, the war wasn't over yet.

My book was published in German, and I had never expected Sooriya to hear of it, wherever he was living, be it the U.S. mainland or Hawaii or somewhere else. Then one chilly winter day my telephone rang.

"Hi, this is Sooriya calling from Hawaii."

*

At the time he called me, Sooriya had still not returned to his beloved Sri Lanka where the civil war still continued after all these years. Occasionally he took a plane to India and traveled to the sacred mountain of Arunachala in the southern state of Tamil Nadu. There he had stayed with sadhus when he was a young man. He liked to visit the ancient temples. With the help of meditation and yoga he would travel back in his mind to the beginnings of his life's journey, when his sadhu had sent him away.

A few of his former travel companions, and people he had met on his way to Europe, were still his friends, such as a Swiss man Sooriya knew from India.

has come," Sooriya said on the telephone.

The Swiss traveler had carried a copy of my book from Europe to India. He had bought it because he had visited Sri Lanka several times and wanted to know what I contributed to the topic. He was surprised to read about his old friend.

"I thought I had lost the address and telephone number you had given to me in our cave," Sooriya said. "Recently when I returned to Hawaii from India, suddenly there was the little slip of paper."

My mother's number had been the same since 1983. She had never spoken any English, but Sooriya spoke to her in German. As soon as he told her his name, she knew who he was. She had read my book in detail. She promptly gave him my landline number. Sooriya got through to me even faster than my mother.

He had read parts of the book, Sooriya told me on the phone. After so many years, he still remembered a lot of his German vocabulary.

"I intend to make a trip to Germany, and I'd like to visit you," I heard him say. "Back in Colombo I told you we'd meet again, you remember?"

Only a few weeks later, I welcomed him at the station in my hometown. He was wearing trousers, shirt and shoes - no lungi or bare feet this time. His long curly mane had turned a little gray. Time had left its marks on us, but it felt so familiar to look into each other's eyes and embrace.

It was early summer in Germany, and we were sitting in my little garden. He had taken off the Western clothes and put on his lungi and a Hawaiian shirt. We didn't know where to begin to catch up – so much had happened during the past 25 years.

"I always pictured you among blue cornflowers," Sooriya said as we sipped tea.

My eyes lit up in amazement – this flower is typical of Germany. You saw them very rarely nowadays.

Sooriya walked around the hedge and pointed at the neighboring garden.

There they were in full bloom: blue cornflowers I had never noticed them before. As for me, I had always imagined Sooriya together with the pink bougainvillea growing at his temple in Arugam Bay.

My daughter Aline was prepared to have a guest, but she was a bit shocked at the sight of a wild-looking stranger with dark skin and long hair. She had never seen a man in a lungi before. Bravely, she tried to converse with Sooriya in her broken English.

"Your mother and I have known each other for many years," he said to her, smiling. "You look very much like her."

Aline forgot her shyness sooner than I had expected. When I returned from the kitchen, they had already started to do some yoga exercises in the living room.

"Why haven't you ever shown me, Mum?" she asked almost reproachfully.

Everything Sooriya said or did was exciting to Aline, who recently had become a teenager. And as Sooriya could see, she didn't know everything about her mother.

After Aline went to bed, Sooriya and I talked for many hours about what had happened to each of us throughout the years. Our feelings for each other hadn't ceased.

He and his wife had separated years ago, he told me.

"We had a good married life together in Hawaii, and we took good care of our son," Sooriya reflected. "But sometimes you meet for a certain period and to serve a certain purpose. Then each one has to return to the path intended for him."

Sooriya had left their house near the beach and moved back to the farm community. During all those years the Bodhi tree he had planted shortly after his arrival had grown huge. In the back yard he equipped a workshop in order to pick up the craft he had studied in India when he was young: Sacred Copper Art.

For Father Phil's chapel on the farm, he manufactured a copper door – a fine work of art. At last he was able to repay the priest for helping him get settled on O'ahu.

In consequence, he received several orders from Christian parishes to create ornate altars.

"I give all my power and belief to it until I have the right intuition, what the altar has to look like," he explained.

Sooriya had become well known in Hawaii for his copper art. One of his works hangs in the international airport in Honolulu. Many of his pieces adorn the buildings and garden paths of the Wai'anae Coast Comprehensive Health Center, which perches on a hillside overlooking the ocean. He showed me many photographs.

Whenever he could over the years, he had helped members of his family get out of Sri Lanka to escape the civil war. The first out was Sri, his youngest brother. In Hawaii, he got the opportunity to attend college. After some twelve years, Ram, his wife and their three children succeeded in escaping. They spent a few years on O'ahu where Ram became the favored cook in the farm community. Nevertheless, he and his wife longed to return to Arugam Bay, though their eldest son, Ranjith, preferred to stay in Hawaii.

"Ram tries to visit us in Hawaii once a year," Sooriya said. "I'm so glad he survived the tsunami!"

In addition, brother Jothi arrived at the farm on O'ahu.

Next Sooriya took a flight to Sri Lanka to meet his mother in Mannar. She still had no exit visa. The civil war was still going on, but Sooriya's American passport allowed him to return to Hawaii at any time. At the airport, Sooriya bribed the officer in charge with a lot of dollars.

"Haven't you also got a mother or a sister?" Sooriya asked him.

His plan worked, and although he deeply despised the procedure, he handed the money to the man in an airport toilet stall. But in the end, both he and his mother were permitted to board the airplane to Hawaii.

There, she lived in Sooriya's home together with his wife and his son for several years. Caroline wanted to resume her job, and Sooriya's mother took care of little Sai. Over the following years, with the help of his wife, he was able to arrange for his three sisters with their children and aunts to leave Sri Lanka and immigrate to Hawaii. In all, he arranged for eighteen family members to leave Sri Lanka for the U.S.

"By now they make a decent living and have become good American citizens," he told me.

His mother had moved in with her youngest son, Sri. Sooriya's son Sai had grown up and no longer needed his grandmother's care.

Sooriya had planned to stay with us for a few days. Each day was full of emotion and endless talk. Exhausted, we had to admit that a quarter century of experiences can't be summed up in a short time. Sooriya took a nap one afternoon while Aline and I sat on our terrace – me sorting out my mind.

Suddenly loud chaos erupted. Countless crows descended on my neighbor's garden, a small meadow surrounded by a wall. The birds were fluttering about as if in panic. The noisy spectacle didn't wake Sooriya but it frightened Aline. I hesitated to explain to her Sooriya's relationship with black birds. When he woke, I asked him what he thought of the occurrence.

Composed and smiling, he answered: "Don't worry about it. They have been greeting you."

This incident deeply impressed my daughter. I had never told her much about Sri Lanka, and nothing about what the black birds meant to Sooriya.

She was sad when her new friend had to leave us. Sooriya wanted to visit his brother, Shiva, who was the only family member to emigrate from Sri Lanka to Germany. In the meantime, Shiva was married and lived with his wife and children in the northern part of my home country, I learned. Sooriya would make a stop to visit his old friends who had named her daughter Suria. The girl was curious to meet the extraordinary man who was responsible for her name.

Aline said good bye to Sooriya, who asked her to visit him in Hawaii when she was older.

I felt deeply unhappy during our ride to the station. To see him off after such a short visit was depressing. A big thunderstorm was brewing; I had to leave Sooriya in a hurry because Aline had gone to the public pool and would be waiting for me to pick her up and take her home. The instant she jumped in the car, big hailstones started pattering down from the sky.

"Strange things keep happening since Sooriya arrived," Aline stated. "I've never met a person like him."

What could I have added? I only nodded. At home, our terrace was covered with ice. I checked my watch: his train had left a minute ago.

Sooriya and I had agreed to keep in touch at regular intervals.

*

From time to time Sooriya would send me a postcard from various places on the planet. Sometimes he called me from Hawaii. Sending emails was not his way of communication.

Meanwhile, Sooriya was undertaking a new project. He planned to found a big new farm on O'ahu, growing agricultural produce biologically. People from all nations would be welcome, and an art village was to be established. Social projects would be called into being.

Sooriya had become a well-known artist, even beyond Hawaii. On the Internet I looked for and discovered articles about him over and over again. No matter what occasion, he was always wearing a lungi and walked barefoot. Never was I having any doubts, that he would make his vision of the farm come true.

Again, years went by. Eventually I found out that he had purchased a big farm in the Wai'anae Valley of O'ahu. Located at the foot of volcanic mountains, the land had had lain fallow for years and was now, completely covered with head-high grass.

One day I received a postcard from New Zealand. In modest words, Sooriya described making a work of art for Tuheitia Paki, the Maori King. The King had invited him to his South Pacific island state

Back on O'ahu, Sooriya prepared and hosted a big ceremony to inaugurate his farm. Hundreds of guests took part. Supervising the music was Eddie Kamae, Hawaii's famous ukulele player, singer and film producer

– one of the founders of "Sons of Hawaii," a group dedicated to reviving ancient Polynesian culture. Father Phil, a Catholic, and a Hawaiian spiritual leader consecrated the ground. Numerous public figures took part in the celebration including the Big Kahuna himself, Kamaki Kanahele, who is dedicated to the preservation of Hawaiian culture and traditions and who, as director of a big center for traditional healing – the Wai'anae Coast Comprehensive Health Center – employed Sooriya as the Center's esteemed copper artist in residence. The income helped Sooriya fund the farm. He called the farm "Mouna," meaning "inner silence" in his mother tongue, Tamil.

It was hard work to make a fertile oasis from the rugged terrain of the Wai'anae Valley, in a place that had been long overgrown with tall grass. The land had to be cleared. Paths and living quarters had to be built, and trees and vegetables planted. After much hard labor, Sooriya would be able to realize his vision of staging social and art events for children and adults. On the telephone, he told me that he and Mouna Farm would be featured in a documentary film, "Ola – Health is Everything," about healthcare projects in Hawaii.

Another turning point in my life lay ahead of me. My daughter decided to move out to attend university in France. She was an adult by now. Mothers who have been raising their children on their own let go with great difficulties. I felt very sentimental about her leaving and recalled my mother's fears and worries when I set off to Asia in my early twenties.

"She will do fine, I'm sure," my almost ninety-year-old mother tried to reassure me.

Then, one night, Sooriya called from Hawaii. He sounded very sad. His brother Ram had suddenly died. The brothers had been very close.

For the first time since he had come to Sri Lanka to get out his mother and bring her to Hawaii, Sooriya returned to his native island. The civil war had come to an end in 2009 after more than 25 years. It is said that 80,000 to 100,000 human beings lost their lives in the conflict. He still felt uneasy upon arrival at Colombo's airport – and on the overland trip to Arugam Bay.

Much had changed, but Sooriya wasn't inclined to dwell on the past. Again, it was the eldest brother's duty to ignite the flames at Ram's cremation, the way he had done for his father a few decades before.

A few days later, he took a flight back to Hawaii.

"I want you to come to Hawaii," he told me on the telephone. "I would like to show you where my life's uncertain journey has been leading me since I've left Sri Lanka. Back then, you helped me to go this way."

I hesitated to leave my hometown, because my mother wasn't feeling well. She had supported me all my life. Could I really leave her on her own?

"Please book a flight to Hawaii and to Sooriya," she implored me. "This is your life, and I want you to live it. I don't need your help at the moment. Don't worry about me, please. My love for you will persist forever, even when I'm gone."

She caressed my hair as she had done when I was a little girl. This time I didn't go – my dear mum sent me away.

Mouna – "inner silence," – that was exactly what I was looking for. Distance, and taking a look on your life from the other side of the planet, may do one's soul good.

Another turning point on our journey showed me the way to Sooriya. I decided to fly.

Chapter 9

Many years had passed since I had taken a long-distance journey. About thirty hours, including stops along the way, lay ahead of me to reach Honolulu, O'ahu. Part of it was a six-hour flight across the Pacific Ocean from Los Angeles to the northernmost of the South Sea Islands – Hawaii, the fiftieth state of the USA. I was so excited! On the plane, I conversed with a nice woman who asked me why I was traveling to Hawaii.

"That's an incredible story," she said when I told her my tale. "You have to write it down."

I nodded agreement.

I had departed from Germany on a winter day. Stepping out of the airport in Honolulu, a wave of hot air hit me. Then I saw a huge copper flower adorning the building's outer wall. This had to be Sooriya's work! Sure enough, he had come to the airport and was waiting for me.

"Aloha, welcome in my second home," he greeted me. In Hawaii, everybody embraces – very different from Sri Lanka. I was so happy to see him again.

A man named Ken, who worked on Mouna Farm now and then, was driving the pick-up truck. We climbed in and then were on our way on wide, modern streets passing Honolulu's skyscrapers. Everything looked quite American. For the time being, I saw no South Sea postcard-idyll. Happy to be with Sooriya, I cared not the least.

Our 30-mile ride took us west, to the dry, leeward side of the island at the foot of the Wai'anae mountain range. From the coastal road we turned toward interior O'ahu. It had grown dark, and when we arrived at the farm, I could perceive little of the surroundings except palm trees, tall papaya trees and banana plants silhouetted against the night sky. Countless stars shone much brighter than any I had seen back home. I smelled sweet flowers and tropical vegetation, and the silence of the farm made me forget the typical American feel of Honolulu. This farm felt distinctly different.

A group of people of different nationalities welcomed me to Mouna Farm. Sonia, born in Hawaii, is of Japanese descent. She placed the traditional Hawaiian lei around my neck, fragrant with plumeria blossoms. Plumeria also adorned my bed for my first night on the farm. Their smell was bewitching.

In the morning, I made my first reconnaissance of the premises and immediately felt taken back to Sri Lanka. Sooriya had created a paradise, reminding him of the country of his birth. As a result of Sooriya's hard work and persistence, in only a short period, the long-fallow, hardened ground of his new property had blossomed into a green and fertile oasis.

"My brothers and my friends have been helping me," Sooriya emphasized. "One finger alone cannot hold a glass. Only with all my fingers I can do it. With their help it was possible to reach our common goal."

The men and women on the farm had paved wide paths and started to grow all sorts of vegetables in small fields. Palm trees gave shade. Numerous banana plants bore ripe fruit. On a few trees I recognized longish vegetables – in Sri Lanka, the locals called them "drum sticks," I recalled wistfully. My mind returned to Hawaii. The valley was surrounded by black mountains of volcanic origin. From afar, I could make out the relief of a cold lava belt.

Not surprisingly after the long and strenuous journey, I slept late. By the time I got up, everybody else had eaten breakfast long ago. The kitchen building, which was located amid lush greenery, had only three walls; the open side was open to the gardens. In the middle of it sat a long wooden table. A wooden sign engraved with the name Anna Poorani hung by chains from a tree. Sooriya had named the kitchen after his mother. She had taught him to be grateful for food at all times, however simple the meal might be.

Taking a closer look at the kitchen structure, I realized that it was a used shipping container with one wall cut out. Sooriya and his companions had added a wooden terrace. The big table on it could accommodate many guests. The container was furnished with several propane stoves and a vast number of pots, pans, dishes, glasses and cutlery. A sink unit and water supply had been installed outside.

"The kitchen dedication will be celebrated by my family soon," Sooriya explained to me.

He prepared breakfast for me as I watched. Still another familiar situation – as if we hadn't been separated half our lives – was the way he moved barefoot through the kitchen. On a propane stove, he boiled black tea, milk and herbs for fresh chai. A plant bearing ripe passion fruit was practically growing into the kitchen.

After I had relished the freshly picked tropical fruit, Sooriya showed me around, and only now I discovered how large the farm was. Mouna wasn't just a vision any longer – it had become a beautiful reality.

Another little house served as a bathroom with showers, washbasins and toilets, but Sooriya wanted his own shower Sri Lankan style: without a roof and protected from sight only by wickerwork. He still didn't like closed rooms. And, last but not least in that part of the farm, I discovered a library packed with books on religion, spirituality, nature, Hawaiian culture and many other topics – and among them I noticed my book was standing on a shelf.

Sooriya had his own, private area on the farm, surrounded by so many palm trees and fast-growing banana plants that it felt secluded from outsiders. He dwelt in a small, cozy wooden cottage erected on pilings. Sooriya never needed much in the way of comforts; most of the day he spent outside in the open country.

A short distance away, on a large wooden platform open to the elements on all sides and topped by a vine-covered roof supported by posts, he had set up his workshop. Here he created his copper works of art. In the seclusion of his private area he was able to concentrate on his tasks and his artwork.

"Art is a way of expressing love, a gift of beauty," Sooriya said to me. "If you let the energy of your heart flow in your work, you will bring the spirit of love to life."

A brightly-painted, 1960's-vintage school bus stood out among the greenery, resplendent with colorful flowers and bearing the words "Peace & Love" in big, bold letters. The bus had been the first place of accommodation on the farm, when there was nothing else on the land but grass and brushwood, so I was told.

A cement bridge crossing a large drainage canal led to the rear area of the farm. The property here is situated near the foot of a brush-covered, weather-worn volcanic mountain. I noticed a striking octagonal wooden house with a little garden situated off to the left, surrounded by plants

"A very special friend has built it for himself," Sooriya told me. "You'll meet him soon; you've heard of him before."

It was Peter, who was American student Sooriya befriended long ago in Sri Lanka. Peter and several fellow former students had made it possible for Sooriya to immigrate to the USA. Now, Peter helped to organize the farm.

In a small greenhouse, I discovered a familiar face: Sooriya's brother Jothi. He was cultivating young plants for the vegetable fields. What a joy to see him again! Jothi recognized me at once and welcomed me with a big smile.

Jothi and his family lived in Honolulu, but he came to the farm almost every day to help. With his profound knowledge of farming, he had done most of the initial planting. When Jothi was a boy in Mannar, his father had taught him a lot. Later, Jothi studied farming and agriculture. A big round herb bed added to the variety and abundance of edible plants on Mouna Farm.

A Bodhi tree was the first thing Sooriya planted on the farm. By now it had grown tall, and beneath its many heart-shaped leaves was hidden a small Buddhist temple. An elderly Buddhist monk wearing a brownish cloth was solemnly decorating the statue of the Buddha with flowers. A second temple stood a little apart, visible and accessible to everyone. Attached by strings, many small prayer flags of different colors fluttered in the wind.

Sonia had an own small house and garden next to the neem-tree nursery by the farm's front gate. Sonia Her "house" was actually another re-purposed shipping container, covered with vines and surrounded by lush greenery. Sonia had inherited a love for gardening, and especially for cultivating flowers. A well-known TV producer in Hawaii, she nevertheless had given up her apartment in Honolulu and moved to Mouna Farm.

While she still produced films in Honolulu, she liked helping Sooriya with bureaucratic issues, emails, appointments and scheduling. He was very happy to be released from these tasks and called Sonia the "Mother of Mouna Farm." She had a special relationship with the birds on the farm, especially the zebra doves. Sonia fed them every day, and at her whistle, crowds of loud twittering birds would invade her little garden.

Sometimes young visitors came to the farm to stay for a few days, weeks, or months. Called WWOOFers after a program most of them were enrolled in - World Wide

Opportunities on Organic Farms – they helped in the fields and gardens, contributing labor in exchange for food and accommodation. Since hotels in Hawaii can be very expensive, this was a popular way to experience Hawaii on a small budget. The additional help made it possible to maintain and grow the farm. Of course, the Mouna Farm community wasn't representative of the typical Hawaiian lifestyle.

The Buddhist monk I saw at the Bodhi tree on my first day here was a permanent guest on the farm. Everybody just called him "Monk" He was more than 90 years old and led a modest, monastic life. The monk took no part in the farm routine or the common meals. He had a small garden that provided him with enough food for himself. A little rice would complete his sole meal a day, Sooriya told me. He never ate more.

Sometimes we would see Monk walking along the paths. We never bothered him. His only regular guests were the farm's chickens. They seemed to enjoy his small garden. I never found any eggs on the farm – Monk had created a nest where the chickens laid their eggs.

At first Monk ignored me. Had he taken a vow of silence?

One day as I passed his garden, I was surprised to hear him speaking in an unfamiliar language. Had someone come for a visit? When I came closer, I saw that he was speaking into a cell phone. He looked happy and waved at me. From now on, he greeted me whenever we met. But we never had a real conversation – Monk spoke almost no English.

The old monk regularly surprised me. One day I saw him walk to the parking lot at the front entrance of the farm. I never imagined him driving, but he got into a car and sped off rapidly. Obviously, I had underestimated him. A few hours later he reappeared and dragged a big sack of rice from the car to the kitchen. He set it down and bowed his head in greeting to Sooriya and me. Sooriya did the same, and Monk retreated in silence to his quarters.

"People give Monk the rice for free, you know," Sooriya explained. "He keeps only as much as he will need for the moment – the remaining stock of rice is for our community. He likes to give – more than to take."

Another day, Monk returned from a car ride bearing a calendar with golden images of the Buddha, which he donated to the community; he himself paid no attention to boundaries such as weeks or months, or even days or hours.

One afternoon, I thought I was going to be all alone on the farm. Everyone was going out, including Sooriya, who had to meet an "important person." I felt a bit insecure.

"Monk will be guarding the premises," Sooriya assured me as he got in the pick-up.

Sooriya could drive, but he didn't really like to. I watched him leave.

As soon as I was alone, I saw Monk walking around, talking to himself in his language.

When Sooriya wasn't on the property, Mouna Farm seemed different. It felt so empty without him, and the birds appeared to be much noisier.

I doubted that the frail and peace-loving Monk would be able to defend the farm and me against any intruders. Even so, I felt fairly safe with him making his rounds. Anybody passing by the farm's gate would see that the premises weren't deserted.

Shortly before sunset, Sooriya returned. When he heard the jeep pull up, Monk disappeared to his hut. I told Sooriya how Monk had been protecting me.

"Although he doesn't say much and hardly speaks any English, I know quite a bit about him. We understand each other without speaking many words."

Monk came from Laos; he had been in the army and fought in a war. After hearing about Sooriya and this special place, he and several other monks visited Mouna Farm. Monk decided to stay.

*

Mouna Farm was planned for far more than growing vegetables, herbs, and fruit. Its full name was Mouna Farm Arts and Cultural Village. Accordingly, Sooriya had realized many projects and community events on the land.

Organized group visits were a regular occurrence. The next day, for instance, a group of young teachers arrived for a visit. In the shade under a giant tree, the ground had been raked and seats were arranged for the occasion. Sooriya, in his lungi and with bare feet as always, welcomed his fifteen guests. After Sonia had offered them locally grown fresh fruit, Sooriya asked us all to stand in a circle.

"Aloha" was the common Hawaiian greeting. Each participant spoke a few words. The young educators had seen the film "Ola - Health is Everything" in the cinema with its depiction of Sooriya and Mouna Farm and were keen to meet this extraordinary person and experience the farm. Sooriya had told about this film, shot by a film director named Matthew Nagato. He promised to show it to me later.

A further reason for the teachers' visit was that Mouna was the only farm of this kind in Hawaii. They had graduated and started their teaching careers only recently and wanted to learn if the farm with its special spirit might be suited for school class projects.

Sooriya introduced me. They were very interested to hear that I had made such a long journey from Germany to visit Sooriya. I explained to them that we had met many years ago in Sri Lanka.

"I come from a small island South of India," he told them. "My life's journey has led me to Hawaii."

From the beginning, the atmosphere was very relaxed. Sooriya was not only lecturing, but also joking with the young people, who were captivated by his easy way of communicating. They clearly enjoyed his narrations about his childhood and early youth in Sri Lanka. Sooriya introduced his brother Jothi to everyone. Jothi had brought a tremendous know-how about planting and farming from Sri Lanka to Hawaii.

Laughing and chatting, we started our excursion across the farm, guided by Sonia. Sooriya and Jothi went to the kitchen to prepare a very special meal with many tasty dishes for their guests.

"One of the first trees Sooriya planted on the farm was a breadfruit tree," Sonia told me. Quoting Sooriya, she said: "For many people on this planet, its fruit is the bread of life."

This year the tree bore fruit for the first time.

"On the farm we are in the habit of harvesting the first fruit with a little ceremony, in order to show our gratitude. You may harvest this tree's first few breadfruits today."

Our group was now passing a neem tree, whose seedling Jothi had brought along from Sri Lanka. Sonia explained the healing effects of its fruit, bark, and leaves. They have been used against all kinds of illnesses in India for thousands of years. The plant contains antibacterial and other healing substances. Sonia invited us to try the leaves and the fruit. I recalled that, back in Sri Lanka, Sooriya often cleaned his teeth with neem tree leaf stems. Chewing on the stems releases the natural oil that mixes with your saliva. Neem tree oil is used in many products, including soap and toothpaste. The trees are prized by sadhus and yogis in India and Sri Lanka who like to sit under them and meditate.

Sonia led us past a plantation of mango and papaya trees to show us the herb garden in the center of the farm. Here, many rare medicinal herbs were being cultivated. I noticed the young people entirely enjoying the atmosphere of the farm.

Back at the breadfruit tree, Sonia spoke a few words of gratitude. For the visitors, the event of harvesting the farm's first few fruits assumed a special distinction.

"Never before have I been so conscious of plucking a fruit," one of the young teachers said to me. She seemed almost devout in her words.

In the art village, a section of the farm being set aside for projects and workshops, Sooriya joined us again and invited us to take be seated in the shade of a wooden pavilion.

Sooriya talked about the meaning of his "Sacred Copper Art," which he had first studied in India. To him, the shaping of copper wasn't just arts-and-crafts exercise.

"You must put your soul into it," he declared. "Art will develop from the inner energy and from your vitality."

During the creative process, he didn't want to be disturbed. When he was immersed in his work, he disliked interruptions.

What Sooriya particularly wished his young visitors to know is that the farm's spirit and his art are informed not only by Hindu and Buddhist ideas.

"All religions are united here," he emphasized again.

Sooriya had once created a figure of the Virgin Mary holding her baby Jesus. The framework around the two was a Hawaiian motif, with Maria wearing a lei around her neck. He created sacred motifs of Hinduism, such as the deity Ganesha, but also images of the beautiful Hawaiian and Sri Lankan flora and fauna.

Sooriya approached every new work of art in a special way. He worked with simple tools, including some he had manufactured himself. He would clean and bless them in a little ceremony before beginning.

"I'm doing this, to show my respect and my esteem for the parts they are playing in my work," Sooriya elaborated for us. "From the very beginning of each copper work, up to the end of it, I am in a spiritual process. First I meditate until the idea has been born in my heart. Only then will I start the actual work, during which I chant in my Tamil language. It's more than just music – it's a way to focus on my creativity and concentrate on my heart's feelings. Every piece of my art reflects my inner journey expresses the big joy I want to share with all living beings. To me, copper is the bridge between the Creator, who towers above everybody and everything, and the artist, who has to do the physical work."

His young guests listened with rapt attention to this description of his sacred art.

In the farm's art village, Sooriya offered an assortment of workshops for children and for adults: painting, wood carving, and, stone or metal sculpting. For children especially, a visit on Mouna Farm meant a wonderful experience. Here they discovered creative possibilities and learned about nature all at the same time. Sooriya thanked the teachers for their visit and invited them to return soon to attend a copper workshop and make their own copper bowls.

"Most important in life is not only knowing certain things, but experiencing them with all your senses," he enjoined them. "Urban children are excluded from certain experiences. On our farm, they are able to touch and smell many plants. They can eat vegetables and fruit they have harvested or plucked themselves. It's a wonderful experience for them to plant a tree, water it, and see it grow. They need this close contact to nature in order to be able to love and care for Mother Earth. Who wants to lose his or her mother?"

In one corner of the farm, situated below a huge neem tree, Sooriya had created a temple to the spiritual teacher and yogi from India, Sai Baba. Sooriya invited the young teachers to take off their shoes and sit with him on the ground in front of the small statue of Sai Baba. His teachings concentrate on a moral code of love, forgiveness, helping others, charity, contentment, and inner peace.

When Sooriya was scouting in Hawaii for good land with fertile soil, his path led him to the aforementioned neem tree.

Neem trees are native to India and Sri Lanka, yet here was one growing on O'ahu, on this fallow piece of land. As soon as he saw it, Sooriya knew he had found just the right place for Mouna Farm.

Sai Baba's influence had been with him also when he lived in Sri Lanka, Sooriya told his visitors. When Sooriya settled down in Arugam Bay after his spiritual sojourn in India and his travels through Europe, he retreated into a small hut, there to live all alone for some time.

"The ground was made of dried cow dung," he recalled. The idea of which caused his visitors to giggle and wrinkle their noses.

"Cows prefer selected plants and herbs. To sleep on this ground is healing; the plants will extract everything bad from your body," he explained. "And as the dung is dry, it doesn't smell bad at all," he added with a wink, amused by the looks on his visitor's faces. Clearly some had been born on the "clean" American mainland or in modern Hawaii, not on a farm.

Somebody had gifted Sooriya a picture of Sai Baba, and he has kept it hanging on a wall in his cottage.

Sooriya's narration was so indubitably heartfelt that every one of us hung on to his every word.

"Mouna means inner silence or inner journey," Sooriya emphasized, explaining the essence of the farm. "Mankind is bending over backwards to achieve their inner silence. Some will run, others will swim. Meditation or yoga may be helpful, or prayers."

He told us about the tragedy of his father's murder in Sri Lanka. The teachers had learned this story in the movie "Ola," but were visibly moved to hear it from Sooriya's lips.

"To find my inner silence and forgiveness, I have been walking. I have overcome my sadness and my hatred by walking long distances through India - barefoot most of the time."

"Of course, sometimes I had to wear shoes," Sooriya grinned, "for instance in the Himalayas or in Europe in winter."

It was a good way to cheer us up again.

"Now that I've grown older, I realize that inner silence means to have a relationship with yourself, to follow yourself on your inner journey, and to share your experiences with other living beings. That's Mouna Farm."

Everyone listened in rapt attention as he spoke.

"I have been making my life's journey until today; this has been my education, my school and my university. Maybe you will have a more responsible task ahead of you than I've ever had. Children will be entrusted to you. Nowadays, they are spending more time at school than anywhere else. You will have to be teachers, but also mother, sister or brother. What you will show them or tell them might determine their entire life. Whatever you give them will come back to you. If you change yourselves and your way of teaching, the children will change as well. It's up to you! The Creator may be a different one to each of us, but this Creator picks you to do a certain job. Do it as good as you can. Make mistakes and don't be afraid of making them. They will allow you to advance. The most important thing is: put your hearts into it."

Sooriya never prepared a speech beforehand; he just opened his heart and let the words pour forth from his mouth. Then, all of a sudden, he might leap to a completely different subject.

"Any more questions?" he asked, apparently ready to bring the tour to an end. He patiently answered many questions, then after a while said:

"I would like to talk with you for hours and hours. You have good souls; I can see it in your eyes. But the brain is a silly monkey. This monkey is telling me right now that I have to prepare the breadfruit-curry for us."

We laughed, our spirits high again. While Sooriya prepared the first breadfruit-curry on Mouna Farm, the teachers were free to scout the premises or join in group yoga exercises at sunset.

A surprise awaited me. The yoga teacher turned out to be Sooriya's youngest brother, Sri. I had last seen him in Arugam Bay when he was seventeen years old. I had always enjoyed our friendly conversations. We greeted each other warmly.

Sri had kept his youthful appearance and soft voice. He had come to the farm from Honolulu, where he was living with his wife and little son. The brothers' mother, Anna Poorani, lived with them as well. We revived our old jokes and it seemed as if I had found my little brother after so many years.

Everyone on Mouna Farm contributes what they can for events like this one. From the open-air kitchen, where Sooriya and Jothi lovingly prepared our breadfruit curry, we could look across the property to the big wooden platform where Sri was leading the group in yoga. He looked beautiful and supple, just as he had been at seventeen in Sri Lanka. In the distant background, just before sunset, the bizarre looking volcanic mountains contrasted with the evening sky.

Our breadfruit curry dinner, served with rice and chapati tasted exquisite, especially in the company of so many nice people. Candles and torches had been lit on the yard. We all felt familiar and at ease that night.

Many lively conversations developed, but of course Sooriya received the most attention. His joking let everybody relax, yet in every joke there were seeds of wisdom.

Some of the teachers asked me to describe Germany, about which they had heard little before now, and they wondered how I had met Sooriya, so long before they were born.

I heard one of the young women ask if she might help on the farm during her holidays. She lived in a tower block in Honolulu, she said, but she missed having a direct connection with nature. With a smile, Sonia replied: "Of course, you will always be welcome!"

*

A few days later, the farm would celebrate the naming of the "Anna Poorani Kitchen." Just in time for this event, Peter had arrived from the U.S. mainland and settled into his wooden hut on the far side of the farm. This was my first time meeting him, though it was he who had written the vital letter inviting Sooriya to make the journey from Sri Lanka to America. I had questioned Sooriya's words back then, about the black birds announcing the arrival of the news. But the news was correct: Peter's letter arrived, offering Sooriya the chance to continue his life's journey in Hawaii.

For the kitchen dedication, all of Sooriya's relatives currently living in Hawaii gathered on the farm, including Ram's son Ranjith, who came with his wife and his daughter. The girl played with Sri's little son as Sooriya's sisters arrived, bringing along exquisite Sri Lankan dishes. Friends arrived as well – and then, of course, the guest of honor: Sooriya's mother, Anna Poorani. She had to be more than 80 by now, but she looked healthy and composed. She gave me a friendly smile. Did she remember meeting me in Mannar many years ago? At that time, she had abandoned the white mourning clothes she had worn following her husband's death and returned to wearing a sari. Still, she maintained an inner and outer silence; I never heard her speak.

Sooriya welcomed his guests and as all held hands in a circle, Peter gave a solemn blessing. Sri translated the words for his mother. To monk went the honor of dedicating the kitchen to Anna. Nobody could understand the words he muttered, but this was a minor matter.

For all gathered, and especially for those of us who had been to Sooriya's native land, the gathering had the look and feel of Sri Lanka. All of the dishes were vegetarian and cooked Sri Lankan style, with aromatic spices. To chat and eat together in such company, with such excellent food, gave special emphasis that night. At the table, conversations in English mingled with the sounds of the Tamil language. Being at this Mouna Farm party made me feel I had stepped back into Sri Lanka.

Never had I seen Sooriya work as hard as he did in Hawaii. He divided his energies between the farm and his work at Wai'anae Comprehensive Health Center. There, in addition to creating copper art for the buildings and gardens, he gave lectures on the healing attributes of herbs. He even taught yoga for a while.

"I feel blessed that I'm allowed to work at the health center and be a part of it," he told me one evening. "Whenever I leave the farm for my courses, I relax my head. I won't think about invoices, watering the plants, or any appointments lying ahead of me. As soon as I return to the farm, I'll leave behind everything I've done in the center as well

Ken was a big help on the farm. Born and raised in Wai'anae, he was a highly skilled carpenter, tractor driver, and jack-of-all-trades. Sooriya kept him busy working to expand the art village. When Sooriya met him, Ken was a petty criminal without a job. Sooriya asked him to help out on the farm occasionally. It was a risk, because on Mouna Farm, nothing was locked up. Sooriya put his trust in Ken, and the trust paid off. Ken had become Sooriya's right-hand man.

"Ken has changed. Everyone can," Sooriya proudly declared.

The farm's good spirit must have been the reason for Ken's transformation. Ken could be trusted, and most probably he would defend the farm against any kind of evil. Here, he had found his vocation and a family.

Ken occasionally showed a softer side of himself on the farm by playing ukulele. Sometimes he would play and sing sentimental Hawaiian songs. He was surprisingly good. It turns out he had long associated and jammed with the best native Hawaiian musicians in Wai'anae valley, including IZ - Israel Ka'ano'i Kamakawiwo'ole - one of the most famous and beloved native Hawaiian musicians of all time.

Of course, a woman can't travel from frosty Germany to beautiful and warm Hawaii to spend all of her holidays on the farm! So, I took regular trips to nearby Pokai Bay Beach, always taking along my notepad and pen.

Stepping away from Mouna Farm was like stepping into another world. O'ahu is blessed with natural wonders and a dreamlike climate, but in Wai'anae Valley, at least, the local reality was not at all a South Sea paradise.

I encountered much poverty. People were kind and would smile at me, but many of them were missing teeth. Here, apparently, this was normal; nobody seemed ashamed.

I recalled the TV series, "Hawaii Five-O," on German television. The actors all looked like supermodels or bodybuilders. The Hawaiian reality I observed looked different: in Wai'anae, I spotted even more overweight people than in Germany.

In Germany, the weather often forces people inside. Many Germans don't participate in sports. Not everyone gets enough exercise. And in many jobs, there, you spend most of your day in front of a computer. For these reasons, people put on weight. But the reason for obesity in Hawaii became clear to me one day when I wanted to try a typical Hawaiian dish – but all I could find in Wai'anae were American fast food outlets, one after the other.

The clear water of the Pacific Ocean is gorgeous. To placate its powerful waves, at Pokai Bay engineers had designed a coastal sea defense structure made of stone that dissipates and absorbs the force of the waves. Hawaiian families were sitting in the sand and playing in the calm bay. They seemed to be of many different nationalities, and I hardly ever noticed indigenous Hawaiian characteristics.

All of a sudden, I spotted a small group of wheelchair-assisted patients on the beach. They were obese, and so and had difficulty wading into the ocean. However, once they reached water deep enough to carry their weight, they burst into happy laughter, hopping about in the ocean.

I recalled a video clip of IZ: a tender soul in such a massive body performing such beautiful music with ukulele and voice.

I looked across the ocean toward the horizon, lost in thought. With Mouna Farm, Sooriya had made an island on an island. It was just as he had done before, with his Beach Hut in Sri Lanka.

I intended to catch the bus back to the farm before sunset, but I missed it, so I had to wait an hour for the next one. It was a bit unnerving in this part of Wai'anae. Drunkards passed by the bus stop, and a woman was screaming.

It was very warm outside, and the scene was a bit surreal. Christmas was close. Garlands and colored lights decorated a tower block, and many a plastic Santa Claus climbed its front. Surrounding it all were many palm trees.

The bus stopped near Mouna Farm and I walked the short distance from the road to the front gate. Sooriya came running toward me as I made my way to the kitchen, where everyone was gathered. The farm family had been nervously awaiting my return.

"There is a lot of unemployment, poverty, homelessness and criminal energy in Wai'anae," Sooriya gently admonished me. You shouldn't underestimate this."

He seemed more worried about me here in Hawaii than he had been back in Sri Lanka during the civil war.

For tonight, Sooriya was planning a surprise. He had mounted a canvas screen to show me the documentary film "Ola - Health is Everything," which had recently premiered at the Hawaii International Film Festival in Honolulu.

The movie shows magnificent scenes of Hawaii's nature, combined with an almost hypnotic sound track, but it reveals that amid all that beauty, health issues abound. Poor people, as everywhere in the USA, have insufficient access to decent medical care Rotten or missing teeth, malnutrition, and obesity are wide-spread in the islands as a result.

The film illuminates the connection between nature and the raising and education of children, who are our future. In Hawaii, children have the perfect climate for playing outdoors, but instead, they increasingly watch TV or play videogames while eating junk food. The film appeals to common sense and a natural way of life.

One segment of the movie profiles Sooriya, allowing him to narrate his story, showing his respect for nature, and how Mouna Farm project developed.

As we sat watching staring up at the big screen outdoors in the dark, Sooriya's image towered above us, an impressive and moving sight. The movie's director, Matthew Nagato, had done a very good job.

On screen, Sooriya talks about his childhood and how he had been taught by his parents to esteem nature's generosity. He also expresses his gratitude for having found this wonderful property for Mouna Farm. The film describes projects in which Hawaiian children come to the farm to plant their own trees. They are welcome to visit the farm at any time to see how much their trees have grown. The children learn that the vegetables come from the fields, and that they are used for meals prepared in the community kitchen. At the end of the visit, visitors share a meal with the farm family. For some attendees, this experience stirs a continuing interest in stimulates their eating healthy food.

Living on the farm has enriched him with a wonderful community and so much happiness, Sooriya declares in the movie. Moreover, the community of Wai'anae and the people of O'ahu have given so much, he feels a great desire and responsibility to return the favor.

His moving words touched me.

Sooriya kept in contact with many influential personalities in Hawaii. Mouna operated as a nonprofit organization. It derived income from the sale of art works and fresh produce. Jothi and Sonia understood the task of selling vegetables to natural-foods markets and restaurants in Honolulu. Whatever they couldn't sell went to feeding everyone on the farm.

Every now and then, journalists from Hawaii and the U.S. mainland came to report on Sooriya and Mouna Farm. One day, a journalist announced herself unexpectedly. As usual, Sooriya didn't just give a short interview, he took the time to demonstrate something special.

"With everybody who visits us, I share a meal," he explained as he prepared food in the kitchen. "This is the most important thing that I've learned from my parents. Before my father would sit down at the table, he would have a look up and down the street, to see if someone was poor and hungry. Only after everyone had eaten would my father have his meal."

A cat came running into the kitchen. Sooriya placed a little bowl of leftovers in front of the animal.

"I share with everybody," Sooriya laughed. "Even with the cats."

He then returned to kneading dough for the journalist's meal.

A clay oven had been built in front of Sooriya's wooden house, beside his workshop platform. While Christine interviewed him, he kept baking chapati - flat bread spiced with tasty herbs. Monk was there too, helping silently. Sooriya wanted the Buddhist to be in on any photographs Christine took. The peaceful co-existence of all religions was an important part of Sooriya's message to the world. Christine not only received an interesting story with unusual photographs of what looked like Sri Lanka in Hawaii, but she enjoyed a splendid afternoon with delicious food. Once she had gathered enough material for her article, she and I had a nice chat about our journalism careers.

Never before had she been given such a long interview, Christine laughed. She had long since packed away her note pad, voice recorder, and camera in order to just soak up the experience.

"A book should be written about this unusual man," Christine said, and asked me why I had come to Mouna Farm from Germany. I told her how long I had known Sooriya, and that in fact there was a book about this unusual man - namely the one I had written about his former life in Sri Lanka.

"Too bad there isn't an English translation," Christine responded, a sentiment I shared.

The sun had long since set, and a cozy fire crackled in a big copper bowl. A huge full moon lit the place, and Christine, Sooriya and I relished this wonderful evening. Ever the charming host, Sooriya cheerfully chatted with Christine. He welcomed her and every visitor on the farm as a friend.

*

Sometimes, when Sooriya was busy with farm matters, Sri would take me in his car for a trip across O'ahu. One day, we visited Father Phil's community – Sooriya's first home in Hawaii. The community's organic farm also ran a little restaurant. Ram's son, Ranjith, who I knew when he was a boy in Sri Lanka, worked as a cook there, together with his wife. Sri showed me the wooden house Sooriya had built on the property years ago. This Father Phil's community served as the first address for several of Sooriya's family members ever since they started arriving in Hawaii, one after another. Sri had lived there as well.

The Bodhi tree seedling that Sooriya had planted shortly after his arrival had grown into a huge tree with a magnificent canopy. The small Buddhist temple at the base of the tree reminded Sooriya's family of Sri Lanka. The family members were allowed to cultivate plots garden with their own vegetables and herbs. Ranjith's wife was took good care of their plot. A neem tree and another temple completed the private setting.

As Sri and I continued our sightseeing tour, I spotted Father Phil's chapel and admired the wonderful copper-art double door, which Sooriya had manufactured – his way of thanking the Father for giving him a home. Sooriya's copper work also adorned the inside the chapel.

Finally, Sri drove us a short distance to the beach house where Sooriya and Caroline had lived with their son and Sooriya's mother. As we drove, we chatted about my life in Germany. I confessed that I felt sad, because my grown-up daughter Aline had moved out of our common home to lead her own life.

"Let's prolong our trip a little: I'll take you to a very special place," he suggested.

Ka'ena Point is the westernmost end of O'ahu. The original inhabitants from Polynesia believed that right here, the souls of the dead leave the island. Sri explained this to me on our way there. But the place was also – and still is – a sacred place for the living: apparently many people come here to let something go and say goodbye to it.

We had to park and walk the final stretch to Ka'ena Point. The waves were crashing into black and bizarre-looking cliffs, and tall jets of sea water darted from gaps in the volcanic rock. I felt small at the sight of this overwhelming force of nature and sat down to take it all in.

At Ka'ena Point – almost at the other end of the world from Germany – I said goodbye to a twenty-year period of my life. The love for my child would always stay with me, however.

Sooriya had a saying: "Everybody has his own life's journey."

Ka'ena Point's black rocks are exposed to the immeasurable power of Hawaii's sunlight and ocean. Huge waves constantly flood them and then retreat – a natural come-and-go.

On our ride back, we stopped at Ranjith's home. He was just 18 when he came to Hawaii. Now he, his wife and their little daughter lived in a modern house with Western comfort: they were even had an ice machine for cold drinks! Ram's granddaughter sat in front of the TV watching cartoons. Their lovely garden was full of toys.

I received a very heartfelt welcome. Ranjith had prepared an excellent dinner combining traditional Sri Lankan recipes with Western ingredients. Afterwards, we looked at many images of Ram on Ranjith's tablet. He had even saved a photograph of Ram holding my first book in his hands! A German traveler to Sri Lanka had brought a copy for Ram. Ranjith had discovered the photograph in one of the social networks. His uncle Sri looked rather skeptical.

"That's the new generation," he said in the car on our way back to Mouna Farm. "Our sons won't follow our old traditions any longer. What will our grandchildren do? They're losing their roots. But isn't it a fact that a strong tree needs strong roots?"

On our arrival at the farm, we came upon a little ceremony in progress. A Japanese woman who worked at the health center had recently lost her husband. She came to Mouna Farm to plant a tree in loving memory of him. At the dedication, Sooriya said a few caring words, and everyone took part by laying a flower under the newly planted sapling.

In a short speech, the woman said she felt joy because her husband's suffering had now come to an end.

Sooriya invited her to visit her tree over time to watch it grow, or whenever she might want to be near her husband. The woman smiled gratefully, placed her palms together, and bowed her head.

*

Whenever Sooriya had free time - when he wasn't expecting visitors - we would sit under the palm tree at his art workshop in the evening for hours. Those warm nights, close to a fire in the big copper bowl, enhanced the intimacy of our long chats. I was planning an extended version of my book, describing what had become of this wonderful man after he left Sri Lanka in 1984.

Every morning, he lit the fire in the copper bowl. The element fire means a lot to him: Sooriya is convinced that he receives his strength and energy from it. Sometimes he had difficulty explaining such matters to me. Words describing his way of thinking are not easily found.

In those nights he loved to recall many big events in his life, but he also revealed intimate details of his life's extraordinary journey. It had been more than thirty years since I had met him in Sri Lanka. He had profoundly influenced my own life's journey; I had always kept him in my heart and mind.

We talked about old times, but also about his recent life. He showed me photographs of his visit to the Maori King, and of the work of art he had been creating for his majesty.

He frequently stayed in touch with the Prince of Samoa. One of his future projects was to invite handicapped artists to Mouna Farm and promote their work. Sooriya had met a deaf Samoan artist who was well known for his marvelous works of art. If he could reach a greater audience, the proceeds from his work could be spent on social projects in his home country.

On one of Sooriya's numerous trips, a young man with a partial paralysis attracted his attention.

"With his beautiful hands, he was able to create the most magnificent sculptures," Sooriya sounded rapturous.

One of his many plans was to expand the farm's art village, where currently workshops for children and adults took place. He had so many ideas, he was brimming over with energy and enthusiasm.

Sooriya often received invitations to attend big official festivities.

"Sometimes, I go barefoot, wearing only my lungi and a shirt," he grinned.

Over the past few years, Sooriya had become the subject of many published articles. He didn't want to brag about them; he just handed me a pile of newspaper clippings to see for myself. While I was sorted through them, he went to the kitchen to fetch us something to drink.

I learned that Sooriya had been honored with the "Hero of Forgiveness Award," which is granted once a year on Hawaii International Forgiveness Day. Another article described the murder of his father, which resulted in Sooriya's long travel through India to find forgiveness in his heart. Many other articles praised his internationally known spiritual copper art and his social programs for children on Mouna Farm.

On his return from the kitchen he was chuckling: "O, I forgot to mention: They made me a knight! Wait, the certificate must be somewhere in my hut."

He came back with a diploma and a chain with a cross. Both items had been awarded to him by the "Orthodox Order of Saint John Russian Grand Priory," "M. Sooriya Kumar. Knight of Honor," it said in artful letters. This order goes back to St. John in Jerusalem, who founded the first hospitals for the ill and wounded. All patients were treated equally, no matter what race, religion or social status they belonged to, the certificate was explained.

Sooriya had been honored in a solemn ceremony. But he was not vain about it: for him, this certificate meant doors might open for him, which could help him realize his social projects.

"I wouldn't have been able to do anything of value if I had been a prisoner of the civil war at Beach Hut in Arugam Bay. I'll never forget the people who risked so much to help me escape," Sooriya said. He gazed at me, then, and added: "And I'll never forget our good times in the Shiva-Ganesh-House and in the cave on Crocodile Rock."

But now he wanted to tell me about the big new project he was planning.

"We will build the biggest copper whale this world has ever seen!" His eyes shone with enthusiasm. "Children, school classes, adults – anybody can participate. I'll gather more than one-thousand people. Actually. the sculpture will consist of two figures – a mother whale and her child. On Mouna Farm, we have plenty room to realize it. We will rouse the public from inactivity. Everybody who wants can watch humpback whales in the Pacific Ocean from Hawaii's coasts. They come here every year to give birth to their babies and raise them. We humans have to protect them during this life, while we are here on this planet. I'm so grateful that I can be part of it."

In Sri Lanka, his energy and his creativity would have wasted away. Sooriya seemed to know what I was thinking.

"I was crying, and my tears froze, when my sadhu in India told me that I couldn't be a sadhu, that I had to carry my light into the world. He was the one who has sent me on my life's sacred journey. I have to perform my duty."

All of a sudden, he switched to being lighthearted.

"Do you remember that Sri Lanka wasn't only civil war? That there were also so many beautiful and unforgettable moments?" He smiled at me. "Good memories will never die."

His eyes looked at me the way the young Sooriya had.

"Authors from the U.S. mainland have been asking me if they might write my biography," Sooriya said. "But why and how should I tell a stranger what my life has been? What do they know about my Sri Lanka and my India? You have to trust someone from the bottom of your heart before you tell them your story. What if they make something totally different out of it?"

I felt that it must be me he should allow to write down his journey. I was his old friend and had been accompanying him for a while.

It would take some time to gather all the facts and take all his personal emotions into consideration. Of course, during my time on the farm, I couldn't count on him every day. Sooriya was much too busy with his ideas. He often found peace by meditating, and his art allowed him to switch off the "silly monkey called reason." When he was immersed in that zone, you definitely had to leave him alone.

It was nice to hear him working the copper sheets in his workshop, the hammer beating like the rhythm of a heart. He created a panel of taro plants in relief. I saw the fire glowing when he heated the copper with a flame, which led to amazing changes of color. I knew Sooriya was in his element.

What a beautiful place - here on Mouna Farm - to work on the book.

Chapter 10

I had taken a flight back to Germany in order to finish and publish my book. It is such a grand feeling to put an end to hard work! My thoughts were still back in Hawaii when my telephone rang.

"Hi, it's me, Sooriya," I heard him say. "I'll make a journey to Sri Lanka soon, and I'd like you to come with me ..."

It had been a long time since I set foot on the island where I met Sooriya more than thirty years earlier. I had never wished to go there again because Sri Lanka would seem deserted without Sooriya. I wanted to preserve my memory of the island and Arugam Bay just as they had looked then.

But abruptly I decided to travel there once more, together with Sooriya. Of course, the country wouldn't look the same. I knew that from German travelers, who had read my first book. They wanted to stay in touch with me through social networks and they kept me updated.

"A film team from Hawaii will accompany me," Sooriya told me on the telephone. "They will make a documentary about my life. Of course, they have no idea about Sri Lanka during the civil war – but you have."

Immediately, I stopped every activity to publish my book – obviously life hadn't finished the story yet.

A whole group of people would meet up in Colombo at an agreed-upon date. We would travel from Hawaii, the American mainland, Canada, Spain and Germany, Sooriya said. He would travel in advance and await us in Arugam Bay. Shortly before I left Germany, he called to inform me that the film team had decided to travel ahead and that he had gone with them. Soon enough, I would see him again.

As my plane landed at the Colombo Airport, black birds flew up, startled by the noise on the runway. As soon as the stewardess had opened the door, a blast of moist hot air hit me. Déjà vu, I thought, and was reminded of my first arrival in Sri Lanka. In 1983, everything had been new. Now, in 2016, I was an old hand. Peter was there to welcome me, and together we waited for our group arriving from the various countries, one after the other. When at long last all had assembled, minibuses took us across the island to Arugam Bay.

I had almost forgotten the chaos on Sri Lankan roads. The minibuses were much more comfortable and faster than the old "Midnight-Express," which needed ten hours to drive from one side of the island to the other. But our trip would be much quicker because our minibus driver seemed to have one rule: only losers step on the brake.

First, we had to get out of Colombo, whose streets still were congested by cars, motorbikes, tuk-tuks and very old red busses. Noise and fumes dominated the city. Maria, a young veterinarian from Madrid, and her boyfriend, Gonzalo, were horrified by our driver's way of snaking through the streets. The stripes marking pedestrian crossings seemed to be there for decorative purposes only.

The two Spaniards were about the age I was when I first came here in 1983. Peter and I were older and wiser. I smiled and to my amazement, I was no longer scared by the breakneck trip to Arugam Bay.

I was much too busy to take in everything around me. You can only love or hate Sri Lanka. Everything outside was dirty, noisy, muggy and chaotic. But for me, the air smelled of familiar exotic odors. It felt like coming home after many years.

My anticipation to see Sooriya increased by the minute as we were approached Pottuvil. The town had grown considerably, but still small, single-room shops prevailed. One of them bore a sign saying, "Fashion House."

Actually, it seemed to be a garage. Dresses made of ballet tulle in candy colors hung outside. In front of another shop, big sacks of rice were piled up. In contrast to the past, many shops now sold electronic devices.

The old stone bridge from colonial times, which once connected Arugam Bay with Pottuvil, had vanished. It had been replaced by a modern two-lane concrete construction.

Practically the first thing I noticed upon arriving at Arugam Bay were the tall transmission pylons for mobile phones and internet towering above the palm trees.

Arugam Bay's streets had been paved with asphalt. And all the bends and bumps had been removed. Hooting tuk-tuks dominated the traffic and chased tourists off the streets. The drivers demonstrated supremacy behind the wheel that perhaps they would never achieve in other walks of life. Only when a paying guest approached would they turn friendly. This was one thing that hadn't changed in Sri Lanka during all the years.

Shops lined the main street, one after another. Even a "supermarket" had been established in Arugam Bay.

Looking at all the sights, I nearly missed the entrance to Sooriya's Beach Hut.

The place wasn't the same. The long, narrow property had been partitioned in three plots. The restaurant's foundation walls were still visible. The old roof made of palm leaves had been replaced by a new one made of corrugated iron. Ram had only kept a little place off the loud and busy main street. Our bus stopped at a sign saying, "Ram's Library." He had always loved books.

To meet Sooriya once again was overwhelming. Even his brother Jothi had come from Hawaii. They introduced us to Alex, the cameraman, and Lisa, the assistant director. Sooriya had arranged rooms for everyone either on the premises or in neighboring guesthouses.

The old place at Beach Hut had turned into a new site. Ram had built a comfortable, two-story brick and wood house toward the back side of the property. He had intended to move in there but had died just when it was finished. On the ground floor there was a kitchen and a restaurant for guests. Numerous books occupied shelves in the main room. They had been collected by Ram over many years. Many had been destroyed by the Indian Ocean Tsunami of Dec. 26, 2004, which had destroyed much of Sri Lanka's East Coast. Happily, my first book, Crocodile Rock, stood on the shelf in Ram's library; a German visitor had given a copy of it to Ram.

The bedrooms on the first floor had been provided with separate showers and toilets. On the second floor there was a spacious room with several beds for guests. Arugam Bay had become westernized. The old well – our former bathroom – had been filled with dirt.

The only old building still standing was the little Shiva-Ganesh-House house on the front of which Sooriya had painted the images of Shiva and Ganesh in the early 1980s. I was surprised to see it intact. I was told that the tsunami had destroyed it. Almost by a miracle, the front wall with the paintings had resisted the devastation. Ram had rebuilt the house even more solidly. To look at it now brought beautiful memories. The lush vegetation that had been wiped out by the tsunami had completely recovered, and Sooriya's place now had many trees and a garden. No signs of the catastrophe remained.

Quiet waves of a turquoise ocean were washing up on the shore of the dreamlike bay. As before, fishing catamarans lay in the sand, ready to be put out to sea. In spaces between them, many beach chairs had been put up for the now innumerable tourists. I had forgotten how warm the water was. After so many years, the sight of the glittering Bay of Bengal simply overwhelmed me. That a raging tsunami had wreaked havoc in this paradise a dozen years ago was hardly imaginable.

Peter knew Ram had experienced the horror of the tsunami. They had talked about it when Ram visited Hawaii.

"Ram had noticed a few people running to the beach," Peter told me. "He thought maybe they were watching an incident with the army. Then he noticed that there was no noise at all. It was totally quiet."

Ram was working that day on building his new guest house. The first floor had only just been completed.

"Suddenly people came running back across the street in panic, and then he heard the water coming. He wasn't able to see it yet, but he knew something big was happening," Peter recounted Ram's story.

Ram called to his wife, but he got no answer from her. There was no time to look for her. In a hurry, he grabbed their son Ranjith and both climbed on the roof of the first floor, which was about three yards above the ground.

Immediately the full force of the tsunami wave was gushing over the place. The flood reached up to the height of the platform; father and son were spared by only a few inches.

Ram's wife was more than half a mile inland when the flood reached her. As the water surged around her, and then as it retreated, she managed to hold on to a tree. As she later recognized, it was a neem tree that saved her life.

The family had survived. Beach Hut, however, was completely devastated - except, miraculously, the front wall and mural of Sooriya's Shiva-Ganesh House.

The house that had saved Ram and his son's lives now belonged to someone else. The entire middle section of what had once been Sooriya's Beach Hut was now run by another person. I visited this neighbor to see how the building and property had fared since the tsunami.

At first, nothing reminded me of the old times. Then, simple cabanas made of palm leaves had stood there. But in the middle of the property, pink bougainvillea blossoms were growing rampant up a tree, eager to reach the sunlight. At one time these bougainvillea had covered Sooriya's little temple, which had long since vanished.

Neither the vandalism of civil-war times nor the tsunami - nor even the current crush of tourism - had impeded the progress of this beautiful and persistent plant.

*

The Beach Hut, scaled down to an intimate size, survived. And now that he had returned, Sooriya was being monopolized by everybody: by his travel companions, many visitors and, of course, the film crew. Everybody had a different relationship with him, but no one knew what role I had played or was still playing in Sooriya's life. Was I his biographer? A long-standing friend? Or was there even more? I recalled when we had to keep our relationship secret during the civil war and its hostilities, also against foreigners.

I remembered how he used to ask me in the old restaurant, if I was tired, yawning himself.

"A bit," I would answer.

"Good night - see you later," he would say to everybody, meaning me, I knew.

A little later, we would meet at the Shiva-Ganesh House.

Nobody except Ram and his other brothers seemed to have registered then what kind of relationship we had. Or, at least no one disclosed what they were thinking.

Peter, who had been an essential help in getting Sooriya out of Sri Lanka in 1984, had stayed close to him during all these years. He and I had known Sooriya the longest of his Western friends.

A member of our group named Mark, who lived and helped out at the farm sometimes, woke everybody on the place each morning by playing songs on his flute. He had been invited to come along to Sri Lanka as well. Shortly after sunrise, we woke up to the melody of Cat Stevens' song "Morning has Broken." It was a beautiful start into a new day.

Darcey had arrived from Canada. His interest in biological farming and art projects had led him to Mouna Farm.

"I was drawn to Sooriya immediately," he told me.

Many a night back on Mouna Farm, Sooriya and the Canadian had talked for hours on end. The actor and single father of two sons had returned to Vancouver, trying to adjust his life to the personal reality of his three-men family. But he came back to Mouna Farm periodically. For him, as for so many people, life changed upon meeting Sooriya.

"I had been feeling so empty, and had run out of ideas," Darcey told me. "Sooriya pushed me in another direction. Obviously, I had been waiting for someone to show me a new point of view."

Darcey saw Sooriya as a teacher and visited Mouna Farm many times. Sooriya had invited him to come and experience the country where he had grown up. To accompany Sooriya to Sri Lanka was part of Darcey's lesson.

Maria, the young Spanish woman, had come to Mouna Farm as a "WWOOFer" meaning a volunteer with World Wide Opportunities on Organic Farms. There, Sooriya gave her the opportunity to travel to a distant country on a limited budget. She was very young, but she had already received a university degree in veterinary medicine. Maria wanted to see something of the world. On Mouna Farm, she had found an atypical but informative place to experience life. She asked if her friend Gonzalo might come along to Sri Lanka, and Sooriya was happy to have him join the expedition.

"Now I know what Maria meant when she told me that Sooriya is a special man," Gonzalo said one day, his warm and curious eyes registering delight after his first few days in Sri Lanka.

Alex and Lisa, members of the documentary film crew, hung around Sooriya all the time. This was not a holiday – this was Sooriya's Sri Lanka, never disclosed to ordinary tourists.

One day, all of us went along to a fishing village called Karaithevu where Sooriya was to be the guest of honor at a big ceremony. He had agreed to help the villagers build their own temple. It would be the first fishers' temple on the East Coast. Sooriya knew the swami of this village, a fisherman himself.

This swami liked to visit Sooriya and hang out at the old place. He always slept on a bast mat on the small porch in front of the Shiva-Ganesh House. He and I were unable to have a conversation since he spoke neither English nor German and I spoke no Tamil. The swami, with long hair and naked except for his lungi, had no possessions except for a mobile phone, which he constantly held to his ear. Even so, the swami was a highly respected man, though his social ranking was far below Sooriya's. His behavior toward Sooriya was almost submissive.

It was an honor to accompany Sooriya to the ceremony. Almost the whole fishing village turned out for the occasion. Some children had never seen Westerners before. Tourists rarely came to this village.

"Many of the children are orphans or have lost one parent," Sooriya pointed out. "They lost many family members as a result of the tsunami."

Tragically, of course, the fishermen and their families, living close to the ocean shore, had been the first to be hit by the tsunami.

Now, however, spirits were high. Everywhere there were splashes of color – all the little girls in bright dresses and boys wanting to impress with cool t-shirts.

All the inhabitants of the fishing village welcomed our delegation with much respect, especially for Sooriya. We saw the children's eyes sparkling with joy, and their parents smiling at us, graciously inviting us to feel at home. They had set up a canvas shelter to protect us from the sun, and we all sat on the ground beneath it.

The villagers had prepared a program of dance and song for us. First a graceful little girl performed a traditional dance. She was about eight years old and her command of the choreography was perfect in every detail. Every movement of her hand was had a special meaning. Her dress was beautifully embroidered, and her face was made up with golden dots. She wasn't nervous in the least. She seemed to be married to the art of dancing.

More girls appeared, dancing as boys chanted hypnotically, one boy beating drums in the background. The villagers were rightfully proud of their talented children. And the children, of course, relished our applause.

The village mayor gave a speech, as did Sooriya, both speaking Tamil. Clearly, they all agreed to something as all of them wiggled their heads in consent. Then he turned to us Westerners and kindly spoke a few words in English.

Sooriya had brought orange trousers for the fishermen and for our group, orange lungis with borders. Orange identifies the pilgrims. The big Perahera Festival would be taking place in Kataragama soon, and thousands of believing Hindus would take part in a pilgrimage there, including Sooriya and most of the villagers.

The Mayor guided our group to a structure with a canvas roof. At the entrance, we took off our shoes. Many villagers knelt to wash our feet. This demonstration of respect for us made me feel rather ashamed. The swami painted sacred ashes on our foreheads, and a crimson dot. Women strung flower garlands around our necks. Not surprisingly, Sooriya received the most attention and was adorned with the most beautiful flowers.

They invited us to sit down on mats. The villagers went to great trouble to make us really feel at home. In front of us, and the ground, they placed big banana leaves, onto which they doled out servings of rice and curry. All of them paid close attention to us. As soon as one of us finished a dish, somebody would approach to serve more. After we finished the fruit dishes, a few men brought fresh water in bowls, so everyone could wash the hand they had eaten with.

In an adjoining area, the villagers gathered to partake of their own meals as well. Now it was Sooriya's and our group's turn to serve dishes to the villagers. Giving and receiving food is an essential way to show respect and care for somebody. As we served, Mark played his flute – the sounds were unusual for the people here, but the songs were a special part of the festivity.

Sooriya, our group members, and some other guests returned to the tent-like room. There, drum beats and chants accompanied a woman who was dancing herself ecstatically into a trance. She ran through the room, yelling wildly and throwing up her arms, her eyes wide open, and her incredibly long tongue hanging out of her mouth. We Westerners had to stay open-minded and accept this culture. This was no performance for tourists. Sooriya threw inquiring glances at me; he knew my inner fight between rational thinking and emotional experience very well. Sooriya liked to expose the people he loved to uncertain situations. He was convinced that this might enrich their ways of thinking and make them more open-minded.

Someone carried around a candelabra blazing with flames. Swami fanned the heat and the smoke, and everyone crowded around him to receive the energy radiating from the flames. It was an honor for us to be allowed to take part in this rite, which tourists aren't allowed to witness. Our hosts were counting on us to respect their religious traditions. I looked at my fellows' faces and saw fascination, doubt, amazement, insecurity, gratitude, or simply fatalism at being confronted with a situation. Only Sooriya could arrange this for us.

So many people had gathered that it would have been impossible to leave. In the crowd, our cameraman, Alex, had great difficulty finding the right position for shooting this unreal scenery. He was lucky to have come across such exclusive movie material in a little fishing village in Sri Lanka.

The air was boiling beneath the canvas roof. Fisherman Swami softly touched the forehead of the woman in trance. She broke down within a second. Totally exhausted and calm now, she had sunk to the ground.

We left the enclosure, feeling completely overwhelmed by what we had witnessed. The fresh air outside, even though it was hot, did us a power of good. Maria was quite pale. She had intended to go to the beach with Gonzalo for a while. But on this day, no privacy could be expected. A flock of children came running after them. The kids had quickly grown fond of our friendly and always-smiling Maria. They had no common language, but there they were, Maria and the children playing together on the beach, the children laughing and shrieking with glee as waves washed over their feet.

The rest of us were being monopolized by the adults. Despite all the old traditions, everybody seemed to own a mobile phone. We were a welcome attraction in the fishing village, and people taking countless selfies with one or several of us was unavoidable. We all had fun, though no coherent conversations were possible because of the language barrier.

Meanwhile, Sooriya was having a talk with the Mayor. None of the locals would have dared to interrupt them. Alex remained in the background with his camera. In Tamil, the Mayor and Sooriya were discussing his plans for a new project in the village. There was so much passion in Sooriya's eyes!

Only much later, we learned that a reporter had written an article about Sooriya, the ceremony, and our group that appeared in a nation-wide Sri Lankan newspaper. Being a journalist, I would have liked to read the article. The man had described us as "American Hindus," I was told. It is correct that we all wore those orange lungis for the occasion. But we had come from various distant nations, not only from the USA. And nobody can convert to Hinduism just like that. You must be born a Hindu. Sooriya couldn't be bothered by this article. Media reported on him all the time, in Hawaii and on the U.S. mainland. Only the realization of his temple project in the fishing village was of any importance to him now.

*

It was so amazing how Sooriya commuted between the cultures. He was so different in Sri Lanka and with his local friends, compared to the other Sooriya in Hawaii. The old roots and energy were re-growing, so it appeared to me.

At night, back at Beach Hut, I felt exhausted from this exciting day and the heat. But Sooriya was already entertaining us on the small terrace. He was joking and narrating episodes of his eventful life. And he described our common adventures in Arugam Bay - painful, but also very beautiful memories.

Maria and Gonzalo were very curious about how I judged my time with Sooriya when I had been about their age.

"O, we were young then," I tried to stay vague. Maria burst out laughing.

"And we still are," Sooriya added with a wink.

"I would like to have experienced the hippie area and the traveler scene," Gonzalo said. "Unfortunately, I only know about it from various narrations. I bet those were exiting times."

He tried to visualize the old Arugam Bay, before the village had become a tourist site. But although the main street outside had degenerated into a busy shopping mile, our place had kept its good old atmosphere, which Peter and I now enjoyed. Sooriya's energy and presence pleasantly dominated our private surroundings.

"It's exactly the way it is on Mouna Farm in Hawaii," Darcey exclaimed. "Only Sooriya is capable of generating this atmosphere."

In the evenings we sat together, feeling happy, and Sooriya was able to relax, surrounded by his friends from the Western world. But his mission and his projects always remained in the foreground. It must have been terrible for this agile man to keep quiet and passive during the civil war. I recalled the soldier who had warned him to refrain from any activities.

Sooriya - born a Tamil Hindu - had never wanted and still didn't want to spread his religion or to fight others. His vision was tolerance and peace among all ideologies.

For the following day, two visitors had announced themselves. A highly respected monk, who was born in Thailand and now served as head of a big Buddhist center in Hawaii, had requested to see Sooriya. Having been in Colombo on business, he and a local monk made the long trip to Arugam Bay in a dark limousine. The villagers of Arugam Bay paid much attention to this visit, for it concerned both Hindus and Buddhists. Some of the villagers were not so pleased. Surely some Sinhalese Buddhists were asking why the Tamil Sooriya was given the honor. Sooriya wasn't wasting any thoughts about this. He preferred to live according to his firm principles and convictions.

Sooriya and the monk had known each other for a long time and were bonded in a strong friendship. They had had long conversations and discussions back in Hawaii. We, being Sooriya's Western friends, were invited to spend the evening with them. The monk spoke to us in English.

"First of all, you have to forgive yourselves in order to find peace in your hearts," he said.

He wasn't preaching, just chatting with us about our Western lifestyle.

"A car needs fuel from outside, otherwise it won't move. Our own fuel, that will enable us to move ahead, we must draw from our inside."

The friendly monk invited us to join in a communal meditation. People with the ability to switch off their minds and achieve a state of complete relaxation are to be admired. I've never been able to do it. I'm always watching and taking notes in my mind. But I felt a pleasant calmness in looking at my friends while their eyes were closed. Sooriya had taught not to dismiss something just because I didn't understand it. The monk gave me a friendly smile, as if he knew my thoughts.

Finally, our Buddhist monk friend blessed each of us and tied a red friendship bracelet around our wrists. At the same time, the muezzin began to call from the nearby Muslim mosque's minaret. It was a small but significant demonstration of what Sooriya's vision of tolerance could be like.

Only the camera team would accompany Sooriya on all of his trips in Sri Lanka. One day, Sooriya went to Colombo to give a TV-interview. From there, he traveled to the north of the island to spend a few days in Mannar, where he had been born. The camera was aimed at him the whole time. During their absence, I was sorted my notes and continued writing my book. Sitting in the warm sand, in the shade of palm trees and near the ocean shore, was more inspiring than any modern office.

At my leisure, I paid a visit to Fred, whom I had last seen in 1983 or 1984. He had been living in Arugam Bay for about forty years, running a restaurant with guest rooms for nearly thirty of those years. Fred had discovered my book in the internet, and from then on, we kept in touch by email. I don't think he ever thought we would meet again. He was so surprised to see me! And I was surprised to see Fred holding a little boy with dark curls in his arms.

"Baby number 12," he said with a wide grin. He had few occasions to speak German, and his English accent was unmistakable. I smiled. Back then, when we were young, he and I had been the only white people in Arugam Bay for some time – defying the monsoon and the civil war.

Fred and his Tamil wife had separated, meanwhile. She had been the reason for him becoming an Arugam Bay resident.

"They shot six of her relatives during the civil war," he lamented. "Here and in Jaffna."

Meanwhile, Somlak, a Thai woman with African roots, was living by his side.

"Yes, I've moved around a lot in my life," said Fred, who fathered twelve children with seven women.

The mothers and their children lived in the Philippines, Kenia, Brazil, Papua New Guinea, and Sri Lanka, he told me.

"All of them are really fine," he emphasized. This was very important to him.

He hadn't supported the mothers directly but had helped them to set up their own enterprises. One of them was running several internet cafes in Kenia.

I wanted to hear how he had experienced the tsunami in 2004. We were sitting on his terrace with a grand view of the ocean.

"That was an interesting day," Fred replied tersely.

I was surprised.

"We had recently completed a few new bungalows. Very comfortable, with air conditioning and flat-screen TV's. Most probably, it was the best hotel on the East Coast – for two days."

On Christmas, Fred, his family, and their guests were having a forty-eight-hours party. Everybody in the hotel was asleep in the early morning of December 26.

Outside, a gardener saw the sea retreat, and he quickly woke everyone in the guesthouse.

"Then the wave was coming – it had built up to more than fifty feet in height," Fred recalled. "All of us survived: my family and me, the personnel, and our guests. But in Sri Lanka, about 35,000 children, women and men lost their lives that day."

Fred, an engineer for bridge building with a doctorate degree, had designed and built the restaurant on the upper floor, which allowed the flood to shoot through the floor below.

"We gave all of our provisions to villagers, who were worse off than us. Too bad that all the liquor was gone," Fred mused, now pouring himself a glass of beer. "But on New Year's Eve, we had our first party in the midst of chaos."

He had long since completed all the repairs on the hotel. Its restaurant was quite an unusual construction. He had left open several holes in the floor and the ceiling to allow the huge old trees to grow on. Their crowns afforded shade to the terrace on the top floor.

"We haven't killed a single tree, ever," Fred said, almost indignant, when I asked him why he had built the house around the trees. "We also leave alone the cobra family in our garden. The snakes have been living here for years, and they never have harmed anyone. Only the tourists are panicking, after they have disturbed them. In Sri Lanka, more people die of coconuts falling on their heads than of snake bites."

Of course, Fred had heard that Sooriya was back in Arugam Bay. People talk. Ram and he had become friends with the passing of the years.

"This isn't the rule around here," Fred emphasized. "Envy and resentment are two bad diseases in Sri Lanka. Sooriya was lucky to be able to leave this country. Who knew if he was still alive? Even I have been threatened with murder, when my restaurant was doing well -- even my children! Sooriya and I weren't close then; but please give him my regards. Ram's funeral was the biggest ceremony we've ever seen in Arugam Bay and Pottuvil. Sooriya and all his family had arrived from Hawaii."

It was late afternoon by now - high time for Fred to look after his bar.

"O, by the way, you have to publish your book in English," he called out to me as I left.

From then on, I frequently showed up at Fred's restaurant, and so did almost everyone else in our group. We all liked his place. We had good times there at night. The sound system played '70s and '80s rock music. Sometimes Fred invited live musicians. It was unusual for me to see local rock musicians in torn jeans. Meanwhile we waited for Sooriya to come back from his trip to Mannar.

One evening, a few locals stopped us on the stairs to Fred's restaurant.

"Those are the people who have come here with Sooriya," somebody said.

Another man patted my shoulder: "Sooriya good, Ram good," he said in broken English.

Darcey was standing beside me, and I saw his eyes go wide; all of us knew that Sooriya had left Sri Lanka and Arugam Bay more than thirty years ago. We were slightly embarrassed when the men put their palms together and bent their heads. Obviously, Sooriya still was a well-known man.

*

By now, Sooriya and the film crew had returned from Mannar. Everyone felt how important it was for him to go back to his roots. For so many years, it had been too dangerous for him to return home.

In Mannar, he had been developing another new plan. Sooriya wanted to establish a place like the old Beach Hut in the north of Arugam Bay – a place where friends from all over the world might come together, and also spiritual seekers would be welcome. Art would play an important role there, just as it is does in Hawaii on Mouna Farm.

"There are so many things I have to do in Sri Lanka," he said.

For Sooriya, Mouna Farm on O'ahu is a good place to live, – but he holds out the possibility of someday returning to his home country, Sri Lanka.

"Maybe, you'll want to live here one day, too," he said to me.

Arugam Bay had become a tourist site, and he didn't like it. What had been his "place" was past now. Ram had been able to preserve the old spirit, but now that most of the place had been leased, only Sooriya was able to revive the past for the short while we were living at what was left of the old place.

As usual, Sooriya was restless. Every year thousands, of believers went on their pilgrimage to the Perahera in Kataragama. On their way to the ancient temples in the southeast of the island, they would make a stop at the temple in Pottuvil, as well as in many other Hindu temples along their journey. With our help, Sooriya wanted to provide them with food and medical care before they went to sleep. Many of them were very poor and couldn't afford the travel expenses. Our group went with Sooriya, all of us wearing the orange lungis Sooriya had given us.

Hundreds of pilgrims had gathered within the Pottuvil temple grounds, all of them wearing orange. Some of them slept on tarps spread on the ground, finding shade under trees. But there was also a vast hall that afforded shade. Ram had built it years ago. It was supposed to serve as a resting place for pilgrims. Even an artist had been assigned to decorate one of the walls. It had fallen into disrepair over the years, and now Sooriya decided to order a renovation of the building.

Goats were grazing everywhere, monkeys were jumping from one tree to the other, and agile mongooses ran along the temple walls. It is said they fight even against cobras. The pilgrims liked them, because the mongooses protected them from snakes.

Here, as well, Sooriya was welcomed with much respect. First, the head of the temple spoke to the believers, who sat on the ground, and afterwards it was Sooriya's turn to speak. Together, they all stretched their folded hands toward the sky. I didn't understand what he was saying in Tamil, but the pilgrims were hanging on his every word. For them, he was a holy man.

Then Mark was playing his flute - unknown sounds to the believers. A long queue of hungry people formed in front of the mobile kitchen. They patiently waited for the women to fill their tin bowls with rice and curry.

At Sooriya's urging, Peter had brought along supplies for a makeshift first-aid station. Just before sunset, we Westerners began ministering to the pilgrims, who lined up for our service. Among us, Maria stood out for her service; in fact, she was the only one of us with professional medical training = as a veterinarian. Minor foot wounds had to be cleaned and disinfected. We had plasters and dressing material. Children and old people had splinters in their feet. Most of them were walking the long pilgrimage barefooted. Some of the pilgrims needed painkillers or a foot massage. As darkness set in, we continued working by the flashlights of our cell phones until everyone had been treated.

Sooriya had decided to walk a certain distance on the Pāda Yātra to Kataragama. Six days was the estimated time. The camera team and almost every one of our group joined him.

We got a ride to Okanda, the last temple before entering Yala National Park. From there, the path leads through the jungle. En route, we saw a few elephants crossing the road, and we watched monkeys cavorting in the treetops, and water buffalos cooling off in shallow rivers. Green and sand were the primary colors.

From the moment we arrived at the temple site, where Sooriya and companions would begin their six-day march, the glowing orange of the pilgrims' clothes dominated the jungle colors.

The believers sat on bare ground. Women were preparing meals over small fire pits, while their children slept in the shade of ancient trees. Old, frail men and women slowly dragged themselves across the square. Traders were there selling tin plates and cups.

The believers carried all their provisions on their shoulders or on their heads. The army provided drinking water in big tanks set up along the pilgrimage route. On the path that lay ahead, no one could buy anything. Thousands of pilgrims on the move through the jungle had to be entirely self-sufficient.

In the temple area, we received many invitations to share meals. We were the only Westerners in attendance.

The believers welcomed Sooriya as a holy man. Believers were knelt down to be blessed by him. Patiently, he would pay attention to each one. Swamis and other Hindu dignitaries approached him to have serious conversations. On those occasions, I preferred to stand aside. It was quite surreal for me to witness this other aspect of Sooriya. Occasionally he cast reassuring glances in my direction.

Do not instruct, but let good deeds speak for themselves; this was Sooriya's credo. Litter, for instance, was meaningless to the locals, but had always been a big problem. Litter was scattered all over the area around the temple, especially empty plastic bottles, among other residual waste. Nobody seemed to feel responsible for cleaning it up. However, Sooriya had brought along many empty rice sacks for refuse disposal. Completely taken aback, the locals watched as Sooriya and his Western friends spread out to pick up litter from the sacred site. Silently, a few pilgrims began to help us. Perhaps they felt ashamed. After a short time, we had cleaned up the place, and a pickup truck carried everything away. In Sooriya's eyes, the litter had been a desecration of the temple site, but he didn't waste a single word lecturing about it.

I didn't join Sooriya for the six-days' walk through the jungle to Kataragama. He would proceed with the camera crew always by his side. He treated it quite naturally, as if it was the most normal thing in the world. For my own part, I returned to Arugam Bay. I felt urged to write down what I had been allowed to experience recently.

I decided to visit Crocodile Rock. The old path guided me to the cave, to which I was bound by such wonderful memories.

"It's a magic place," Sooriya had said then. There, he had decided to walk in a new direction on his life's journey. This decision had turned him into the person he was today.

In Arugam Bay, hotels and restaurants now lined the bay from one end to the other. The little hut where surfers had deposited their boards overnight was gone. The once lonely spot was crowded with many tourists.

I could hardly remember the impressive landscape that awaited me. In my mind, the old gray-haired Swami still danced on the beach. Sooriya still walked the same path, full of doubts and worried about the people he loved. I pulled a lungi out of my bag and put it around my shoulders to protect them from the broiling sun.

En route to my destination, I recalled, I had to pass the first of the black-rock formations. Whether it was called Crocodile Rock or Elephant Rock didn't matter; I pushed on to find our cave. Never had I imagined that I might walk this path once more.

Inevitably, monkeys were shrieking in the trees of the jungle. Very cautiously, I approached the lake at the foot of the rock. Thank God there were no crocodiles to be seen anywhere! I climbed up the smooth rock face to reach the ledge.

The view from there onto untouched nature was grand: open ocean in one direction, jungle in the other – and I let my thoughts wander back to the past. At this spot, at least, nothing had changed. I had been young and so sad to lose Sooriya. But what might have happened to him and his family had he had stayed in Arugam Bay? I hadn't anticipated that our lives would stay connected, and that we would meet again.

On my way down, I saw a crocodile dozing in the sun, but I decided to ignore it. An elephant crossed my path, but as I was obviously not threatening it, the huge animal turned away. Thinking about the civil war, human kind had turned out to be the most dangerous of beasts.

Soon, Sooriya and our group would arrive at Kataragama. They would see the famous elephants covered with brocade blankets, their legs tied up with iron chains. They always had been the main attraction of the religious festivities. Sooriya wouldn't stay there for a long period. For him, the way through the jungle had been his destination.

*

Exhausted but happy, they all safely returned to Arugam Bay after several days of adventure.

They had had to ford seven rivers, because there were no bridges. In places the water had been quite deep, and for our cameraman, Alex, it had been a serious challenge to get his equipment to the other side in a dry state.

Each day of their journey, they had had to get up before sunrise and walk until to noon, when they took their first break in the blistering heat.

Wild boars and a bear had crossed their path. Every now and then they spotted water buffalos trying to cool off in the water. Of course they encountered monkeys - lots of monkeys! Word was that a group of pilgrims had been hurt by elephants near one camp site - the people had made the mistake of sleeping on the animals' path. Two people had to be taken to hospital.

The pilgrims had walked across a dried-up lake, its mud cracked. Often the ground was hot and sandy. Sooriya led our group, walking barefoot, as always. The pilgrims built temporary camps beneath trees every night, and with simple means they prepared rice and curry.

"Everyone was sharing; it was overwhelming," Darcey proclaimed.

Every night, swamis came to Sooriya to show their respect for him.

"They treated him like a big religious leader," Darcey added. "All of them wanted to spend some time with him. Sooriya was encircled by them all day long."

To cope with all of this demands a lot of strength and stamina, I thought to myself. Once they had committed, there was no turning back. And the walking - this man had endured a strenuous time.

"They seemed to drain him - to take away his energy in order to make themselves stronger," Darcey said of Sooriya's many petitioners.

Being Sooriya's friend and student, Darcey shouldered as much of the load as possible. He was about forty-five and healthy. Sooriya was glad for the help as he had other duties.

"Pilgrims were throwing themselves in front of his dirty and hurt bare feet," Darcey told me. "It is hard to describe what was going on."

Looking at me with his big blue eyes, Darcey asked: "You know what I am talking about, don't you? Sooriya didn't intend to just talk to me about these things in Hawaii - he wanted me to see them!"

Indeed, I understood Darcey's emotional turmoil only too well. Sooriya didn't insist on anything, but he always planted the seed. Then he would turn to something else, trusting that the power inside the seed would make it grow into a strong plant.

Darcey hadn't been prepared for so much devotion; this was more than he had ever seen with Sooriya in Hawaii. This was at a whole new level: wherever Sooriya was, he seemed to draw people like a magnet. How did so many people in Sri Lanka know him, even though he had left more than thirty years ago? Had information about him been passed on to other pilgrims and to younger people?

Or did they acknowledge his status by the white ashes of a sadhu on his forehead and his skin?

Swami Jeebakran from the fishing village kept close to Sooriya at all times, and it was he who would restore Sooriya's ashes after Sooriya bathed in a river. Swami and Darcey together took good care of Sooriya quite naturally. If the night got a little cold, they would cover him with a blanket. If he wanted to wash, Swami poured buckets of water over him. While showering or bathing, Sooriya always wore his lungi, the way he had done since he was a little boy. There had never been private bathrooms. One day Alex, the cameraman, asked him how much of his privacy he was allowed to invade and Sooriya answered:

"You want to shoot a film about my life? This here exactly is my life. Decide for yourself."

In Kataragama, the pilgrimage reached its peak at the Perahera, before the exhausted group set out for Arugam Bay. Their feet were aching, but it seemed they had acquired a new kind of energy on their way through the jungle.

Sooriya had never been a guru to me. No matter if he was a holy man in Sri Lanka – or an artist and a socially engaged personality in Hawaii – he was my beloved friend, and forever a part of my life.

He still is a man – a man who wishes to cross borders. He doesn't bother about the color of somebody's skin, their nationality or religion. Long ago I accepted that Western thinking has difficulty finding a logical explanation for his special features. I am his friend and I want to describe him simply the way he is. In my book, I've tried to point out his many good facets.

"The rational mind is a silly monkey sometimes," Sooriya had said to the young teachers in Hawaii. "Some things you can only understand with your heart."

At the Beach Hut, I was sitting at a little table in the shade of the palm trees, writing and breathing the warm tropical air. The place was quiet. From the terrace I was able to see the Shiva-Ganesh House.

While sitting there, I watched a movie in my mind. A younger Sooriya was crossing the place: sometimes calm, sometimes furious, but always full of energy and keen to realize his ideas. Often he was desperate because the civil war was slowing him down; or he was sitting on a mat, narrating.

I was so deeply lost in reverie that I didn't hear Sooriya come to the table. Smiling, he followed my eyes to the Shiva-Ganesh House. It was late afternoon and the weakening sun was spreading a warm light.

Together we walked to the simple house that had stood the test of time. We listened to the black birds. Sooriya put his arm around my shoulders – a familiar gesture. Our wheel had come full circle.

*

Sooriya got the news from O'ahu that the Buddhist temple Honpa Hongwanji Mission of Hawaii had chosen to bestow upon him the prestigious title of "Living Treasure of Hawaii." The honor, part of an annual tradition in Hawaii dating back to 1976, would recognize Sooriya for embodying the philosophies of forgiveness and healing and for his connection with others through self-reflection. "He takes life experiences and transforms them into mantras for compassionate change and unconditional love," the temple declared.

Sooriya flew back to O'ahu, and I to Germany. We stayed in touch. On the phone he told me that the Love

Peace Harmony Foundation and the United Nations Association of Hawaii honored him as an "International Peace Builder." The ceremony commemorated the United Nations International Day of Peace.

After some time, he called and told me he had started the whale project he had been planning for so long.

"Koholā Ola is the whale that gives life," Sooriya said. "The whale is the mother of our oceans and we must love her now and listen to her whale song."

A few years earlier, Sooriya had a dream in which he was shown a whale as a symbol of peace and unity on this planet. Having lived in Hawaii for more than 35 years, Sooriya knows that to Hawaiians, whales are sacred for their grace, intelligence, and beauty; they are revered as the Kinolau (physical form) of Kanaloa, the god of the ocean. These large creatures of the sea visit the west coast of O'ahu where Sooriya lives.

"They live in community and harmony, and teach us that we can do the same," he says.

In the same way that these beautiful sea mammals take nutrients and their newly born from Hawaii to the rest of the world, Sooriya saw in his dream that the copper whale he would create would bring the message of Aloha, love, oneness, and care for the planet to all the world.

After having revisited this dream for many years, Sooriya at last was bringing his vision to life through the creation of a life-size copper whale sculpture, a 45-foot-long makuawahine (mother whale) and her keiki (calf).

"The mother and child motif is a significant one," Sooriya said, "for it exemplifies unconditional love, care, trust and comfort. These qualities are urgently needed at this time on Earth. Humanity has become separated in so many ways, that now is the time to heal the separation between people of the world, and by healing this separation we can then help heal and care for Mother Earth. We are living in critical times and it is important now that we all come together to make a positive difference in the world."

Sooriya called the project, "Ke Koholā No Ma Maluhia Honua" -"The Whale for World Peace."

"All people have heart," he said. "Children and kupuna of all ages, all spiritual beliefs, and all ethnic backgrounds must come together to bring world peace, unity, and healing through art. All are needed. All are welcome to build and share in the spreading of this whale's message. Art has the ability to heal. Art has the ability to transcend boundaries and separation. The same way the whales teach us to live in a peaceful co-existence, so does art have the ability to bring us together in unity, peace and harmony."

Toward this end, Sooriya invited the local Nanakuli Community as well as the greater community of O'ahu to participate in the creation of the whale sculptures. Over the course of several months, nearly 1,000 children from the local schools came to Sooriya's Artist Village in Wai'anae to pound on the whale and give it shape. Community leaders as well as members of all the different political, religious, spiritual, and business communities came together to contribute their mana - their energy - to the project. Ohana (family) Days saw people from all walks of life, races, religions and cultures - from Hawaii and around the world - pounding on the copper sculpture, coming together to exemplify the message of community, support, and peaceful co-existence.

"In the art process, judgments are suspended and eyes are opened to see all as beautiful," Sooriya said. "Seeing beauty, gratitude arises, and this allows us to connect to all of our relations. When we feel this connection, we feel our Ohana, our family, among all people. When we come together anything is possible and it is up to us to pave the way into a new level of connection, one that supports the life and well-being of all the planet as a whole. This is the message of the Whale Song."

In January 2020 the whale sculpture will be unveiled at the Dr. Agnes Kalaniho'okaha Cope Community Center in Nanakuli on the West Coast of O'ahu.

Dr. Agnes Kalaniho'okaha Cope, known as Auntie Aggie, was a long-time resident of Nanakuli and a champion for Native Hawaiian health, education, culture, and the arts. She was also Sooriya's ohana and spiritual mother. It was a great honor for him to have his whales displayed at the Nanakuli Community Center, which was built in memory of Auntie Aggie and her contributions to the islands of Hawaii.

"Koholā Ola is the Whale's Song for World Peace," Sooriya said. "It will continue to share its message with the world. It is a gift from my heart to the islands of Hawaii and to the world for harmony, unity and peace."

It was the last big project he wanted to realize in Hawaii. For months, he was very busy and put all his energy into the project.

After completion, Sooriya planned to return to Sri Lanka, where his eventful life journey began. Peter, who many years ago helped Sooriya to leave the country's civil war, would take care of Mouna Farm. For a long time, Peter lived there and helped relieve Sooriya of organizational tasks.

Inevitably, I thought back to the day in 1983 in Sri Lanka when the dripping postman brought Peter's letter from the USA to Sooriya's Beach Hut. In it, Peter laid the foundation for Sooriya's departure from Sri Lanka and his further life. I smirked at my confusion and skepticism when he said that morning, "Someone or something will come to us today. There will be a change. The black birds have told me."

I had long since stopped wondering about such statements from Sooriya.

Sooriya had no desire to return to Arugam Bay. The former fishing village had become too loud and touristy for him. But very close to Arugam Bay, at a wonderful beach, he had found a place that was still untouched by mass tourism. He told me that everything had been arranged to set up a place where friends from all over the world would be welcome, as they once had been at Sooriya's Beach Hut. He wanted to maintain the exchange of ideas with Hindu sadhus and swamis, as well as Buddhist monks that had always been a part of his life.

Of course, he was not a person who would sit around idly. In Sri Lanka, there is a great need to set up social projects, especially for the Tamil population, many of whom still live in poverty. Sooriya would travel to India, to the lonely mountainous regions, and to the temples where he found his inner silence and learned the Sacred Copper Art. In a square in Sri Lanka, he would find more time to devote himself to his art.

There, Sooriya Kumar, son of the sun, I'm looking forward to see you soon.

***

To the author:

Claudia Ackermann was born in Stuttgart in the South of Germany in 1960.

In 1983 she traveled to Sri Lanka and other Asian countries for the first time.

Later she studied German language and literature and cultural anthropology in Cologne.

She works as a journalist and editor and is the co-author and author of several German books.

1983: Sooriya at the beach of Arugam Bay, Sri Lanka

In India, he lived as a sadhu for several years

Copper art work: Sooriya manufactured a door for Father Phil's chapel in Oahu, Hawaii

In Hawaii, Sooriya is honored several times. Beside him the famous Hawaiian ukulele player Eddie Kamae